A S

There was one empty parking space in the postage-stamp lot sandwiched between the Harrowleigh Clinic—still busy at 8 P.M.—and a tiny park. Charlie paused to look into the tangle of trees and shrubs, feeling the pull of wild things even in that small place.

Locking the Volvo's door, he glanced down where something had caught his eye. He bent, and there, at the edge of the park, was a bloody handkerchief. Charlie told himself that he was near a medical clinic and it was probably the result of a bloody nose. "Blood and medicine go together," he said aloud in a strange voice, for now he was thinking like his grandfather. His senses told him that something was very wrong; he felt the violence in the air around him. He clutched the handkerchief more firmly, knowing that it had blown over the ground. He stood undecided at the edge of the trees for only a moment, then pushed into the tangle of branches, certain of his path.

The body lay only a few feet away.

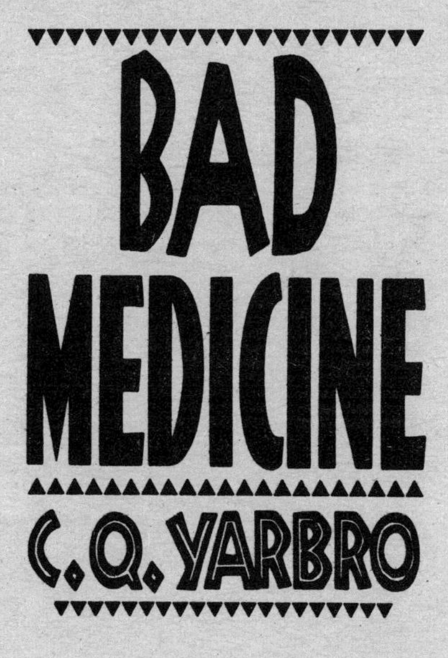

PUBLISHED IN HARDCOVER AS *OGILVIE, TALLANT & MOON*

JOVE BOOKS, NEW YORK

This Jove book contains the complete
text of the original hardcover edition, as revised by the
author. It has been completely reset in a typeface
designed for easy reading, and was printed
from new film.

BAD MEDICINE
Published in hardcover as *Ogilvie, Tallant & Moon*
by Chelsea Quinn Yarbro

A Jove Book / published by arrangement with
the author

PRINTING HISTORY
G. P. Putnam's edition published 1976
Published simultaneously in Canada
by Longman Canada Limited, Toronto
Jove edition / September 1990

ISBN: 0-515-10399-3

Jove Books are published by The Berkley Publishing Group,
200 Madison Avenue, New York, New York 10016.
The name "JOVE" and the "J" logo
are trademarks belonging to Jove Publications, Inc.

PRINTED IN THE UNITED STATES OF AMERICA

10 9 8 7 6 5 4 3 2 1

Most affectionately dedicated
to my sister
Ann Christine Kokonmaa

ACKNOWLEDGMENT

The writer wishes to thank Frederick Douglas Gottfried, attorney-at-law, practicing in Oakland, California, without whose expert advice this tale would be riddled with errors.

For the second edition of the work, she would also like to thank Robin A. Dubner, attorney-at-law, for providing advice and assistance since Fred Gottfried's death.

The Indian dead will rise to eat the grave meats
left for them when the white man's dead
rise to smell their flowers.

—INDIAN PROVERB

I

March

Thursday Evening

EVERYONE ELSE HAD gone home when the phone rang. Charlie Moon stopped in the door, one hand on the light switch.

The phone rang again, a frightened sound in the dark office. In three more rings the machine would record the caller's message.

Charlie hesitated, listening to the urgent ringing. Then with a sigh he put the lights back on and walked to his desk. "Ogilvie, Tallant and Moon," he said. "Charles Moon speaking."

The voice on the other end gave a little cry. "Charlie. Thank God I caught you. I've got to see you. It's very important."

"Miranda?" He had never heard her this upset. "What's the matter?"

"I was afraid you'd gone home already."

Frowning, he picked up a pencil and pulled his note pad nearer. "What is it, Miranda? What's happened?"

"The Weed boy died on Tuesday," she said abruptly, then waited. Charlie pictured her biting her lip as she always did when she was worried. "His parents are suing me. Just like that. Their attorney called the clinic today. They'll serve me tomorrow."

"What are their grounds?" He tried not to anticipate.

Miranda gave a mirthless laugh. "Malpractice." Then her voice broke. "Oh, Charlie, what am I going to do?"

It took only a moment for Charlie to flip through his desk calendar. "What's your schedule like?" he asked.

"Same as always, for the time being."

"I'm in court tomorrow and Monday. How about Tuesday? Can you make it by the office around two?"

"I've got a staff meeting at one."

Again Charlie consulted his calendar. "Make it eleven then. Eleven on Tuesday. Got that?" He jotted down the appointment, circling her name.

"Yes, but what about now?" Irritation had crept into her tone. "I'm in trouble now, Charlie. I don't think the Weeds are going to wait."

Charlie chuckled. "The law is very slow, Miranda. We have thirty days to respond." When he heard her swear softly, he went on: "Tell me about the Weed boy. What did he die of?"

"Apparently he died of Parkinson's disease."

"Apparently?"

Miranda was calmer now that she was on familiar ground. "Parkinson's disease is controllable with L-dopa. Since I've had him on the drug, I thought it was under control. He was responding to it quite well."

"Any reason to think he wouldn't continue to?"

"Well, he was pretty young, and that's always chancy. He did occasionally resist the drug. When that happened, we increased the dosage until he responded."

"Okay. That's normal, I take it?" He heard her murmured assent and went on. "Anything unusual about the case? Anything that required special attention other than your regular service? Was there anything peculiar about his particular case of the disease?"

"Not really." Miranda hesitated. "Can I see you, Charlie? I . . . I don't want to talk about Sparky. Can't it wait?"

"Not for long," Charlie said firmly. "I'm tied up this evening, Miranda," he went on, somewhat gentler. "What about Saturday? I'm planning to go hiking out at Point Reyes. Some cartographic firm over in Oakland's got a good map out of the place. It looks like fun."

"What time?" She sounded harried. Charlie guessed she was still at the clinic. "I've got two appointments around four. But it would be so good to get away for a while."

"I'll pick you up at nine thirty. I'll bring the lunch if you'll bring the beer." He forced cheerfulness into his voice. "The weather report looks good. Take a sweater just in case."

"All right, nine thirty Saturday. But, Charlie—"

"We can talk about it then, if you want to." He flipped the page of his memo pad. "You did say Parkinson's disease, didn't you?"

"Yes. Parkinson's."

"Good. See you Saturday." He scribbled "Parkinson's disease" on the pad, putting a question mark after it. "Don't let them rattle you, Miranda. Don't say anything; don't volunteer anything; don't mention or discuss the case in any way. If you get hassled, tell them that your attorney is a bastard and he insists you do it this way. Okay?"

He could hear the beginning of a smile in her voice when she said, "Okay, bastard. I'll be ready at nine thirty."

"Right."

"Thanks, Charlie."

Charlie Moon was still Indian enough to find thanks awkward. "It's my job. That's what I'm here for." He hoped that would stop it, for the repayment ritual for gifts and thanks was long and uncomfortable. "Saturday, then."

"Saturday. Good night." Her end of the line went dead.

Charlie weighed the receiver in his hand before he hung up. Malpractice was very, very sticky. He did not want to believe Miranda was guilty.

On the way out he left a note for the receptionist.

"Lydia," it read, "find out everything you can on Parkinson's disease. What is it? What does it do? Who catches it? Why? When? I need the material—he almost wrote tomorrow—tonight. I offer dinner at the Blue Fox and the show at McGoon's as a bribe. Charlie."

Friday Afternoon

NOT EVEN THE weather had gone his way. The morning fog had burned off about half an hour before the afternoon fog came in. The judge had been sick, and his opposing attorney had been unable to produce the witnesses he needed in the afternoon session. Charlie glared out the window of his office at the Transamerica Pyramid. "Damn building should have a radical architectomy," he remarked to the air.

The intercom on his desk buzzed. "Mr. Moon," said Lydia Wong in her special voice, reserved for impressing clients. "There is a Dr. Fritz Bjornsson to see you."

"Bjornsson?" He scowled as he asked. What was Miranda's boss doing here? "I can see him in about five minutes, Lydia. I'll buzz when I'm free."

"Very good, Mr. Moon. But remember that Mr. Carpenter is coming in half an hour." Mr. Carpenter was the favorite fiction of Ogilvie, Tallant & Moon. Whenever an appointment proved difficult, the invaluable Mr. Carpenter would appear promptly.

"I remember now. Thanks for reminding me." He flicked the machine off and rose angrily to his feet. He knew that there was something wrong, something more than Miranda had told him. He did not like knowing half the truth. And he did not like being pressured.

More than six minutes had elapsed when he buzzed Lydia and told her to send Dr. Bjornsson in.

Dr. Fritz Bjornsson had the lean, ascetic look that might once have been worn by a monk. On a surgeon, it was even more effective. His lined, careworn face was belied by the cold ferocity of his pale-blue eyes set like ice below his finely arched brows. As he crossed the room, he extended one impeccably groomed hand. He smelled faintly of expensive European cologne.

"Good afternoon, Dr. Bjornsson," Charlie said as he took Bjornsson's hand, repulsed by the cold, reptilian skin.

"Good afternoon, Mr. Moon. I realize that you're a busy man, so I won't keep you." He smiled with his teeth as he sank into the chair on the other side of the desk.

"Not at all," Charlie said, as determinedly urbane as his caller. "What can I do for you, Doctor?"

"It's my understanding that Miranda Trobridge has contacted you about this unfortunate Weed business."

"She has. You realize that I am not at liberty to talk about her position with you." Although his tone was slickly professional, Charlie knew that Bjornsson would recognize it for the challenge it was.

"Naturally. I admire your conscientiousness. It's just that I have some information you might not have run across yet. I felt that you should have all the facts before you commit yourself to her case."

"Dr. Trobridge and I have not had our first meeting. Officially I have no information."

"I realize that, too. I believe she's coming in on Tuesday morning." Slowly he stretched out his long legs, crossing them at the ankle. "You might not be aware that she has been . . . shall I say, unwise? . . . in the past. One of her patients died under rather questionable circumstances about five months ago."

"Questionable circumstances?" What was Bjornsson up to?

"As you may know, persons with degenerative diseases are often obliged to take ever-increasing amounts of drugs in order to slow the effects of the disease. Sometimes the body will reject a drug entirely, and then death results. And sometimes a physician will discontinue the drugs if it appears they can no longer be of use."

"You mean a mercy killing?" Charlie tapped impatiently on his intercom. "You're trying obliquely to tell me that Miranda decided that the boy couldn't make it."

"Not precisely." Bjornsson gestured carefully, dismissing Charlie's words. "It's not like that. But there is the case of Mrs. Margolis, and I must keep that in mind. Let me put it this way: The Harrowleigh Clinic is not prepared to support any physician on its staff who has decided to practice euthanasia on his or her patients."

"You are certainly direct," Charlie said after a moment, his sarcasm lost on Fritz Bjornsson.

"Yes," the surgeon said seriously. "I felt you should be aware of the situation."

As he rose to leave, Bjornsson turned eagerly to Charlie. "I am not asking you to violate any confidence given you by your client, of course, but if it should turn out that Dr. Trobridge has perhaps intervened in the Weed boy's case, I trust you will not insist that the clinic operate in the dark."

"My responsibility is to my client," Charlie said stiffly, rising to see Dr. Bjornsson out the door.

"Naturally. But you do understand my position, I'm sure." With a last false smile the doctor left.

Charlie closed the door, then wandered over to his bookcase, staring unseeing at the titles. A soft knock on the door brought him back from his reverie. "Come in," he said as he rubbed his forehead as if to clear his thoughts away.

Lydia Wong came into the room with a file folder in her hand. "Excuse me, Mr. Moon. I have that information you requested."

He took the file she held out to him and flipped it open.

There, on five single-spaced typewritten sheets, was her report on Parkinson's disease. With an appreciative whistle, he said, "Great. I didn't expect it so fast. What about your bribe?"

"I can't tonight. What about some evening next week?" From the way she said it, Charlie knew she was turning him down. Next week there would be some reason it was impossible then, and for the week after that.

"I appreciate it," he told her. "If you want some other bribe, you can let me know."

Her reply was prompt. "Tell Willis Ogilvie that I could use a raise."

"Okay. Anything else? How much of a raise?"

Lydia looked startled, her eyebrows lifting incredulously. "You'll do it?"

"If that's what you want. What's the figure?"

"One hundred fifty more a month." She waited to see his reaction.

"What will you settle for?"

"The hundred, but eighty rock bottom. My rent just went up."

Charlie nodded. "Okay. What about Annie and Janis?" He knew that the firm's two secretaries were well paid, but he also knew that Willis Ogilvie would not spend one cent more than he had to, and with a new law clerk and two new associates coming in next week, he was already complaining about the high cost of salaries.

"They could use fifty each. We were talking about it a couple of weeks ago. Inflation, you know. And Annie's husband's been laid off."

Charlie knew only too well. "I'll do what I can," he promised her, and was surprised to see Lydia smiling. "You're worth the money, Lydia."

"I'm glad somebody other than me knows that," she said as she left his office.

* * *

Driving home out Geary, Charlie found himself frowning over the things Fritz Bjornsson had told him. Looking briefly at Kaiser Hospital while he waited for the light into the tunnel, he remembered what it had been like when his father had gone there to die. A compassionate doctor had saved Daniel Moon from weeks of suffering by discontinuing medication for a few hours. Charlie had always thought of that doctor with kindness. But this was different. This time it wasn't a question of when death would occur, but if it would occur.

Ahead the lights changed, and the rush-hour traffic crawled forward, the setting sun shining mercilessly into the eyes of the homeward-bound drivers. A thin film of fog made the light glary, turning the disk of the sun into a bright smear dead ahead.

Charlie slid his Volvo a few feet forward and, adjusting his sunglasses, waited once more for the light to change.

Across the street an ambulance wailed as it darted away from the hospital, threading its way through the lighter traffic in the other direction. As he watched it go, Charlie found himself thinking that it must be very easy for a doctor to make a wrong decision. So much of what they were faced with was immediate life and death. The stress must be all-consuming. All the doctor had to do was make one wrong assumption. Perhaps Miranda had done that. He knew that she dealt with chronic and degenerative diseases; watching people die by inches would get to her. Maybe that was the answer.

But he knew it wasn't. Miranda was too careful and too competent. He tucked the idea away in his mind for the moment. With the next change of lights, Charlie made it under Masonic and was out of the bottleneck, headed for home.

* * *

It was almost midnight when Charlie sat down with Lydia's file on Parkinson's disease. He had pulled a few books from his shelves, prepared to search farther if he had to.

PARKINSON'S DISEASE

Known also as quaking palsy or St. Vitus' Dance.

Generally a disease of the middle-aged and elderly. Rare in young; when contracted before age seven, generally fatal. Being a disease affecting the nerves, it is aggravated if vitamin B is deficient in the diet. There is some indication that certain aspects of the disease are psychogenic, although this is disputed. Standard treatment of the disease is L-dopa. Long-term results are not presently known. Laser surgery is used occasionally, but not in pediatric cases.

Symptoms: involuntary muscular contractions and spasms resulting in uncontrollable trembling. In advanced cases, all muscles are or can be involved. Breathing and bladder functions are impaired. Walking unassisted is impossible; eating and swallowing become palsied, as does the function of the gastrointestinal system. Failure of any of these normal functions can result in death. . . .

Lydia had been thorough. The close-written pages revealed the scope of Parkinson's disease, its characteristics, its history and what was being done about it. As he read, Charlie wondered what it must feel like to have a disease that would insidiously rob him of his strength and the control of his body, to know that in the end he would be incapable of doing even those simple things any normal baby can do.

He also knew now what it was Miranda had been

fighting, and he knew how she must have fought it, willing the boy to respond when she could not hope.

When he got up for coffee, he was aware of how much he took for granted. Rising from his chair, walking to the kitchen, and taking the things he wanted from the shelf, never considering what his muscles were doing, never worried that they might not do as he wished—they were so automatic. Until recently no one with Parkinson's disease would have shared his confidence in the workings of his body. L-dopa had changed that.

Charlie tried to imagine what the Weeds had gone through, believing that L-dopa would save their son from surrendering to the demands of the disease until he died. With the promise of control, how senseless his death must have seemed. He understood how they would want to lash out, to insist, demand that someone take the blame for Sparky's death.

Rufus whined, sensing his master's concern. He thrust his muzzle into Charlie's hand and licked the fingers, his intelligent eyes troubled. He was a large dog, part highland collie, part husky, with a broad head and a compact, strong body. He waved his plumed tail uncertainly.

Quickly Charlie knelt. "What's the matter, Rufus? Huh? Getting housebound? Is that it?" He rubbed the dog's ears affectionately. Rufus was special. Charlie valued him not only for the fine dog he was, but because Rufus was one of the few gifts he had ever received from his grandfather; the pick of the litter from the old man's Seeing Eye dog. Looking at Rufus, Charlie could feel the strength of his grandfather, and remember.

Reassured, Rufus wagged his tail, making soft yelps of pleasure as Charlie found that one spot between his shoulders that always itched.

"Okay. We'll have a walk." Charlie straightened up, wishing for a moment that they were back in Canada, on the

Iron River, with the stark wild beauty around them. The city thrummed with life, and Charlie liked it, but at night he felt the tug from the wild places.

It was late, and the fog hung wetly over San Francisco. Charlie glanced out the bay window, then went for his coat.

Saturday

CONTRARY TO THE weather report's promise, the morning was cold and sodden. A drizzle that was more than fog and less than rain clung to the hills; out in the Bay the foghorns mooed. The wan morning light shone off the slick street side by side with the ghosts of electric signs.

As he finished his second cup of coffee, Charlie reminded himself that if he were on the old reservation, he would have ignored the weather and gone off for the day. But he was in California, a long way from northern Saskatchewan, and even the Iron River tribe lived in snug houses in their new location. Not that the ferocious winter blizzards there were anything like the soft, civilized mist outside.

The phone jangled in the hall, a sudden sound shattering the morning. Charlie swore as he got up to answer it. "Moon," he said brusquely.

"It's Miranda."

"Hi," he said, irritation melting away. "You've looked out the window?"

"Yes. You can go ahead if you like, or you can bring your picnic over here, but I am not going to Point Reyes on a day like this." Though her tone was cordial, her words were sharp, her tone preoccupied.

"I don't blame you." He was about to ask what was

wrong, but instinct warned him not to. "Can we make it a late picnic?"

"Why?"

"Well, I *do* want to go to Point Reyes. I'll need thawing out and drying off when I get back, and a picnic inside would be great." He was frowning as he spoke, wishing he knew what had upset her.

"I'd love to, but I have a meeting with Fritz this afternoon." She said it bitterly, and Charlie knew he had found the reason for her irritation.

"Tell him you can't make it."

"What?"

"Tell him you can't make it. Say that your lawyer insists that you do not discuss the case with anyone until a settlement has been reached." He smiled to himself, thinking of Fritz Bjornsson's smooth, impeccable manner.

"He won't like it." She sounded uncertain.

"Of course he won't like it. He's not supposed to like it. You stick to your guns and put all the blame on me. It won't hurt me, and it'll take the heat off you."

"He's already set up the meeting."

"Cancel it."

"But, Charlie—"

"If you don't want to, give me his number, and I will." He hesitated. "Look, Miranda, this is going to get a lot worse before it gets better. You're going to have to shift a lot of your hassles to me, or you won't be able to work. So get used to doing it. What's Fritz's number?"

On the other end of the line she sighed. "It's in the book under his wife's name."

"Which is?"

There was a suggestion of a giggle before she answered. "Swanhilda."

"Christ." He scribbled the name on his phone pad out of habit; he knew he would not forget Swanhilda Bjornsson.

"What time will you be back, Charlie?" Miranda asked

quickly, as if she wanted to forget everything to do with Dr. Bjornsson.

"Four? Say four."

"Picnic at four then, if you're sure that this meeting with Fritz is a bad idea." This last was skeptical.

Charlie knew how Miranda's brow furrowed in doubt, and he could see her over the phone. She must be sitting in her basket chair, her knees drawn up under her chin, her face intent and the frown deepening. "Miranda, you don't have to worry about this; worrying is my job. You're hiring me so that you can get your own work done. Remember that." He waited for a response, hoping she would be kinder to herself.

"I'll see you around four. 'Bye."

"Okay," said Charlie and hung up.

Swanhilda Bjornsson still had a strong accent, although it had disappeared enough to be hard to place. She said, with hushed awe, "My husband, you know, is very busy. I will give your message to him."

Charlie took a firmer stance. "This is Charles S. Moon of Ogilvie, Tallant and Moon. It is imperative that I speak with him."

"Moon," she said reflectively. "A Chinese gentleman? What do you want with Dr. Bjornsson, sir?"

"Mrs. Bjornsson," Charlie said to the phone with a patience he did not feel, "I am an attorney. One of Dr. Bjornsson's colleagues has retained me. I must tell Dr. Bjornsson that it is not possible for Dr. Trobridge to meet with him this afternoon." That was putting it more bluntly than he might have, but he knew Swanhilda would understand him now.

"Oh. Dr. Trobridge." She said it as if she were identifying a noxious odor. "Dr. Bjornsson has been very reasonable with her."

"That may be. But I cannot allow her to discuss her case

with anyone at this time. And that includes your husband."

Swanhilda sniffed aristocratically. "Dr. Bjornsson's schedule does not permit him to attend meetings easily, Mr. Moon. But I will tell him. Perhaps he will call you later."

Charlie stopped her, putting down the phone with: "Tell him that if he tries to cut Dr. Trobridge out of the clinic before we go to court on this charge now, he himself will face a suit for damages. Thank you for your attention, Mrs. Bjornsson. May you have a delightful afternoon." He grinned as he slammed down the receiver. Chinese, indeed.

Then he turned his attention to his day at Point Reyes.

There were few people on the road once he left the freeway for the winding complexities of Highway 1. He was glad of it, for it gave him the break he needed, the illusion that he had left civilization behind. One glance at the expensive watch on his wrist reminded him that he carried civilization with him, but he did not look at the time; he looked at the watchband, a wide band of silver and turquoise with rim accents in cinnabar. It was one of the few ever made by the Hopi jeweler Charles Loloma, and it had cost Charlie every cent of his first two fees to buy it.

The road crested, then began its winding descent to Muir Beach, which lay hidden below in the fog.

There were fewer buildings here, and the mists shut them out. For the moment Charlie felt alone, alone by choice. There were other times, too many times, when he felt alone by insistence. He could remember being a boy in Vallejo, often ignored because he was an Indian. How certain he had been then that going back to the tribe would rid him of that feeling. And then, at six, his father took him back to Canada, and Charlie found out abruptly how very Californian he was. At first there had been a sense of relief, for these were his people, and they spoke his language. They looked like him, eyes dark, black hair straight, skin the color of wheat. He felt he had cast off the shell of himself and was renewed as a snake was, as a bear shedding its winter coat. But the other children looked at him with guarded eyes, his neat clothes and expensive jacket out of place among those scruffy rugged youngsters. Two things had ended his agony: his cousin James Raven Feathers had taken a liking to him and made the others stop their pestering—the outcast from the Vallejo shipyards and the best athlete in the tribe became friends. The other and more profound change came when his grandfather had discovered that Charlie possessed magic and had begun to train him as he himself had been trained more than sixty years before.

A deer stood on the highway, its delicate ears turning as Charlie's Volvo appeared. In the back Rufus let out a yelp and jammed his nose into the space left by the unlatched window. Charlie braked, making an effort to bring his mind back to the present. The car swerved on the wet pavement, and Charlie forced himself to ignore the steep cliff falling away on his left. The deer looked startled, then sprinted away up the slope, its long, graceful bounds carrying it swiftly into the cover of brush.

Charlie watched it go and let his memories slide away from him. "I owe James a letter," he told Rufus musingly, thinking that James, now the young turk of the anthropology department at McGill, was in his own way as far from the tribe as Charlie.

He parked near the stables, enjoying the rich, warm smell of the horses. Rufus scrambled out of the backseat barking joyfully, his tail waving, the long leash trailing from his collar. Neither the cold wind nor the ominous clouds dampened his delight as he capered around Charlie.

"In a minute, you," Charlie said as he pulled on his jacket. When the zipper was secure, he pulled a small leather bag from his pocket and touched it in a certain way, humming under his breath, softly repeating the monotonous words his grandfather had taught him as he stroked the bag.

They set out several minutes later, Rufus leading the way, sniffing excitedly at the damp earth, pulling on the long leash.

But Charlie moved more slowly, carefully. Occasionally he would stop to pick up things. Once it was a broken acorn, another time some wood fungus; once he substituted a redwood cone for the pine his grandfather used in spirit bags.

By the time it started to rain the little bag bulged.

When he left the wilds of Point Reyes, Charlie was happily soaked to the skin. He had tramped over ten strenuous miles, had had the satisfaction of seeing no one but a mounted ranger, and had completed the spirit bag with the proper ritual. He was content. Walking alone like that with his thoughts and his dog, living through his senses and his pores; he remembered that this was one of the many things Lois had not understood. But that was over. It no longer mattered that Lois did not understand.

Coming back to the parking area, Charlie made the unpleasant discovery that his right rear window, which he had not secured, had blown open and the rain had soaked his towel and the change of clothes he had brought along.

"Damn," he said without anger. With a resigned sigh he opened the car for Rufus, cringing as the dog shook himself briskly, spattering everything.

"So we drive back wet," Charlie said. "It's only an hour. We can stand it."

The rain was heavier as they drove through Stinson Beach and headed south. Mud oozed from the cliffs, forcing Charlie to slow down. He was thoroughly fed up by the time a Highway Patrol car came along, lights and siren going, to stop every car.

"What is it, Officer?" Charlie asked the big man in the uniform after he strode up to the idling Volvo.

"There's a washout ahead. You'll have to turn back. You can cross Mount Tam into Mill Valley or go back through Samuel Taylor Park into San Rafael. Mill Valley's a little faster if you're going to the city."

"Gr-eat," Charlie said dryly, hating the thought of another hour in wet clothes and wondering what he would say to Miranda when he arrived late for their picnic. "Any idea when the slide will be cleared away?"

"Not for some time. It took some road with it, and we can't fill until the rain's over." The officer glanced in the car. "Good-looking dog you got there."

"Yeah. Well, thanks for telling me about the slide." He watched the man amble back to his black-and-white car. "I guess it's Mill Valley," he said philosophically.

He had been in the shower almost ten minutes when Miranda called. "Where are you?" she demanded.

"It's kind of hard to explain," he said, watching the hot water pool at his feet and turn cold. He crossed one arm over his chest as gooseflesh rose on his skin.

When he had told her, she said, "Poor Charlie. Do you still want me to come over? Or is that off?"

He laughed. "A house call? You don't have to."

"I know that," she said happily. "But I'll bring the beer, how's that?"

Inwardly he knew he wanted to be alone with his aching muscles and stuffy head, but he had the spirit bag, and Miranda sounded better than she had in the last three days. "Okay. Come ahead. But I'm terrible company—fair warning."

"I'll remember."

"You aren't a bad cook for a lawyer," Miranda said as they sat amid the ruins of their picnic. Her short brown hair glowed in the firelight, and her face was faintly flushed from the heat.

"I'm not a bad cook for an Indian either." Charlie, inspecting the last bit of chicken marsala, decided against it.

"I didn't mean that."

After a moment he turned to her. "I know. Force of habit, I guess. Like your feelings about being female probably."

Her brows raised above the thin gold rims of her glasses. "Oh?"

"You know, imagined insults that aren't meant because so many insults are offered." He paused long enough to sneeze. "I'm not usually this touchy."

"That's because you don't usually have a cold," Miranda said authoritatively. She reached out for his hand in a businesslike way. "Hot and dry. You're probably running a fever. You should be in bed, Charles Moon."

He waved away her diagnosis. "I'm fine. I just overdid it today." He remembered the spirit bag. "I have something for you," he said, getting to his feet. When he came back into the living room, she had moved to the window seat. "Here," he offered, holding the leather pouch toward her.

"What's that?"

"It's a spirit bag. My grandfather taught me how to make them." He handed it to her. "Don't open it."

She stopped toying with the thongs holding it closed. "Why not?"

"You'll let the magic out," he said seriously, hoping she would not laugh.

"All right. Thank you." She rubbed the bag as if trying to identify its contents by touch. "Is that why you went to Point Reyes?"

He shrugged. "One of the reasons. I have to get away sometimes, that's all. Too bad I picked such a lousy day."

"You need rest," she said, back on familiar ground. "You should have said you weren't feeling well."

"I feel fine," he protested, not believing it any more than she did.

"Well, fine or not, you are going to bed." She got to her

feet, holding out her hand to him. "Come on. Doctor's orders."

With reluctant gratitude he took her hands as he got up, saying, "You're the boss about this. But remember, I'm the boss about law."

She paid no attention to him, pointing him down the hall toward his bedroom. Her grip was steady, and her fingers were strong on his arm. "I like a woman who knows what she's doing," Charlie said to cover his embarrassment.

Sensing his discomfort, she asked, "What is it?"

He stopped at the door to the bedroom. "Miranda, there are some things I am very Indian about. One of them is modesty. I promise you I will get undressed and into bed, but will you leave me alone while I do?"

She nodded. "But why?"

"You are not my lover, Miranda. It isn't right for you to see me naked. My grandfather would say," he added uneasily, "that it is bad magic."

"Is that like medicine?" She said it clumsily.

"Medicine, magic, same thing." He shrugged. "Do you mind?"

"All right. I'll be back in a couple of minutes." Frowning, she walked away.

Charlie changed quickly, feeling the chill of the room like insects on his skin. He stored his clothes neatly and pulled on his heavy dressing robe before getting into bed, thinking as he often did that the king size was too large for him now that he was alone again.

"Ready?" Miranda called from the hall.

"Ready. Come on in."

She was carrying one of his mugs and a flat packet. "I took the liberty of making you some bouillon. And here's something for what ails you." She held out the packet and the mug. "Go on. Take them."

"What are they?"

"Cold pills. A new kind. Supposed to be the best around."

"Where'd you get them?" he asked as he took the mug.

"I had them in my purse. We had some samples lying around the clinic, so I took a few. Most of us do." She handed him the paper container with six capsules. "This should get you through the weekend."

He nodded as he took one.

"You should stay in bed tomorrow, Charlie. You want to get rid of this bug."

He laughed, thinking of his days at Iron River. "I'll sleep in tomorrow."

She shook her head professionally as she straightened the covers. "You should take better care of yourself, Charlie." She took the proffered mug.

"Okay, what's bothering you, Miranda?"

"Nothing," she said unconvincingly as she turned to go.

"Is it this case?" He was curious, eager to know.

"Not exactly."

"What then? You'd better tell me, if you think it could interfere with what the textbooks call our lawyer-client relationship. Out with it." If only his head didn't ache.

Miranda bit her lip, her face showing strain. "Charlie, how come you haven't made a pass at me?"

He bit back a retort. "I distinctly remember making a pass at you three months ago. You turned me down as I recall," he added, sinking back on his pillow.

She leaned toward him. "But you continue to see me. And you're defending me."

"You'll get a bill," he assured her.

"That's not it, Charlie, and you know it. What do you want of me?"

Cautiously he reached for her hand, feeling her fingers unyielding. "Look, Miranda, I've been divorced three years now, and it still bothers me. I'm a lousy celibate, but I don't like fucking strangers. I admire women who are doing things with their lives. I told you that when I first met you."

"God, I was scared," she said, remembering.

"Why? Because you had the good sense to have an attorney read your contract with the clinic before you signed it? Why is that scary? What's scary is what might have happened if you hadn't had me read it. That one clause about extended hours was iniquitous."

"They took it out," she said, her face flushing. "I didn't realize what it meant." She sounded as if she were accusing herself.

"Hey." Charlie reached for her again. "It's no sin to be ignorant as long as you don't insist on acting in ignorance. You didn't. And we've had some good times since then." He wished he sounded more reassuring. "Miranda, look, so I made a pass at you and you turned me down—I still enjoy your company. And I sure as hell am not going to have an affair with you now, with this suit pending. We'll be tangled up enough without that."

"And after?" She had pulled her hand away from his and was tracing the design on her woolen slacks.

"I don't know. Neither do you." He recalled too many times when the end of a case was also the end of a friendship. "We'll find out when it happens. That's too far ahead to deal with now. Go home, Doctor. I'm a sick man, and I need my rest."

"All right." She got to her feet and looked down at him. "I wish I knew what you were really thinking about, Charlie."

He had heard those same words from Lois too often and felt the same pang. "Go on," he snapped. "Get out of here." Then, regretting his abruptness, he gave her a rare smile that turned his dark eyes into bright slits.

"I'll see you Tuesday. Sleep well."

"I will. I'll use the medicine." He tapped the packet.

She was at the door. "Well, it's free. When you run out, I'll get you more. The drug salesmen hand 'em out."

Then she was gone, and the flat felt empty. Charlie heard the door slam. He wished now that he'd slept with her when they had met the year before. Too bad it hadn't worked out. He put her out of his mind as he turned on the light over his bed. He had a lot of reading to do before he would be ready to take the Guttierrez case to court.

Tuesday

CHARLIE HESITATED BEFORE asking his next question, dreading Miranda's answer. "Was it a mercy killing? It does happen, doesn't it?"

Miranda turned on him angrily. "I'm supposed to keep people alive, remember?"

"Then how the hell did you get yourself into this, Miranda? You say that you were aware of the gravity of the boy's condition, that you saw him twice a month, and that's pretty damn often. Now that he's dead you've got a malpractice suit hanging over you and your clinic, which carries your malpractice insurance and has a lot to lose, is hedging its bets. Help me, Miranda."

She pulled nervously at her short brown hair, thoughtfully nibbling one stubby fingernail. As usual, she was wearing slacks and, because it was chilly, a fisherman's sweater. "I don't know," she said after a moment.

"What about the clinic? Bjornsson insists that publicity about this could ruin it. And even though they can't fire you unless you lose the suit, they can make life miserable for you if you just let them ride roughshod over you. You know that."

Sighing, Miranda pushed out of the chair and began to pace. At the window she stopped, looking three stories to the street. It was a rare clear March day, sun-washed. The people below her moved like confetti on the wind. Watching them, she did not hear Charlie's next question.

"Miranda!" This time he rapped out her name, his black brows snapping together over flinty eyes.

She turned. "I'm sorry, Charlie. I keep thinking about the kid." Reluctantly she left the window. "I keep trying to figure out why we lost him. Parkinson's is tricky, particularly in kids. You have to watch the drug levels and you can't use laser surgery. I never thought it would happen to me, not in clinic work," she said in quiet anguish. "Malpractice. Shit."

"Look, Miranda. Sit down." He pointed to the chair opposite his desk and waited while Miranda slumped into it. "You've had a bad time at the clinic."

"They're acting like I had leprosy and this was the fourteenth century."

He nodded. "Okay. Let's do this one step at a time. I want you to tell me what happened—everything you can remember about the case. Take your time." He leaned back, his copper face deliberately blank.

"But I've told you—"

"Tell me again. Details, people, everything. Everything."

"Let me think." She was very still, a distant frown on her face. "We saw him first, oh, eighteen months ago. His father had been in aerospace and was out of work about three years. He did part-time library chores; cataloguing, that sort of thing, in Daly City, and filled in nights at a local liquor store.

"Kirsten, his mother, does those hand-embroidered shirts they sell on Union Street. Well, they had too much money for welfare and not enough for a doctor. So they came to the clinic when Sparky started having attacks. They thought he had epilepsy."

"Give me the boy's full name," Charlie interrupted, his pen poised.

"Chisholm Harris Weed. Born February 27, thirteen years ago, in San Jose. I can get the name of the hospital if you want it." She reached into her pocket and pulled out her cigarettes. Until recently she had not smoked. "Got a match?"

Charlie tossed her a book of them. "Those things are bad for you, my doctor tells me." He pushed the ashtray toward her.

"Rotten," she agreed, and lit up. She exhaled smoke and tossed the matches back on the desk, buying time. "Name and age. Father is Weiland Rudolph Weed, PhD in physics. He'd probably be an alcoholic right now if he could afford it. Herr Professor is a very twitchy gentleman. He brought Sparky in the first time; Kirsten has a horror of disease. She even had trouble admitting Sparky . . . had . . . allergies."

"Allergies can't have helped much. Do you think she could have bungled the treatment? Did she want him to die, subconsciously?" He tapped his pen impatiently, waiting.

Miranda shook her head. "No. She felt too guilty to do that. She isn't the perfectionist in the family; Herr Professor is."

Charlie changed the subject. "What about MediCal?"

She gave a sarcastic laugh. "Dr. Weed doesn't approve of socialized medicine. He doesn't really approve of the clinic. We tried to get him to see the people up at Cal Medical. Let the interns see Parkinson's in the young. But Herr Professor wouldn't allow it. So sometimes we got Max Wannermahn down from Cal to take a look at him unofficially. Herr Professor didn't like that either. He's never got used to being poor. His father was rich, his grandfather was rich, and his great-grandfather was. He's one of the elite. He's never forgiven the government for cutting back on the space program; he takes it personally."

"Sounds charming," Charlie said dryly. "Would he be a mercy killer?"

She examined her fingers. "I don't think so, no."

"You don't think so, but you aren't sure."

"No, I'm not." Again she was up and moving restlessly around Charlie's office. "Sparky got Parkinson's young. And the younger they are, the harder it hits them. Kids under eight don't last long, no matter what you do." She leaned across the desk, her light-brown eyes on his dark ones. "Charlie, I worked on Sparky over a year. I had him under control. I really did. He was getting better all the time. Even his allergies. Truly." There was a plea in her voice.

"Okay, Miranda, you didn't do anything deliberately to cause his death. I believe that, but what I believe doesn't matter. We have to prove it."

"There's a record of everything," she said wearily. "Even the freebie drugs we gave the Weeds to save them a little money."

"Freebie? Like the cold pills?"

"Sure. We put those things to good use, Charlie. We get L-dopa along with other things. L-dopa's standard for Parkinson's, but it runs about twenty dollars the hundred if you're lucky. Sparky was on four a day."

"You say you have records of that. Drugs as well as examinations?"

"Of course." She bit another fingernail.

"Okay." He felt more secure about the case now. Records could be produced in court. "What about the treatment? Was it unusual? Is four L-dopas a day a heavy dosage?"

Her eyes drifted back toward the window. The sun was slanting through the curtains, revealing swirling dust motes in the light. "That's part of the trouble," she admitted. "Doses are an individual matter. Most adults take two, sometimes three a day. Children can take higher doses, depending on the severity of the disease."

"Which means?" When she did not answer, he said,

"Miranda, I can't make this up out of thin air. What are you holding back? If it's important enough to conceal, you can damn well bet that the opposition will use it against you."

"It's just that sometimes we'd order dosage increase over the phone—"

"You have a record of that?"

"Yes, certainly. Everything is on his chart. Visits, calls, all changes."

"Was he taking anything besides L-dopa?"

"B vitamins. Nervous diseases often respond well to B vitamins. And calcium lactate, of course."

"Why of course?"

"Sparky was allergic to milk, so we gave him a calcium supplement."

"Is that unusual?" His patience was waning.

"It depends. Some doctors don't use vitamin therapy, and some might not consider additional calcium when milk sensitivity was indicated. But it's a matter of personal opinion. I'm in favor of vitamins, minerals, hot baths, prayer meetings, or anything that helps. I don't care how my patients get well, Charlie, so long as they do get well."

"But you could be criticized for the vitamins and the calcium?"

"It depends," she said slowly. "So much of medicine is a matter of . . . of"—she looked for the word and found it—"personal *style*. It's hard to say who will do what and what results he'd get."

"It doesn't sound very scientific."

Miranda stopped and regarded him measuredly. "It isn't."

Charlie accepted this. "Fair enough. I gather Parkinson's is unpredictable. Did you make any special provisions for this? Say, instructions with his teacher at school?" Perhaps there had been laxness at that end.

"Hell, the school has a complete copy of his records."

"Oh?" This was unusual. "Did they get it with a court order or what?"

She swung her foot. "Well, no. In cases like this one, the parents sign a blanket release so that the records can be made available on a moment's notice to anyone who needs them." She saw the question in his face. "Look, Charlie, a couple of times it saved his life."

"Why?" He paused. "Give me an example."

She glared at him. "Aspirin and L-dopa don't get along well together. If he'd had aspirin at the beginning of an attack, it would take longer for the L-dopa to work, and sometimes we can't afford that waste of time."

"Could he have taken aspirin before he died? Would that have made a difference?"

"Yes, of course it would." She stared out the window again. "I don't think the Weeds would have been that foolish. No one at his school would have given him aspirin. . . . They have his records, remember."

"What about the swim team? Would the coach know about it?"

"Damn right he would," Miranda said with some heat. "He'd know about it, and he'd pay attention. When Sparky was in good shape, swimming was great, but if he got into trouble in the water, that was very serious. He could drown quickly if the coach didn't keep an eye on him."

A thought occurred to Charlie. "Miranda, about that release. Is it blanket enough for me to get a copy of the boy's records?" He scribbled on his pad. "I can get a court order to release them, but that takes time, and I don't think we have a lot of it."

"I could get you a copy if you want," she said hesitantly.

"If you can give it to the principal of the school, I think you can give it to me. Do you recall the wording clearly?" He was poised to write.

"Oh, yes." She wrinkled her nose. "It says 'For purposes of consultation.' "

"Well, that's okay; you're consulting me."

"That's true," she agreed. "And anyone who saw Sparky at all got copies of all his records."

"Who else followed his case?" Again Charlie was looking for his chance.

"Well, when Sparky was in really bad shape and Herr Professor was scared out of his aristocratic wits, Wannermahn would see him. Most of the time we'd fill him up with L-dopa and wait for a break." She began to pace again.

Thinking back, Charlie asked, "Did Wannermahn approve of your treatment?" It would help to have such prestigious backing in court.

"Most of it," was her circumspect answer.

"What didn't he like?"

"He's not very keen on vitamins." She looked for a sign in Charlie's impassive face. He surprised her by changing the subject again.

"Were you the only person at the clinic treating him?"

"He was my patient, if that's what you mean. When I wasn't available, the rest of them took care of him. Fritz saw him several times. So did Chris Hannlin last year while I was back East. You can't wait with Parkinson's. That's why his records were so freely available. Everyone at the clinic knew who Sparky was and what to do for him." She stubbed out her cigarette, annoyed. "I was thinking about the L-dopa. There wasn't anything wrong with him the last time I saw him: that is, anything *else* wrong. Wannermahn and I were going to run tests on him Wednesday."

"Tests?" Again he readied his pencil.

"Standard series. His condition was stable. I gave him a couple of packs of L-dopa and told him to take them same as always."

Charlie scribbled. "Who gave him the medication, his parents?"

Miranda laughed. "Sparky took his own medicine most of the time. He was a very reliable kid. He learned to be responsible so he could survive. Kirsten certainly wasn't any help, and Herr Professor resented the disease. It made sense for Sparky to take care of himself."

"Okay." He paused. "What was your prognosis on the case? Honestly."

"Honestly?" She stood very still, hands limp at her side. "I think the Weeds waited too long to get him help. I doubt he could have lived another five years. We kept the disease at bay, but that's all. He was a tough, bright kid; the disease had its hooks in him too deeply."

"So his condition was degenerating." His eyes hardened. "What made him die?"

Quickly she lit another cigarette, having leaned across the desk to get the matches. "I saw him last a week ago Thursday. He had a regular appointment. He was run-down, and things were rough at home. His father was sulking again. I checked Sparky over, made my notes, reminded him about Wannermahn, gave him the L-dopa because if Herr Professor hadn't been working, I didn't want them to economize at Sparky's expense. Then I went out and had my monthly conference with Kirsten. She was almost hysterical. I gave her a sedative. They left. That was it."

"What about the mother? Was something wrong?"

"Not really. She was upset. I didn't want Sparky under more strain."

"What happened then?"

"It's only secondhand," she warned him.

"Tell me anyway."

She nodded. "Well, they must have got home about half an hour later and had their usual dreadful evening. Sparky got his bedtime pills. He had a good night and was up at seven fifteen. He complained of feeling badly, but Kirsten found out that he didn't have a sore throat or fever, so he went to school. Apparently he took his breakfast and lunch pills, but he didn't feel any better, so he took his dinner pill early."

"Is that unusual?" Charlie asked.

"A little. About eight he had a mild attack. Kirsten called Fritz about ten. He said Sparky should have another pill immediately and to check with him again in two hours if there was no improvement. Kirsten says that he didn't want to see Sparky; Fritz insists that he did. He'd saved an appointment for Sparky with a note to call Wannermahn. Kirsten might not have understood. She gets a little crazy when she's under strain."

Charlie held up his hand. "Why weren't you called?"

"Fritz says"—and bitterness poisoned her words—"he was concerned about Sparky and wanted to talk to his parents. He felt that since he is older, spelled m-a-l-e, that the Weeds would pay more attention to him."

"I see. What happened to Sparky then?"

"Kirsten gave him the extra pill and put him to bed."

"She didn't bring him to the clinic?" Charlie's face was as puzzled as his voice.

"Well, *I* would have seen him, but Fritz thought this was more of the same resistance pattern we'd seen before."

"But they didn't use the appointment the next day either." Charlie tapped his pencil. "Why?"

"Sparky got better. Sometimes that happens, like the calm before the storm. He slept well and felt fine. He'd been shaking and vomiting the night before, but he stopped." Miranda ground her cigarette out and folded her arms. "So, Kirsten called in, reported his condition, and canceled the appointment. Sparky took his pills and went off to school."

"On Saturday?" Charlie asked, wondering if he had got the days wrong.

"Swim club. He liked to swim, and it was excellent therapy."

"Was this what he did most Saturdays?"

"If he felt okay. Kirsten does her shopping on Saturday morning and left Herr Professor in charge of the kids."

"Kids. There are others?" Perhaps this was Charlie's missing link.

"Elaine, age fourteen, and Mickey, age seven. Both girls. What about them?"

"Mickey is Michelle?" He smiled in spite of himself when Miranda nodded. "We'll come back to them later. Tell me more about Sparky."

She sighed. "He was okay Saturday, but Sunday he got worse. Shortly after midnight they took him to San Francisco General. They called the clinic earlier. For some reason I'll never understand, Hartman told them to go to General Hospital. Hartman's only been with us a couple of months, and he's still pretty green. So the Weeds took Sparky down to Army Street. He died before there was any chance to save him."

"Did you see him?"

"At SFG? No. I tried once, but the Weeds refused."

"Even though you'd been his doctor?" The lead of his pencil broke; exasperated, he took a pen from the mug on his desk.

"They decided it was my fault. They wouldn't let me near him. I asked the administration for clearance, but the okay came through too late."

"Who admitted the boy at SFG?"

"Dr. Raymond G. Raymond. I've dealt with him before. He's sensible. I went over his report, and I agree with about eighty percent of what he did."

"Eighty percent. What about the other twenty?" Charlie was hopeful. Improper treatment in emergency receiving might get Miranda off the hook.

"Just little things. Twenty percent of what a doctor does is a matter of style, as I've said. Ray did a few things I wouldn't have, but nothing crucial."

Mentally Charlie cursed. "What about the other children?" he asked, returning to the family, looking for an answer. "Diseases? Emotional troubles?"

"The younger one, Mickey, is asthmatic. Considering her home life, it isn't surprising. She's terrified of her father and doesn't trust her mother. Kirsten is alternately protective and bossy with her, which doesn't help." She put her hand to her eyes.

"What's the other one like?"

"Elaine? She's healthy as the proverbial horse. She's a large, strapping Brünnhilde type. She wants to play baseball with the Giants. She might do it—"

Another dead end. Yet he knew there was something missing. He beat a tattoo on the desk with his pen.

"Raising the spirits, Charlie?" she asked, trying to smile.

"That was my grandfather's job," he told her. "Very powerful medicine, spirit walks. The remedy of last resort." A glance at his desk clock gave him the time. "Let me buy you a sandwich," he offered, closing the subject.

"No. I've got to get back to the clinic. The Harrowleigh Clinic for the Treatment of Chronic Diseases is recruiting today, and the residents from Cal are coming down. We're short of doctors . . . maybe short one more in a couple weeks."

"Don't take that attitude, Miranda," he said sternly. "You're going to have a hard enough time without running yourself down."

She looked at him. "All right. I was unfair. If there's anything to be done, I know you'll do it." Having said this, she slung her purse over her shoulder and started for the door.

"Don't give up, Miranda. This is just the beginning."

She didn't wait to hear the rest. The door slammed behind her.

When she had gone, Charlie sat for some moments, staring straight ahead, his face masklike. He was more concerned than he had admitted to Miranda. Malpractice was always a bad business, for both doctor and patient. If there was a case against her—and he was afraid there was—he would have few options for defense. Damn, this was more a case for Willis Ogilvie, who was better at bargaining then he was. Even if Miranda were found responsible, Willis could do more for her when it came to the settlement. . . .

Shaking his head, he brushed the thoughts aside. That was for later. He checked his card file and began to make calls.

Alex Tallant was in the hall when Charlie came out of his office. Apparently he had been waiting, for he cleared his throat and asked, "You going to lunch now?"

Puzzled, Charlie said, "Yes."

"Mind if I join you?" Alex was certainly uncomfortable. His usually unruffled manner was gone, and even his tawny hair was mussed. "Thought maybe we could talk, you know. Business."

"About what?" Charlie was guarded. Alex almost never asked anything of him, and on those rare occasions when he did, Charlie had learned to be wary. He was also curious.

"Tell you all about it at lunch," he said, beginning to collect himself. "Where were you going?" He started down the hall, impatient now that he was sure of Charlie's attention. "What about Elbert's?"

Charlie liked to avoid places where the sandwiches cost upwards of four dollars, but knew Alex well enough to know that he would not go to the *dim sum* place he had in mind. Too much Eastern money and Ivy League in Alex for him to unbend that staunch Protestant spine long enough to jostle for the stuffed Chinese buns Charlie loved so well. "Elbert's it is," he agreed, and followed his partner into the elevator.

The restaurant was elegantly crowded, and the waiters were haughty enough to sniff at turtlenecks and sweaters. But they were also efficient and unobtrusive, showing a carefully scaled deference to those who ordered the right wines. Alex, seated at his usual table, declined the menu and recommended the medallions of beef.

"Out of my style," Charlie said as he studied the sandwich list. He wished now more than ever he had gone for *dim sum*. When the waiter materialized at his shoulder, he ordered the steak sandwich, then sat back to hear what Alex had to say.

"That malpractice suit—you're handling it?" For Alex it was an awkward opener. "Sounds like a loser to me."

"I'm handling it. Why?"

"It's this Mayling estate. Been wrestling with it for months. No one in the family knows beans about it. It's utterly chaotic." He smoothed his silk regimental tie.

"How? What about it?" Charlie sipped slowly at ice water, wanting to remove the lemon slice that floated in it.

"They had a pharmaceutical house. Small, specialized. Down on the Peninsula in Menlo Park. They did mostly heavy drugs, you know, the ones with the high narcotic content. The FDA checked 'em out, of course, and they come nosing around sometimes, you know how they are."

"So?" Charlie's face revealed nothing.

The waiter appeared with their salads. Alex jabbed his fork into the greens as he went on. "Something's wrong. Books don't make any sense. Can't get word one out of the directors or the distributors. FDA says it's okay, that their drug records all check out, but there aren't enough records for me to make any sense of, not to settle the estate."

"Why tell me?" This was the question Charlie had been longing to ask as much as he had been dreading the answer.

"Well." He wiped his mouth meticulously. "You've got the malpractice suit on your hands. Could do a little snooping on the side. Ask around. Get the low-down. Find out if there's any scuttlebutt about Mayling, anything out of line; bad feelings, bad experiences. Something's being held back."

"Any idea what?"

"Not yet." For Alex, that was quite an admission.

"It sounds like you haven't had any luck." Charlie hated being Jordan Alexander Tallant's errand boy, and if it took time from his own work, he would refuse. It was one thing to be the firm's tame Indian, but Alex was pushing it.

"Not even bad luck. Just a blank."

"Is the estate contested?" Charlie stirred the lettuce on his plate, wanting to be anywhere else. His head was still stuffy from his cold. Then he remembered the cold pills he had tucked away in his wallet. As he swallowed the pills, he repeated this question. "Well? Is the estate contested?"

"Not yet. But there's Howard, you know, Jared's younger half brother, and he's up to something. We're going to have to come up with the right material. Jared Mayling was the most secretive man on the West Coast. He didn't tell anyone more than he had to." He sniffed the wine their waiter offered. "Very nice."

"Is the will okay?"

"On the surface it is textbook perfect," Alex answered disgustedly. "But we can't take too many close questions—not enough information. That information has to be somewhere." Exasperated, he plunged his fork into the last of his salad. "Charlie, I'm stumped. And there's nothing to go on. Can you help me?"

Though he hated to admit it, Charlie was interested. He was also angry with Alex for dragging him into the case, but now he was hooked. Privately he wondered if he could turn it around into a smoke screen to save Miranda. "Okay. Give me the details, and I'll ask around when I have the chance."

It was late afternoon before Charlie began making calls for Miranda again. His two o'clock appointment had been more complicated than he had anticipated, and the deposition afterward took more time than it should have. Even during those appointments he had been bothered about Miranda; he knew he had overlooked a little, obvious thing. Finally he called the coroner's office and left a request for results of the Weed boy's autopsy. As an afterthought, he added, "Will you make a note of the amount of L-dopa in the body?" With all the pills Sparky was supposed to have taken, his tissues ought to be saturated with the stuff.

"Is that Dr. Trobridge's patient?"

"Was, yes."

"Dr. Trobridge," the secretary said knowingly. "She was the one who gave that extra sedation to Mrs. Margolis, isn't she?"

Did everyone know about that incident? "I have no information on that case, Maggie. Where can I find a record of it?"

"There's no record." Her words were sour. "But we all *know*."

"It has nothing to do with this case," he said, wishing it were so.

"Do you have information Dr. Coners should have about the Weed child?"

Charlie laughed, hoping it would put Maggie's nose further out of joint. "All I have is a hunch."

On the other end of the line Maggie gave a disbelieving sniff and hung up.

There was one empty parking space in the postage-stamp lot sandwiched between the Harrowleigh Clinic—still busy at 8 P.M.—and a tiny park. Charlie paused to look into the tangle of trees and shrubs, feeling the pull of wild things even in that small place.

Locking the Volvo's door, he glanced down where something had caught his eye. He bent, and there, at the edge of the park was a bit of mottled cloth. Charlie reached for it, his expression changing as he touched it. The handkerchief was bloody, and the blood was still tacky. Charlie told himself that he was near a medical clinic, that blood and medicine went together, that it was probably the result of a bloody nose. "Blood and medicine go together," he said aloud in a strange voice, for now he was thinking like his grandfather. His senses told him that something was very wrong; he felt the violence in the air around him. He clutched the handkerchief more firmly, knowing that it had blown over the ground, picking up pine needles and dirt. He looked toward the park once more.

He stood undecided at the edge of the trees for only a moment, then pushed into the tangle of branches, certain of his path.

The body lay only a few feet away, screened by the branches. In daylight it would not have been hidden at all. Charlie moved carefully, squatting beside the man, touching the face, which was slightly spongy under his fingers, cool but not cold. The man had not been dead long.

Pulling his key ring from his pocket, Charlie switched on the little flashlight that hung there, playing its pencil beam over the body. The trousers were grass-stained and torn at the knees; he had crawled the last bit of the way. Charlie glanced toward the clinic, saw the parking lot and staff entrance. Was that where the dead man had been going? And why?

There was a spattering of blood on the man's shirt, but very little. Wherever the blood had come from, it had not killed him. The tiny beam of light reached the face.

Charlie retched when he saw it, for the face was as bruised as if it had been crushed under a roller. All the skin showed purple mottling, and the swelling that comes with bruising. Under his nose was a smear of blood. "So it *was* a nosebleed," Charlie murmured as he touched the face, expecting the tissue to give like jelly. Bruising that massive must mean a crushed skull and ruined muscles. But under the soft, obscene swelling the bones were firm. Lifting the eyelids, Charlie saw that the whites were suffused with red.

Curious now, Charlie lifted one arm and noticed that the

hands had the same heavy mottling, deep bruises, and soft swelling without any sign of broken skin or bones. The pervasive stench of loosened bowels combined with the penetrating sweetness of fresh blood. Charlie had seen massive internal injuries before, had seen such mottlings on an abdomen awash with blood, but never anything like this. Bile at the back of his mouth made his taste suddenly sour, and he stood unsteadily.

Tucking the handkerchief into his pocket automatically, he murmured a few words softly over the body before he went in search of a phone.

There was a phone booth on the corner, and Charlie used it rather than the phones in the clinic. His thoughts were jumbled still from shock, and he knew the clinic personnel would find a dead body, particularly one so grotesquely dead, very distressing.

The walk to the corner helped him put his thoughts in order. He used the time to consider what he had to say, especially if the man turned out to be a member of the clinic's staff. He was not ready to face Miranda with another death.

"Yes," he said to the police operator who took his call. "This is Charles Moon. I'd like to talk to Lieutenant Shirer in homicide." He wondered why he was so ready to call it homicide, why he was so sure the man was murdered, why he knew it wasn't suicide or disease. He pictured the body again, the face congested with blood. . . .

"Frank Shirer here," said the laconic voice. "What is it, Charlie?"

"Frank," Charlie said, gathering his thoughts, "I'm at the Harrowleigh Clinic."

"Want to make a complaint about the doctors?" He chuckled.

"No," Charlie said with restraint. "You know that park behind the clinic?"

"Yeah? So?"

"There's a body in it, under the trees. Out of sight."

Charlie had the satisfaction of hearing Frank Shirer draw in his breath before asking, "What are the particulars?"

"Okay. The victim is male, probably Caucasian. . . ."

"Probably?" Frank Shirer's voice was thick with derision.

"The postmortem lividity is too advanced. If it weren't for the fact that he's got no broken bones that I can find, I'd say he'd been beaten to death. His face is purple-blue."

"Jesus."

Having made his point, Charlie went on. "He's about late thirties, maybe five ten, about one ninety, but that might be blood instead of flab. The body is cool, but not cold, and growing stiff."

He waited while Frank Shirer issued terse orders, his hand over the receiver so that all Charlie heard was a few garbled sounds. Then: "I'm on my way. Stay with the body. We'll find you."

Charlie disliked the idea. "How long?"

"No more than twenty minutes."

"I'll be waiting," Charlie promised as he hung up.

The scowl on Frank Shirer's face deepened as he knelt by the body. "Christ." He turned to one of the three men with him. "Get some pictures of this, Harry. Get a lot of them." He stood up slowly, a question in his eyes.

"I've got a client at the clinic," Charlie explained before Lieutenant Shirer could ask. "I should be in there right now."

Frank nodded. "All right. Go ahead. But send someone out. Preferably a doctor."

"My client's the only doctor on duty. I'll bring her out when I'm through." Charlie waited only for the absent-minded nod that passed for a dismissal.

"The ambulance will be here in twenty-five minutes,"

one of the others said. "There's a four-car accident at Sacramento and Taylor."

"I'll be out before then," Charlie assured Frank Shirer as he headed through the trees toward the Harrowleigh Clinic.

Eleven people sat in the waiting room, each in that hunched posture that Charlie had seen in the sick so many times before. He was as much out of place for his easy good health as he was for his copper skin. He knocked on the glass of the receptionist's cubicle.

"Yes?" she demanded hostilely. Her face was so tight and controlled that it looked like a set of sphincters. She begrudged each word that managed to escape from her wound of a mouth.

"Charles Moon to see Dr. Trobridge. She's expecting me. It's urgent."

"Dr. Trobridge is busy. She doesn't have any help this evening. You'll have to wait." Her taloned hand came up to close the cubicle once more.

"I am Dr. Trobridge's attorney. This is an official visit." He had made no move to stop the receptionist, he had not changed his tone, but the woman hesitated, fright in her eyes. The hand withdrew. "I'll tell Dr. Trobridge you're here, Mr. . . ."

"Moon. Charles S. Moon."

"Mr. Moon. I'll do that right now."

"Thank you," Charlie said cordially, and went to sit on the hard, comfortless chair nearby. Curious eyes watched him, trying to spy out what had brought him to the clinic.

Two ancient magazines later Miranda came to the inner door, her wilted lab coat showing more than her face what her day had been. "Come in, Charlie," she said. "I don't have a lot of time."

He followed her down the bleak hall to her cramped office at the back. She handed a nurse three folders before she closed the door behind them.

"How is it going?" he asked, concerned.

The smile that answered him was brittle. "Everyone is being terribly polite." She sank slowly into the wooden office chair on her side of the desk. "You should have been here this afternoon. It was worse than medical school."

"I'm sorry." His throat was tight and the words came out badly.

"So am I."

"I have a favor to ask you," he said carefully. "It's not pleasant, but if you can spare a few minutes when I leave, I want you to come out with me."

"What for?" She fiddled with her cigarettes, wanting something to do with her hands. "Can it wait?"

"No," he said. "There's a dead man in the park back of here. The police are there now. It looks as if the man was trying to get here when he collapsed."

Miranda threw the cigarettes across the room, then ran one hand through her short hair. "Shit." Very deliberately she opened her top desk drawer and slammed it. "Oh, don't mind me," she said in a moment. "I'm going to scream in a minute, but it doesn't have anything to do with you."

"Scream away," he invited.

She shook her head. "No. That wouldn't solve anything. Around here, a scream is all they need. A scream and a body in the park. Great." Ruthlessly she forced herself to change the subject. "You didn't come here to hold my hand. What do you want, Charlie, other than an identification?"

"Two things. I want Xeroxes of the Weed boy's records. Everything you've got, no matter how trivial."

"That's one thing," she said icily as he paused.

"I want to know what happened to Mrs. Margolis." He felt a lingering touch of the miasma of death that had clung to the body outside. It was still with him, almost palpable, a presence. Now to deal with this other death, this woman he had never known, now a partner with the man in the park. He put the thoughts aside, knowing he must not cloud his thinking.

Color had flooded her face, then faded. "That has no bearing on this case," she said stonily.

"I'm sorry, Miranda, but it does. What happened to Mrs. Margolis? Did you consent in her death?"

"If you mean," she said austerely, "did I kill her, no, I did not. She was in the final stages of renal failure. Do you know what that means?" Looking up, she saw the negative shake of his head. "To begin with, she had about forty pounds of excess fluid in her body, and the toxemia was getting to her. Her body was poisoning itself. She had a lot of pain and a lot of family anguish, which was even harder on her. So I left her enough medication to end it if that was what she wanted. I didn't tell her to do anything. Apparently she made up her own mind and died."

Charlie ground his teeth. "How many people know about this?" he asked as flatly as he could. He knew now her case would be terribly difficult to prove, for no matter what she said, the opposition would point to Mrs. Margolis.

"It sounds like the whole city knows about it."

"That's not an answer."

She glared at him. "It's no secret at the clinic here. Maybe it isn't much of a secret in general. Doctors gossip, you know." She said the last with bitter flippancy, then changed, becoming desperate, earnest. "But I'm not the only one who's done this. Really Charlie. Sometimes you lose, and then you have to decide how long you can watch your patient suffer and not at least offer a way out. You should have seen Mrs. Margolis. She was in pain, getting worse with no chance of recovery: she was too far gone for miracles. Her disease was not just killing her; it was destroying her family, ruining them. And for what? Ask anyone here, and they'll tell you there was nothing—*nothing*—we could do for Mrs. Margolis. Sure, she had a pulse, but she might as well have been dead."

"You might not be the only one who does this, Miranda, but you're the one being sued. I told you I have to know everything. Why didn't you tell me about Mrs. Margolis?" He leaned across her desk toward her and was annoyed to see her move away from him, her mouth tightening.

"I didn't think it was important."

"Next time you leave that for me to decide. Are you sure that's all? Are there any more Mrs. Margolises tucked into your closets you aren't telling me about?" He waited.

"I'll order the Xeroxes for you, Charlie," she said, pushing the intercom on her desk. "Thomkins, I want a complete copy of Chisholm Weed's records for Mr. Moon. He'll pick them up on the way out, or you can bring them back here. You'd better include a copy of the Weeds' release."

"Good," said Charlie, trying to restore some contact with Miranda. "I know this is private material. I won't use anything I don't have to."

"Why do you want the charts?" She was suspicious now, and Charlie guessed that she had faced more questions than his all day.

"I'll tell you when I find out. Something isn't adding up, or there's more to this case than we know. So the charts will give me a lead, I hope."

She turned her back to him. "You don't believe me, do you? You think I killed Sparky and I want you to find an out for me."

"Did you kill him?" he asked. "Maybe not directly." Her shoulders hunched. "Okay, not directly. I'll believe that. But did you make it easy for him to die because his condition was degenerating?"

"*No!*" She turned on him, her face distorted with anger. "No, I didn't kill him. I didn't *help* him die. I didn't *let* him die. I didn't do any of those things."

A knock on the door interrupted them. "It's Thomkins, Doctor. I have the Xeroxes for Mr. Moon."

Miranda pushed past Charlie and opened the door, taking the manila folder which was handed to her. "Thank you, Thomkins," she said.

Thomkins looked toward Charlie. "Does Dr. Bjornsson know you're doing this?"

"I don't know," Miranda said sweetly.

"I think he should be informed."

"Look," Miranda said, her eyes dangerous, "Dr. Bjornsson has released this information to a school principal, two hospitals, a pharmacist, and the ambulance company in Daly City. There is a signed release. I was the boy's physician, and for once, I'm going to hand out my own records."

Thomkins made a disapproving cluck. "But this is different, isn't it?"

Without an answer Miranda closed the door and silently handed the folder to Charlie. "The sheets with the triangular tags are emergencies. The circles are for tests and test results. Call me if you don't understand the charts." She stayed near the door, not looking at Charlie.

Briefly he thumbed through the records. "Did you write down the names of the drug companies that supplied the L-dopa, particularly the free samples?"

"I did. I really don't know if the others did. It depends. L-dopa is L-dopa. Why do you ask? Is Mrs. Margolis still haunting you?" This was bitter and without apology.

No more than that body in the park. "Should she be?" he shot back. "No. I'm looking for a pattern if there is one. If I find something that doesn't add up we can file a cross complaint with the drug supplier." He tucked the folder into his zipper case. "Have you heard anything more from the opposition?"

"No, nothing."

"Hammil and Ward, isn't it? Do you remember the name of the attorney who is representing the Weeds?"

"Mellon, Markum, something like that. He's one of their

younger men. He sounded in his late twenties on the phone."

"I don't know him. Young, you say?" Charlie smiled. "Good. Maybe he'll do something dumb and try to rush us into court."

"He sounded like the type on the phone," she said grimacing.

With an intent look Charlie asked, "Is he giving you any trouble? I can make him stop that if you like."

"No, he's just a nuisance. Mostly he wants records, too."

"Hold out for a motion to produce. With this release he might not need it, but see if you can get it from him anyway." He watched her smile.

"A motion to produce—how theatrical." She shook her head. "He's also talking about suing the clinic. The Harrowleigh Foundation isn't very happy about that."

"Well, happy or not, it was to be expected," Charlie said.

There was a rap on the door; then Thomkins opened it briskly. She favored Charlie with one brief nod before saying to Miranda, "We're running late. Mrs. Ellison is here. She's in Room J."

Miranda nodded. "Put her chart on the door. I'll be back shortly," she said as she shut the door on Thomkins. "We'd better go look at that body." She sighed. "You know, Charlie, I see dead people every day, and I've never gotten used to it."

"I know," he said, thinking of the ruined lives she dealt with, and the agony.

Frank Shirer had apparently been satisfied with the photographs, because the body now lay on a stretcher under a sheet, ready for the ambulance. He turned as he heard Charlie call his name. "I was about to come in there after you." His eyes narrowed as he saw Miranda.

Charlie ignored that remark. "This is Dr. Trobridge, of

the Harrowleigh Clinic staff. This is Lieutenant Frank Shirer, Doctor."

Miranda offered her hand without enthusiasm, and Frank Shirer took it perfunctorily. "Yeah," he said, revealing his disappointment in his fading smile as he looked her over. "Well, Charlie probably told you he found a body. He said you might recognize him, if he was part of the clinic group."

"Probably I would," Miranda agreed, her sarcasm lost on Lieutenant Shirer.

"Maybe he was a patient."

"Let me see him," she said, all emotion gone from her voice. "May I open the bag, Lieutenant?"

"He's not a pretty sight, ma'am." Frank Shirer was embarrassed.

"No, very likely not. But I am a doctor, Lieutenant, and I'm sure I've seen worse." She gave him a brittle smile before bending over the stretcher.

"Any identification on him? I guess not." Charlie claimed Frank's attention so that Miranda could do what she had to do.

Frank Shirer shot a look of deferential loathing at Miranda, but said, "No. Could be he was robbed. I tell you, Charlie, I never saw anything like his face, not in one piece. Do you think he was tortured or something? Those marks—"

Miranda interrupted them. "This is Sam Elgin," she said, surprised and saddened.

"You know him?" Shirer asked, shocked by her coolness.

Carefully she zipped the bag. "He's a drug salesman. There are a fair number who come to the clinic. He was here this morning, early." She rubbed her hands on her lab coat. "We were talking about his son. The boy is apparently epileptic: Sam's been very depressed about that. Poor Sam. . . ." She looked back toward the stretcher. "He was worried. . . ." She glanced up at Charlie. "I'm sorry. I'm babbling."

Charlie stretched out a hand to help her up. "Never mind," he said, feeling her hand shake in his. Without turning, he said, "Is that enough, Lieutenant?"

It wasn't. Frank Shirer pulled a tape recorder from his pocket, checking the cassette. Critically he turned it over. "You said the man was depressed. Was it about his kid?"

"Certainly. You'd be—"

Charlie stopped Miranda. "You don't have to answer any questions, Miranda."

"She's not exactly a suspect, Charlie," Frank said, and the warning was plain.

"She is upset. And you know what that can do to opinion, even expert opinion." He put his arm around Miranda's shoulder. "She's had a long, rough day, Frank. Can't you leave this until tomorrow?"

"One question, then," he insisted, his nondescript face suddenly pugnacious.

"One?" Charlie raised his brows, politely disbelieving.

"All right: two." The lieutenant changed his stance, feet set apart and arms crossed. "It's important, Charlie."

Charlie stared at the shrouded figure as the orderlies prepared to load the stretcher into the waiting ambulance. "Okay," he said at last. "Two questions. That's all."

Frank made an irritated sound before asking Miranda, "You said he was depressed. Was that depression getting worse?"

"Go ahead." Charlie nodded. "You may answer that."

Miranda said, "All right, Lieutenant, but remember that I didn't know him very well. I though he was troubled; jittery, gaining weight, unhappy, and pressured. The situation with his child wasn't good, and I know he was concerned about the money; chronic disease is very, very expensive."

"That's enough," Charlie warned her. "What's the next question, Frank?"

"You bastard." He studied Miranda critically. "You're a doctor. Do you think he could have done that to himself somehow?"

"Suicide, Frank?" It didn't ring true to Charlie.

"Let the lady answer," Frank snapped.

"I wish you'd both stop it." Miranda's voice was weary. "Sam Elgin was a drug salesman. He carried a lot of pharmaceuticals. He mentioned he'd been taking Actifeds for his cold—he's had a cold—and there's a lot of drugs he carries regularly. I suppose he could have got a bad reaction or had an allergy. Drug salesmen are usually pretty careful about drugs, or they don't stay drug salesmen long."

"What do you think happened?" Frank demanded.

"That's three questions." Charlie took Miranda's arm, preparing to take her back to the clinic.

"One thing," Frank said desperately. "When did you see him last?"

"Look, Lieutenant." Charlie stopped her. "Dr. Trobridge is involved in civil litigation, and she is not at liberty to discuss any part of her work associated with the clinic."

But Miranda paid no attention to Charlie's tightening grip on her arm. "I saw Sam Elgin this morning. Sam and some of the other salesmen were having doughnuts and coffee with our staff."

"Was he having doughnuts and coffee?" Frank was prepared to take full advantage of her willingness to talk.

Miranda frowned. "No, I don't think so. He had a cold, remember. I think he was drinking orange juice. Shelly was teasing him about it."

"Shelly?" Frank prodded.

"You're pushing your luck, Frank," Charlie said.

"All right. I'll find out on my own." Annoyed, the lieutenant waved them away. "Go on. Go on. I'll talk to you later. You'll probably both be called as witnesses at the coroner's hearing."

"I have a patient waiting," Miranda whispered to Charlie as they stepped onto the asphalt of the parking lot.

"Let her wait a little longer," Charlie said, very tense now.

"What's wrong?" She turned to him, genuinely puzzled. "Why wouldn't you let me talk?"

"Because you might have said something, quite by accident, that could prejudice your case. You hired me, remember? I'm the one who knows about law. Pay attention to me."

The lines in her face deepened. "But this has nothing to do with the Weed business." Her voice rose as she spoke.

"Until that case is settled, everything you do has something to do with the Weed business." He took a deep breath, steadying himself. He felt the death of Sam Elgin clinging to him like an odor. "Look, we're both upset. And that means we're in no condition to give reliable information. If you really want to help, when you get home, make a list of everything Elgin said to you recently. Not things you heard about him, only firsthand conversations."

Her expression was dubious, but she said, "If you think that's best—"

"I do," he said. "And next time, pay attention to what I tell you. That's what you're paying me for."

"Yes, sir. Is there anything else, sir? Do I have to get your permission to leave the room, sir?" Her sarcasm faded as she vented it. "I didn't mean that."

He nodded, smiling, and saw her rigid face soften. "Okay. You're right. Go take care of your patient."

Rufus was waiting for his evening walk when Charlie finally got home. Eagerly he wagged his tail, making appealing noises.

"Okay, in a minute." Charlie put aside his zipper case

and coat before kneeling to ruffle Rufus's coat. "It's been a rotten day, and I need a breather." He went to his bedroom, glad to take off the clothes that felt fetid. On impulse he hung the suit in Lois' closet, feeling slight regret at its emptiness. But Lois was Janos Zylis' wife now, and would not care that her old closet held a contaminated suit. Did she like her Hungarian physicist better than she had liked her Indian? He closed off the question as he changed clothes.

It was foggy, and the sound of diaphones drifted with the night. Charlie remembered his first trip to the Iron River, deep in the Canadian wilderness; there had been fog there, too, but no familiar bleat as he had known in Vallejo. For a time he had felt disoriented until he had realized there were no foghorns in that somber fastness, for the ocean was more than a thousand miles away. He laughed at himself and his memory.

Rufus pulled urgently at the leash as they went from Lake to California Street. Charlie let him tug, thinking it was unfair to keep dogs in the city with nothing but cement, asphalt, and houses. What Rufus wanted was the wild freedom he had been born to.

At Yuri Lanoff's grocery Rufus stopped expectantly, knowing that his master would pick up a few things for supper and something extra for him. He sat obediently while Charlie went inside.

"You're late," the old Russian grumbled as Charlie brought an armful of items to the check stand.

"The fortunes of war," Charlie told him.

But the sturdy old man had not finished complaining. "That's the trouble. No one has any consideration of time anymore. Everything is rush, rush. Then they are all angry because of the rush. So they fight. Eh! If we go slowly," he said, drawing out the words in illustration, "then there is time for everything, for everyone."

Charlie nodded, keeping his thoughts to himself. Perhaps, if Sam Elgin had rushed, he might not have died. . . .

"There's your change. Money and hurry, what a mess it has brought us to." He handed Charlie his bag of groceries. "What am I but a tired old Russian, that is what you are thinking, you Cossack. But we old men, we know things."

Charlie thought of his grandfather and did not contradict.

Shoving Charlie ahead of him, Yuri Lanoff went to the door. "You're the last one, you clever lawyer who worries too much. I am tired. I am going home." As soon as Charlie was out, he locked the door, turned out the light, and went slowly through the familiar darkness to the stairs that led to the flat above the store and his ancient, rotund, comfortable wife.

At home Charlie made his supper and dutifully put Beethoven on the turntable. Lois had loved it, so he had made a determined effort to enjoy the sonorous music. But the morose, formal brooks and well-ordered storms were not part of him, and the music eluded him. Only once had the wilderness of the concert hall rung true, and that had been the wild, lorn *Tapiola* of Sibelius. Lois had told him that Sibelius was second-rate and self-indulgent.

When the *Pastoral* came to an end, he did not put on another record.

Sam Elgin's death rankled, coming so close to Miranda. Of course it was coincidence, but Charlie did not believe in coincidence. "It's wrong," he said to the white brick fireplace. "Damn it, it's wrong."

Later, the dishes done and the flat quiet, he sat down with the folders Miranda had given him spread about his circular oak table. Rufus lay at his feet, head on paws, his eyes half shut. Occasionally Charlie would rub his head as he went carefully through the material, making notes. Once he chuckled and made a memo for Alex. Amid the various records, he found that some of Sparky Weed's L-dopa came from the Mayling drug company. "I don't know what good it'll do him," he remarked to Rufus, "but he might make some sense of it."

Wednesday

THE MORNING BEGAN with a persistent drizzle. Charlie wrinkled his nose at the smell of wet wool which pervaded the offices of Ogilvie, Tallant & Moon when he arrived shortly after nine. Frowning, he added his coat to the others, noticing that Willis Ogilvie was actually in the office for a change; his Savile Row overcoat steamed gently beside Charlie's from Sears.

Lydia caught Charlie's attention. "A Mr. Malton called you earlier. He will call back. The Davids want to see you—more community property trouble, apparently. They're both hopping mad, as usual. And the Department of Public Works is fulminating about that suit you're handling for the Guttierrez family. Also, Lieutenant Shirer will call you sometime around noon."

"It sounds wonderful," Charlie said, taking the slips of paper Lydia handed to him. "And how are you?"

She smiled, and her serene face came alive. "I'm fine," she announced. "Morgan Studevant—the new associate, remember?—arrived this morning. All I need is a raise to make it perfect."

"Okay," Charlie told her, wondering what Morgan Studevant looked like. "I'll do what I can. You don't have to hint."

"Your first appointment is in ten minutes. You've got time for coffee."

"No thanks. I can't taste much with this damn cold."

"Cold? You do sound a little funny," she conceded.

"I got it at Point Reyes on Saturday."

"Are you taking anything for it?" She seemed only a little worried.

"Miranda gave me some pills. She said they're the best stuff around, but they feel about as effective as aspirin."

Lydia motioned for him to wait while she rummaged in her purse. Finally she emerged with a couple of pills in her hand. "Try these. I use them."

"What are they?" Suspicious, Charlie hesitated.

"Good old over-the-counter Dristan. Go ahead, they'll clear you up in no time." With a wide smile she pressed the pills into Charlie's hand. "Now, you'll want to call Malton before your first appointment."

"Do I know Malton?" The courtesy coffee urn steamed pleasantly on the far side of the room. Charlie filled a styrofoam cup, waiting for a moment before gulping down the pills.

"He's the opposition on the malpractice case. Hammil and Ward."

"I thought his name was Markum." He shrugged. "Is he in his office?"

"The number is on the phone card, Mr. Moon."

He accepted her sharpness with a smile. "I'm not functioning well, Lydia. Maybe the pills will help." He remembered the notes in his zipper case. "Is Alex in yet?"

"In and out again. He's in court today."

"Okay." He pulled the memo from his other notes. "Give him this when he comes in, will you? You're very good." That saved him thanking her.

"So this is the other one," said a voice in the hallway in the tone of a livestock dealer sizing up a herd of cattle.

Charlie gagged on the last of his coffee. "Morgan

Studevant?" he asked with a deep sense of certainty. The neat young woman in the tailored pant suit could not be anyone else.

Lydia, grinning merrily, introduced them. "Ms. Studevant, this is Charles S. Moon. You'll be working together."

Charlie held out his hand. "Hello, Ms. Studevant." He could tell by her frozen smile that his reaction to her had been noticed and filed as hostile.

She took the hand in a firm grip. "Hello, Mr. Moon. I understand you're the token minority."

Charlie could feel her fright in her hand. "Just like you," he countered, wondering what this tall, efficient woman would say next. He wished he could start over, introduce himself again, choose what he would say before he said it.

"Oh, no. They knew what they were getting when they hired you. Professor Ruxton told me how to get around Willis Ogilvie. You should have heard my interview. And it's too late now for him to change his mind." She gave Charlie a wide professional grin. "If he tried to fire me, I'd sue the pants off all of you. It'd be worth it."

"I'm not complaining," Charlie said, liking her courage even as his hackles rose. He wondered if she was truly capable or merely audacious.

"I graduated top of my class at Boalt. Did you?" Her eyes waited, guarded.

"No. Second in my class at McGeorge." So long as they were trading credentials, he added, "The top of my class went to Washington last year."

"Why didn't you go to Washington, Mr. Moon? Ashamed?"

"Dual citizenship makes such things ticklish, Ms. Studevant." He wanted to avoid further mistakes with her. "Excuse me. I have some calls to make."

"Giving up?" she asked as she stood aside.

He made no answer and was almost at the door to his office when Willis Ogilvie surged out of his door, moving as inexorably as the ocean. "There you are," he cried in the manner of one discovering a celebrity in a supermarket.

"Good morning, Willis," Charlie said reluctantly. When Willis Ogilvie went expansive, it was a dangerous sign.

"I see you have met Ms. Studevant," he said with a casual gesture suggesting that she was a pleasant surprise. "She's going to make one hell of a lawyer when she gets that tongue of hers going in the right direction." He took a cigarette from his gold monogrammed case. "She reminds me a little of you when you first started working with us. Touchy. Very touchy, but gifted."

"That was five years ago, Willis," Charlie reminded him. "Don't worry, I'm not going to hassle Ms. Studevant. If she had guts enough to stick it out at Boalt, she has my respect. Now, what's on your mind, Willis?"

"I've been wanting to talk to you, Charlie, you know, catch up on what you're doing. I worry about the image of the firm. I want us all to put our energies in the places where they will do the most good. So I keep in touch," he declared, firmly guiding Charlie into his own office.

Stepping behind his desk, Charlie watched Willis take a turn about the room. When the older man came to rest by the bookcases, he said, "Okay, Willis, what's this all about?"

"You're handling the Guttierrez case, aren't you? Lamentable business, truly lamentable. It should never have happened." He shook his heavy head and rumbled disapproval.

"What about it?" Charlie's eyes were slits now, and the angles of his face were more acute. He stifled a sneeze.

"I had a call from the mayor's office this morning. They want the case dropped. It would be a personal favor. But don't misunderstand me," he went on, an admonishing finger raised. "It is our duty as attorneys to see that justice is done. I've assured him of the firm's co-operation. Justice must come first. Let me put it to you this way, Charles, my boy"—Charlie winced—"don't take it into court unless you're dead certain you can win. This one counts. Because the whole case stinks to high heaven." Then he gave an appreciative chuckle. "It *is* a sewer in question, isn't it? No wonder it stinks. No wonder."

"Are you saying that political pressure is being used on you?" He shook his head. "In the Guttierrez case?"

"That is a crass phrase, Charlie. Crass, but quite apt." Suddenly his lavish manner was gone. "See here, Charlie. The reason we're the firm we are is that we know when to fight and when to quit. Don't go riding off on your white horse solely on principle. It won't do. Now, I know we could settle the Guttierrez case out of court, very quickly, very quietly. But if you take it any farther, it must turn into an all-out fight. And if you fight them, you must win. Losing is bad politics. And it's bad press for the firm."

"Do you want me to drop or settle the case then?" Charlie asked, a dangerous hush in his voice.

"Nothing like that. If you know you can win. Otherwise, think it over. We can settle." He rounded on Charlie, the lawyer-politician once more. "You must remember, we're in the public eye. What we do carries weight, Charlie, a lot of weight. It's wise to use that weight with circumspection. And you have another delicate matter to attend to, don't you?"

"You mean Dr. Trobridge."

"Malpractice is a very tricky question, Charlie. It's hard to handle."

"I'll manage."

"I hope you will." He bellied for the door, then turned theatrically. "Keep our talk in mind. Think about it." He pulled the door wide.

"Wait a minute," Charlie said. "I've got to talk to *you* about something."

Willis hung on the door. "Oh?" He had lost his momentum.

"Lydia and the secretaries deserve a raise. I told them I'd talk it over with you."

"Raises? They're well paid."

"I didn't say they weren't. But they work hard, and you know what's been happening to prices. It's only fair, Willis." Charlie turned one hand up in placation.

Willis sniffed, a frown settling onto his craggy face. "We've just taken on Studevant, you know. How much do they want?"

"Hundred fifty."

His face grew rosy. "Out of the question."

"Hundred?"

There was a pause as Willis Ogilvie thought it over. "I tell you what, Charlie: you win the Guttierrez case and get to the bottom of this malpractice suit, and they'll get their raises. It's up to you." With that he was gone.

"Thanks for nothing," Charlie said to the closed door, knowing that Willis would be sure Lydia knew the conditions of her raise before noon. He sat down, thinking. He was aware that Ogilvie thrived on politics and that king-making was his favorite hobby. He wondered what the old fox was up to now. He made a note to himself to call the Guttierrez family later in the day. He'd have to step up the action there.

The intercom on the desk buzzed, and a travesty of Lydia's voice said, "A Mr. Malton to speak to you."

"He's in a hurry. Good. Maybe he'll try to rush us," Charlie remarked as he reached for the phone. "Okay. Put him through."

"Is this Moon?" It was a young, yapping voice that revealed the man's immaturity. He bit the words out as if fighting each syllable.

"Speaking."

"This is James Malton of Hammil and Ward."

Charlie decided on the supercivilized approach. "How do you do," he said gravely. "May I help you, Mr. Malton?"

"You can stop this farting around, Moon. You can gather your evidence, if you can find any, and get this matter into court. No delays, no courtesies."

"All in due time, Mr. Malton. We have thirty days to respond, as I am sure you are aware." As he spoke, Charlie amused himself with imagining how Willis Ogilvie would handle the same call.

Malton's tone got scrappier. "Now see here, Moon. My clients have lost a beloved child, their only son. He died through the criminal misjudgment of your client—"

"First, that hasn't been proved, Mr. Malton, and second, this is a civil matter, not a criminal one." Charlie waited for the next salvo.

The aggressive voice was triumphant. "Hasn't it been proved? You haven't got the results of the autopsy. It seems your strategy misfired, Moon. And that puts your client right in the middle of the hot plate."

"What were the results, Mr. Malton?" Charlie asked with careful sangfroid.

"That boy didn't have enough L-dopa in him to fill an eyedropper, Moon. Your client gave him those 'sample drugs,' didn't she?" His mockery made the words vitriolic. "If the case looks strong enough, we'll press for criminal prosecution. It would be manslaughter at the least."

"I see," said Charlie, suddenly thoughtful.

"Come on, Moon. Save yourself and that doctor a lot of pain. You know the procedure. The Weeds aren't unreasonable people. We could have this whole thing settled, no hard feelings, in a couple of months if you'd let your client's insurance company come to terms with the Weeds."

"Perhaps I could if my client had private malpractice insurance and if she were guilty. But she is not guilty, and her salary from the clinic, as I am sure you know, is slightly more than eighteen thousand a year. And I am also sure you know that all the insurance for the clinic doctors is covered by the Harrowleigh Foundation itself. You are aware of that, aren't you?" The false good humor of his voice fooled neither man.

There was a slight hesitation before James Malton said, "I thought they had private insurance as well."

"Those with their own practices do, of course, but not the doctors like Dr. Trobridge who work solely at the clinic."

"But that doesn't change things," Malton insisted, getting back on the track.

"Doesn't it? Why don't you ask the Weeds? And the next time you try to bulldoze me, Malton," Charlie went on, giving his temper free rein, "get your facts straight before you try." He hung up and buzzed Lydia.

"Yes?" she said crisply. Charlie knew from her tone that she had clients in the outer office. "What is it, Mr. Moon?"

"The next time that ass calls, tell him I've gone back to the reservation."

"I'd be happy to," she said with more feeling than usual.

"What's the matter? Did he get your back up, too?"

"He called me a broad and a chick." Then she broke the connection.

Charlie sighed and glanced at his calendar. Noel Davis was due in fifteen minutes, and he knew he should spend the time between figuring out how to talk the man out of taking his hopeless case to court. But the autopsy report Malton mentioned bothered him. If it were true, it would mean trouble. He coughed experimentally and called the coroner.

"Hello, Ms. March. This is Charles Moon," he began with more cordiality than he felt. "I understand the report on the Weed boy's autopsy is ready. Would you mind giving me the results?"

"Your hunch backfired," the woman told him with grim satisfaction. "I'll connect you with Dr. Coners, and he'll give you the details."

"I'd appreciate it," said Charlie, not meaning it.

"Charlie? Pete Coners here. You're defending that Trobridge dame?"

The voice was rough and amused.

"She's my client, yes."

He gave a nasty chuckle. "Well, you bought it this time, my friend. That kid's drug level wasn't high enough to handle a damn thing. . . ." There was a pause. "Do you know what I think?"

"Tell me," said Charlie, knowing there was no way to stop him.

"I think your gal made up her mind that the kid was too sick to make it and took a hand herself."

"Why do you think that?" Charlie asked for form's sake.

"Well, first off, the kid was sick. Most kids die from it; Parkinson's, once it starts downhill, gets pretty ugly."

"What makes you think he was that far gone?" He picked up his pen and tapped it restlessly.

"Well, from what I saw, he wasn't in very good shape. And I saw the parents. You know how parents are—they hang onto any hope they can long after it's too late. They said that he was degenerating and that they knew he couldn't last very much longer. The parents admitted it, Charlie."

"Did they?" Charlie mused, making a note to himself to check this out.

"And if the kid had got the amount of L-dopa they say he had, he should have been saturated with it. I'd give it up, Charlie. You take this into court, and you are gonna get creamed. Hell, I'd have to say this on the stand, and you know what that means."

"Was there anything in the body that shouldn't be there?" Charlie said. He was prepared to scribble the answer.

"Such as?"

"Oh, I don't know. Other drugs. Signs of another disease that might have knocked out the L-dopa?"

"Not that I could find," Pete Coners said, becoming cool.

"What about the L-dopa? Does it have that limited a life? Could it have gone bad? Was there something that might have made it less effective?"

"Look, every drug has an expiration date. But that's marked on the packages. If you bother to look. Maybe the batch wasn't control-tested," he went on sarcastically. "But the FDA takes care of that. Maybe it got contaminated around the house. Maybe it got over a hundred and twenty degrees in the kid's pocket, and that did it in. Maybe it was counterfeit. Maybe they packaged the wrong drug by mistake. Come on, Charlie. You're way out on a limb."

"Look, Pete, I know this is a bad one. That's why I have to ask questions like this—and you know it." He hoped this last would bring Pete to his side.

"Sure," he said grudgingly.

"Will you do me a couple of favors, Pete?" Charlie asked, pushing his luck.

"What are they?" Resignation crept into his tone.

"First, keep an eye out for any other Parkinson's fatality and see if you can make a comparison with the Weed boy. And send me over a complete report on everything you found on the body, no matter how trivial."

"All right, Charlie. But I think you've got your head up your ass this time."

"Probably. But in this case, you said it yourself, I've got to find everything that there is to find. Malpractice is a bad thing."

Pete Coners made a contemptuous snort. "You didn't have to take the case, Charlie. You should have turned her down."

"Thanks for your concern. I'll want that report as soon as possible."

"Sure," Coners growled. Then, playing tit for tat, "I've

got a couple of questions myself, Charlie," he said, more briskly than before.

Charlie nodded fatalistically. "What is it, Pete?"

"Frank Shirer says you found the body we got in last night. That drug salesman?"

"What about him?" He felt a prickle along his spine.

"How did he strike you?"

Charlie shifted uneasily in his chair, feeling the sense of death once more. "Hideous," he said with great precision.

"Yeah. The widow went to pieces when we brought her in to identify him."

"I can imagine," Charlie said, remembering the body.

"You told Frank Shirer that it looked like a beating."

"I did." Charlie felt that nagging doubt again. "What killed him? Do you know yet?"

"We're into preliminaries. The widow wants the body as soon as possible. It looks like he'd had a massive dose of anticoagulants."

"Shit." Charlie put his hand to his eyes.

"Yeah. I wouldn't want to die like that. Well, I'll do what I can on the Weed kid."

"Okay. Thanks. I'll talk to you later." He hung up carefully. What if Pete was right and there had been something wrong with the drug? He wanted to go over the files again, looking for more on the L-dopa. Or perhaps he should talk to the pharmacist who made up the prescriptions for the family. If Malton had overlooked that possibility—and Charlie was sure he had—then they might have an edge in court. Miranda could then file countersuit against the drug company, and the Weeds would have another complaint to act on.

Sam Elgin's livid body rose unbidden into his thoughts. "I don't like it," Charlie muttered. Damn it, it was too pat. The deaths could be tied together, but he didn't know how. Two deaths, neither of which should have happened. Sparky Weed, Sam Elgin, they should not have died.

He rose and went to the window where spring had lost itself in a dreary mizzle. It was a cold gray day when San Francisco blended with the ocean and Bay. He sneezed twice, cursing softly; he could not afford to have a cold now.

Then there was a knock at the door, and Charlie admitted Noel Davis.

It was early afternoon before Charlie called the clinic, and he waited almost five minutes before his call reached Miranda.

"Yes? Dr. Trobridge. May I help you." She sounded worn-out, beaten.

"Charlie here, Miranda."

"What do you want?" she asked listlessly.

"Trouble?" He was too fatigued to imbue his tone with concern.

"Nothing that getting the cops out of here wouldn't cure. They've been in and out of the clinic most of the afternoon. About Sam Elgin."

Of course, Charlie told himself. And that investigation would be certain to overlap his own. Vigorously he shoved the worry aside. "Look, Miranda," he said, wishing he could talk to her in person, "do you have any of the batch of L-dopa you gave Sparky? Are there a couple of packs left around anywhere? Any more samples from the same drug lot?"

"I don't know. I guess so. We've only got four other Parkinson's patients, and they don't usually come in this time of the month. Why? What do you want?"

"Will you put some aside for me? I'll come by after work."

"I don't know, Charlie. We like to save the samples for our patients. . . ."

"Miranda, trust me, will you? Do as I say? If I find out anything, I'll let you know. But either you're lying to me about your treatment and you did let that boy die, or there was something the matter with the medication, or the parents are implicated in his death."

She resisted. "Sparky took care of his pills himself. His folks were too freaky about the disease. Herr Professor despises anything that isn't perfect."

"Then maybe he got confused. Maybe he held back the boy's medication." It was a long shot.

"After eighteen months? It doesn't make sense, Charlie."

"Then there was a foul-up at the clinic and he was given the wrong medication by mistake."

"Oh, come off it, Charlie," she said as if talking to a frightened patient. "This is a private clinic, remember. We aren't the anonymous big organization. We keep track of our people, and we know what's happening to them."

Charlie cut in. "Do as I say, okay, Miranda? I'll be there a little after six. I want those samples if you can find them." As he spoke, he scribbled the appointment on his calendar.

"I have a staff meeting." She was distant again, reserved.

"Miranda, I can't do this alone," he said, his pencil ripping the calendar.

"Charlie. . . ."

"This might be the only way out for you. The only way. Now, will you have those packets ready for me?"

"After six," she said, capitulating. "I'll see you." Then she hung up.

Charlie tapped the receiver on his palm before returning it to its cradle.

There was a brisk knock on the door, and Alex Tallant appeared. Today he was wearing browns and a cream shirt which set off his skiing tan. "Got a minute?" he asked too casually.

Charlie had just finished taking a deposition for the Guttierrez case; it was almost four-thirty, and he was running half an hour late. "Sure," he said.

Alex came into the room slowly, some of his Eastern bounce gone. "Keep running into problems," he said by way of explanation.

"What about?"

"This Mayling business. You got any more on it?" Alex tried to sound hopeful, but it didn't work. He held up the memo Charlie had left for him. "Is this all? Did you find out anything more?"

"Not yet." When this was met with a deep scowl, he asked, "What's the matter, Alex? Why do you want me to do your legwork for you? Why not ask Studevant to do some of that? That's why we hired her."

"Oh, no. Don't blame me. Willis hired her." He leaned against the bookcase with practiced ease. "She's a clever girl. Too clever."

Charlie lifted his brows. "Why not give her a chance, Alex? She sounds okay," he said, thinking of his run-in with her.

"Let's forget her. I need help on the Mayling estate. I'm not using just you, Charlie. I've got Willis asking questions, too. It's a damn crazy case. There's no answer. The family doesn't know anything. The bank doesn't know anything. The corporation doesn't know anything. And the distributor refuses to hand over some of their records. Smells rotten, but I can't find anything. It's a mess." He was upset enough to ram his fists into his pockets, ruining the line of his suit. Today his tie was Italian silk foulard, just the right width.

"What are you looking for?" Charlie asked reasonably. He felt his hunch growing again and knew that Alex was on to something very big.

"I don't quite know; that's the trouble. Money's missing, no reason. Other money's around that shouldn't be, no reason. The records don't account for it, but Jared Mayling kept a private set of books, and they're honest, as far as we can tell. But the last set is missing, and they're the one place we might find some answers." He ticked off on his fingers each unsolved element of the probate, holding out his hand to Charlie. "That's more questions than I like in a case. This is estate work, not fraud."

"You hope," Charlie said as he gathered up a handful of pencils and his zipper case. "I don't have anything more for you, Alex. I still think you ought to put Studevant on it." He started for the door. "I've got to get down to the Harrowleigh Clinic, and then I'm going home." For emphasis, Charlie looked at his watch.

Alex was not to be put off. "You know, that watch—always admired it. Loloma's work, isn't it? Saw some of his things at Tiffany's. Beautiful."

"Yes, it's Loloma," Charlie said.

"Expensive," Alex mused. "But I guess he gave you a discount." He smiled, his mind at rest.

"Why should I get a discount?" Charlie asked, pausing in his exit.

"Well," Alex said, pleasingly awkward, "you're both Indians. . . ."

"Does a Norwegian give an Italian a discount because they're both Europeans?"

"I only thought. . . ."

Charlie bristled, saying brusquely, "I don't even know the man. He's a Hopi and I'm Ojibwa, entirely different groups: the languages have different roots."

"All right, all right," Alex said, his sensibilities wounded.

Charlie held the door open. "It's late."

Alex stopped and fingered his fashionable mustache. "Charlie, there's something wrong with the Mayling estate. I don't know what it is, and I can't find it. But someone has to know. Keep your ears open, will you, Charlie?"

So that was what Alex had been fishing for. Charlie nodded, resigned. "Okay, Alex. Anything else?"

Alex gave him the quick, appreciative smile that had swung juries. "Thanks. You don't know how much I appreciate this. If there's anything I can do for you, Charlie, you tell me." He slipped past Charlie, striding down the hall to his own office.

At the front desk Lydia stopped Charlie with, "What about the papers for Mr. Davis?"

"Shit." He grimaced. "He did want them today, didn't he? I completely forgot."

"At five," she confirmed with a glance at her record book.

He shook his head. "No way. Not even if I had the time." He pulled his overcoat from the closet. "Where's Studevant? She can do them up for me, can't she?"

Lydia made a neutral gesture. "I'll ask her."

While Lydia buzzed the clerk's office, Charlie asked, "Say, do you have any more of those cold pills?"

"Yes. Do you want a couple more?" She paused, her hand near the keyboard.

"Well, they work better than the others, and I sure as hell have to get rid of this cold."

"Just a moment," she said, then addressed the intercom. "Ms. Studevant? Mr. Moon would like you to prepare some contracts for him."

"How flattering of Mr. Moon," said the voice on the intercom.

Charlie leaned across Lydia's desk, saying, "Isn't it? I'd like the work done by this time tomorrow, please."

"I don't like your tone," Morgan Studevant said, sounding annoyed.

"I don't like yours either, Ms. Studevant. But that has nothing to do with your job. Now I've asked you once. Please come out here and get the file."

In a moment Morgan Studevant appeared, somewhat flushed but with a toothy smile pinned firmly to her mouth. "Here I am," she said defiantly.

Charlie had the file folder in his hand, but he held it for a moment. "Let's call a truce for a moment, Studevant. I've got some advice I think you better listen to." When she started to object, he said, "First, you are in an office of legal prima donnas; we don't need another one—all right? Second, you know as well as I that your position is more precarious because you're a woman. Third, it's dumb to antagonize men who can help you just because you're feeling vulnerable."

The color had drained from Morgan Studevant's face. Some of the hauteur was gone from her stance, and her hands moved uncertainly at her sides. "But I'm not second-rate," she stammered.

"No one said you were," Charlie told her. He held out his right hand, without the file. "Let's start over. I'm Charlie, Morgan. I'm glad we'll be working together."

"I won't be patronized," she said, ignoring his hand.

He dropped it. "I suppose it's useless to say I'm not patronizing you? Okay." Then, handing her the file: "Will you have this ready for me by tomorrow?"

"Certainly," she said, sure of herself again.

Charlie studied her. "That's all, Studevant." But her quick departure did not please him.

"What about Mr. Davis?" Lydia prompted him when the door to the clerk's office had slammed.

"Give Mr. Davis a call and tell him that his papers will be ready tomorrow evening. Tell him my case load caught up with me. Use that as my excuse if you have to. And make a nice apology for me, will you, please?"

Lydia handed him two pills. "And the appointment with the Widow Kendrie?"

"Alex is taking that. I'm doing legwork for him and he's going to take Elizabeth Kendrie off my hands. I'll leave him a reminder, if you like." He pictured the short, massive old woman and her hedge-clipper tongue. "And wish him the best of British luck with her."

Lydia raised her perfect brows at his chuckle.

"Never mind," he told her. "Give Mrs. Kendrie my

regrets and tell her that Mr. Tallant will be happy to take over her case."

"Certainly, Mr. Moon," Lydia said without cracking a smile.

"Exactly," he replied with a rare, wide grin.

Miranda met him in front of the clinic. She had marks like bruises under her eyes, and she walked as if her body hurt.

"Hey," Charlie said as he came up to her. His head ached, and his breath grated in his throat. He knew he should be home in bed where he could sweat the illness out of him. "What's the matter, Miranda? You've had a rough day."

She nodded but made no answer.

"Worrying is my job. You should do your work and leave mine to me."

The smile he had hoped to see didn't materialize. "Charlie, I've been fired."

"Fired? What for? This? The suit?"

"There was a conference about two hours ago, and Fritz Bjornsson told me that the Harrowleigh Foundation does not want to take the risk of my continued association. They're afraid it would entail too much public notoriety," she said, quoting. "They told me to collect my things and be prepared to leave by Friday. . . . No references. No contacts. No recommendations. Nothing." She turned away from him, unwilling and unable to face him any longer. Her shoulders were shaking.

He reached out and caught her arm, twisting her back toward him. "Fuck off, buster!" she shouted, breaking free.

This time he grabbed her, deliberately gripping tightly. He felt her flinch under his hands. "Okay, Doctor, now it's my turn. You are going to listen to me. Do you understand? Do you?" Alarmed, she nodded. "Now, first of all, the clinic can't fire you this way. If they insist on your dismissal, we'll sue them for breach of contract. Remember your contract and stick by it. Second, there is some question about the autopsy, and that means we might have more of a case than we thought. Got that? And third, if you quit now, you might as well settle out of court, because it will be virtually impossible to make a jury believe you. That has to be your greatest concern right now, Miranda. You must keep going."

"You don't know anything about it," she declared sullenly, pulling away from the pressure of his hands. He drew her close against him and felt her muscles bunch as she struggled once more to break away. "Don't give me that lawyer crap."

"Calm down."

Wrenching sideways, she lowered her head and sank her teeth into his hand. "Let go of me!"

Expertly he locked a hand into her hair and pulled. She was very still. "If you'd fight like that for yourself instead of against yourself, we'd have this whole case licked," he said conversationally. "Now, I am going to let you go and you are going to be calm and reasonable. You are not going to make a scene, and we're going to discuss your case rationally. Do you understand me?"

"Yes," she muttered through her teeth.

"Good." He let her go, stepping back and coughing gently. "Now, let's do something useful for a change: what about the L-dopa samples? Did you get them?"

"I didn't have the chance. They didn't want me near supplies." Her words were ragged, her hands shaky as she fingered her short hair.

"We'll have to get them some other way then," he said as he smoothed his overcoat. "I'll need to know what batches we're dealing with. Then we'll find out what's what."

"There's nothing wrong with the drugs," she said uneasily.

"That's for us to find out." He tore a page from his notebook in his zipper case. "You need an ally. You've got to have someone in the Harrowleigh Foundation on your side. And I know a formidable woman." He scribbled an address. "This is Elizabeth Kendrie's home address. The phone is unlisted, so don't lose this. I'll let her know about you. I want you to call her tomorrow morning and tell her what's been done. She's on the Harrowleigh Board of Directors, and unless I read her wrong, she'll raise hell for you. Tell her you need her help, that I haven't done enough for you and there's no one else you can turn to."

"Why?" She took the paper hesitantly.

"Elizabeth Kendrie likes to think she can succeed where others have failed. And sometimes she's right. Talk to her."

Miranda glanced critically at Charlie, changing the subject. "You still have that cold?"

"Yep. I'm going home to take care of it right now. Be sure you phone Mrs. Kendrie in the morning. Promise me you will."

She placed her hands together and bowed over them. "Whatever you say, Charlie," she said in mock compliance.

Charlie had been asleep nearly an hour when the phone rang. He woke angrily, his head throbbing. "Hello?" he said experimentally as he grabbed the phone. Then he cleared his throat and said it again.

"Is this Charles S. Moon, the lawyer?"

"Yes. Speaking."

"This," the man on the end of the line announced, "is Dr. Weed. Dr. Weiland Weed."

Without thinking, Charlie said, "What can I do for you, Dr. Weed?"

"Don't you realize who I am, sir?" the angry voice sputtered. "I am suing your client, sir. She killed my child."

Charlie sat up in bed, his mind clearing rapidly. "Yes. I recognize you, Dr. Weed. But I hadn't expected to hear from you. Your attorney should have advised you not to contact me personally without his presence."

"Of course he did; of course he did. But I want you to know about that woman, Mr. Moon. She is a killer. And this isn't the first time. Oh, no. She has killed before, wantonly. She killed that other woman, that Mrs. Margolis. And she killed Chisholm the same way. You can't defend her, Mr. Moon. It isn't humane to defend a monster like that."

"Dr. Weed," Charlie began gently, "it isn't wise for you to talk to me this way. Believe me, you are prejudicing yourself and your case. I would advise you to hang up."

"No more of your legal fripperies, sir. I have talked to Dr. Bjornsson, and he agrees with me that this Trobridge woman is to blame. He told me himself that she had murdered that other unfortunate patient of hers."

"Did he?" Charlie asked, his spine prickling. "Now, I wonder why."

"Because he is concerned, sir. Because he cares about the reputation of his clinic. He knows that woman is guilty of a criminal act. He is shamed by it. And you should be shamed, too."

"Dr. Bjornsson is a fool to discuss this matter until it is settled. It's irresponsible, for you as well as Dr. Trobridge. I suggest you do not repeat his remarks." Charlie looked forward to a few words with Fritz Bjornsson in the morning.

"He at least cares for the dead. But you are callous, sir."

"Being shamed or callous won't bring your boy back, Dr. Weed." He kept his voice level, neutral.

"No," he snapped. "But you should be willing to give up this hopeless case. What that woman did is murder, sir. Would you defend a murderess?"

"Certainly," Charlie said urbanely. "Everyone is legally entitled to defense to the limits of the law. I have done so. And I have won, Dr. Weed."

"You are a disgrace to your profession!" the man thundered at him. "Do you hear me? A disgrace!"

"I hear you." Charlie was growling tired of Weiland Weed's histrionics.

"I shall tell Dr. Bjornsson of your attitude."

"You don't need to do that, Dr. Weed," Charlie said sweetly. "I'll tell him myself. Be sure of that."

"Impudent Chinese!" Dr. Weed shouted.

Stung, Charlie replied, "I'm an Indian, Dr. Weed. The S. in my name stands for Spotted. I am an Ojibwa witch doctor. And don't you forget it."

But Dr. Weiland Weed had already hung up.

II

March–April

Thursday

CHARLIE'S ZIPPER CASE sailed across his office, landing on his desk with a loud report. Disgusted, Charlie slammed the door behind him, leaning on it as if to hold the world out. "I wasted the whole bloody morning," he announced to the air. "That damn fool Taverner's got for a lawyer. . . ." Angrily he flung himself around the desk and into his chair, where he sat drumming his fingers on the padded arms. He coughed suddenly, sitting forward. His cold was no better.

"Lydia," he said to the intercom when his throat was clear, "is Studevant available? I need more information on copyright infringement of lithographs."

"She's in her office, Mr. Moon."

"Send her in, will you, please?"

Lydia hesitated. "Lieutenant Shirer just arrived. He wants to see you."

"Okay. I'll talk to Studevant when he's gone. You might tell her what I said. Copyright infringement, particularly of lithographs. Taverner's pirating that print, or I'm a Dutchman." He gave a single ironic laugh.

"All right, Mr. Moon," she said dubiously. "But Mrs. Kendrie will be here to see you in thirty minutes."

"Why?" he asked, feeling very tired.

"She wants to talk to you about Dr. Trobridge. She was very emphatic about seeing you today."

Charlie thought that Elizabeth Kendrie was emphatic about everything; he realized he should have anticipated this interview with Elizabeth Kendrie. If Miranda had called her—and he was sure she had—it was inevitable that Mrs. Kendrie would discuss the case with Charlie before she lent her support to Miranda since it was her grant that augmented Miranda's salary. He would have to see her; he owed her an explanation. "Okay. Let me know when she arrives."

"Of course."

"And just out of curiosity, do I have any more surprise appointments this afternoon?" The last thing he wanted was another client. He hoped that the Guttierrez family had calmed down.

"No. That's all, Mr. Moon."

"Amazing," Charlie said dryly. "I'll see Lieutenant Shirer."

In a few moments Frank Shirer knocked at the door and came in without waiting for Charlie to open it. He looked around expectantly. "How's it going, Charlie? Had a rough day?"

"It's going badly. What can I do for you, Frank?" He noticed with some satisfaction that Frank Shirer was haggard, his clothes slightly rumpled as if he had slept in them, and his chin was showing a blue haze of unshaved beard.

"It's about this Elgin thing." Shirer sank into one of the chairs. "God, it feels good to sit down. I've been on my feet all morning. We've been running all the other salesmen down in an effort to find out if they've had similar problems. You know, bad reactions to drugs. We also want to find out how Elgin managed to take that kind of overdose of anticoagulants."

Anticoagulants? Was that it? "Any luck?"

Shirer shook his head. "Just when we think we've got something, poof! no good. Three of the salesmen confirm the man's depression. One of them, Ed Shelly, said he recommended Elgin take some time off and see a shrink.

But Elgin couldn't afford that. Your doctor friend is right—those diseases cost a lot of money. Elgin was in hock to his eyeballs."

"Life insurance?" Charlie ventured.

"Maybe. The autopsy was inconclusive, nowhere near enough indications of suicide for an insurance company, and no certain indication of violence, either, which could mean double indemnity. He had quite a lot of insurance." He rubbed his forehead, and opened his hand to show how puzzled he was.

Charlie studied Frank Shirer's tired face. "Okay, why doesn't it make sense? The man was in debt, depressed, in need of money. Why not take an overdose of drugs and let the insurance money pay for the kid?"

"Look, Charlie. He had lots of drugs in his case. If he wanted to die, there were better ways than the one he took. He could have sold his drugs to street dealers. He didn't have to die, and he didn't have to die that way. Hell, he could have wiped himself out in a couple of minutes."

"Then you'd know it was suicide. No insurance."

"Just whose side are you on?" Frank Shirer was suspicious. He slewed around in the chair, fixing a penetrating look at Charlie. "Are you so sure it's suicide? Is there something you aren't telling me?"

"No." Charlie frowned down at the desk. "It's not that simple." He looked over at the policeman. "I don't know a damn thing. I was only wishing I could get this Elgin thing out of the way. It's cluttering up my case."

"Well," Shirer said, softening. "Clutter or no clutter, I'm going to need you for a formal statement soon. Can you come down to the Hall of Justice tomorrow? Say, around one? It won't take long."

Charlie glanced at his desk calendar. "I don't know. I've got a deposition at eleven, and you know how they go. I could be out of here in half an hour, or I could be stuck for the whole afternoon. Do you want me to give you a call when I'm through?"

"That'd be fine."

"Is there anything special you want? Do you need anything other than a record of how I found the body and what I saw? Will a description do?"

Shirer moved uncomfortably. "That should do it." He paused, then went on: "I found out about the Trobridge woman. Her case wouldn't have anything to do with this, would it? I mean, they both have to do with drugs. There's no connection, is there?"

"No," Charlie said, scowling. "It's just a coincidence." But putting it that way, he didn't like the coincidence any more than Frank Shirer did.

"I didn't think there was any more to it. But you know how bad a thing like this can look. Anything with drugs is real bad right now." He got out of the chair reluctantly, not wanting to give up his rest. "We can't keep it out of the press, but we can try to play it down. We don't want to prejudice your case if we can help it, but well, you know the media." He gestured to show how his hands were tied.

"Thanks." For a moment Charlie drummed his pencil on the desk as anger clouded his face. Then abruptly he stopped and looked up. "Thanks, Frank. I appreciate your coming by. We'll just have to last this out."

"Too bad Elgin had to die like that." At the door Frank Shirer turned back. "You know . . . we found his car parked a block away. It's one of the most unsatisfying aspects of the case. If he'd found a place in the lot next to the clinic, he might have lived long enough to tell us what happened to him. As it is. . . ." He left off with a shrug. "I'll see you some time tomorrow afternoon, Charlie."

"Okay." He added, "You can go out the back way if you'd rather."

"Cops spoil the tone of the place?" Frank Shirer's amiable expression froze as he waited for his answer.

"Of course. You also get to the parking lot faster the back way. Take your choice, though." Charlie was relieved when the stiffness left Shirer's face.

But when the door had closed behind the lieutenant, Charlie cursed quietly and thoroughly before he called the Harrowleigh Clinic. "Dr. Miranda Trobridge, please," he said to the receptionist who worked the switchboard.

"Dr. Trobridge is not available."

"This is her attorney calling. Please connect me." He waited a moment, and when nothing happened: "If you refuse to connect me, I'll be down there in person."

"Just a moment, please," the receptionist said in the standard telephone-operator-imitation-robot voice, the words falling on the phone like ice cubes.

"Hello, Charlie," Miranda's tired voice said when the call was put through.

"Are you with a patient? Can you talk?"

"I can talk. What is it?"

"Lieutenant Shirer was just here. We might find ourselves with some slop-over from the Elgin case. He warned me that the press might give you some trouble. Watch out if they come around."

"The press, the staff, Dr. Bjornsson all give me trouble. Was that all you called me for?" She sounded more tired than angry.

"Then there's been trouble already? Why didn't you call me?"

"That is a really dumb question," she said, annoyed. "I've been busy. I've had patients all day. I can't run to you every time someone makes a remark I don't like. Be sensible, Charlie."

"Okay," Charlie said as he quickly reordered his thoughts. "If you're picking up static there, don't let it hassle you if you can help it. Keep calm; don't talk about either the Elgin case or your own. Tell anyone who persists to give me a call."

"Does that include Channel Five?" She made her voice a mewing, little-girl voice. "I could have fooled them, you know."

"About what? What were they doing there?"

"Well, they were here to take some pictures of the place Sam Elgin's body was found, but they stopped in at the clinic, too, since Elgin had been here, and one of the staff was kind enough to mention my little case to them. The reporter said he'd never take a pretty girl like me for a bad doctor."

"He was trying to provoke you; he wanted to shock a response out of you. You don't have to take that crap." Charlie held the broken end of his pencil and stared at it.

"Who's going to stop them? You?"

"That's my job. Now, look, you take the rest of the day off. Go home. Don't answer the phone. If you've got friends you can stay with tonight, go to them. I won't have this case turning into a circus."

"Dr. Bjornsson would still like to dismiss me."

"He can't do it. Not unless it is proved that you did indeed knowingly contribute to the death of that child, which you say you did not. I'll make sure Elizabeth Kendrie sets him straight on that point."

The door opened, and Morgan Studevant came into the room, one brow raised. Charlie motioned her to sit down.

"*If* she agrees to help," Miranda was saying. "She didn't sound very inclined to when I called her earlier."

"She's coming in this afternoon. I'll give her the run-down and let her make up her own mind."

"Shall I come back later, Mr. Moon?" Morgan asked.

"No, wait. I won't be much longer," Charlie told her. Then, to Miranda: "Look, you come by the office tomorrow evening, and we'll work everything out with Mrs. Kendrie then. In the meantime, do as I tell you and get the hell out of there. Don't talk to anyone. Understand?"

"I wish this whole thing was over," Miranda muttered.

"Miranda, you can't give in now."

"No, I suppose I can't. . . . I'll see you tomorrow, Charlie."

When Charlie had hung up, he turned his eyes on Morgan. She was dressed with well-tailored care in a houndstooth pantsuit, and except for her too-rigid posture, she appeared confident and at ease.

"You look harried," she said.

"I am harried," he said, forcing his mind away from Miranda. "I need information on—"

"Copyright infringement, particularly concerning lithographs," she finished for him. "What's the matter? Who's getting his copyright infringed?"

"Our client," Charlie explained, "is an underground comic artist. One of the local poster outfits is selling a blowup of one of his best panels without payment, permission, or credit. We are, naturally, asking settlement and a hefty amount in damages."

"I'll get right on it," she said, but did not rise to go.

"Okay, Studevant. What is it? There's something bothering you."

"Willis Ogilvie made Lydia's and Janis' and Annie's raises contingent on your winning this malpractice suit, didn't he?" She looked at him directly.

Charlie sighed and decided not to waste his breath on sarcasm. "The news gets around."

"I think that's rotten of him. He had no right." Flushing slightly, she rose. "I'll have all the information you need for the copyright suit by Monday afternoon, if that's soon enough."

"Fine," he said, wondering about her sudden sympathy. He knew better than to ask for what she did not volunteer, but his curiosity was piqued. "Is that all, Studevant?"

"Well," she said uncertainly, "if I can help on the malpractice defense, I'll do anything you think necessary. I understand your client is a woman."

"Yes, she is," Charlie said, and waited for more.

"You won't let her get screwed, will you? I mean, the Male Establishment will put her down if it can, and you have to stop it." Her eyes pleaded with him. She put her hand out to him. "I don't mean that quite the way it sounded."

"No, I won't let her get screwed. By the Male Establishment or anyone else."

Nodding, she said, "I'll have your copyright material by Monday morning." Then she bolted for the door. Charlie watched her go with a bemused expression on his lean copper face.

"I'm getting old, Charlie," Elizabeth Kendrie announced in a voice that would start a cavalry charge. "I don't have the energy I used to, and that's a fact." She shook Charlie's offered hand in a firm, businesslike way, then marched across to the straight-backed chair. After arranging herself properly, she sat. As always, everything about her was precise, from the crisp steel-colored curls to the arrow-straight seams of her silk stockings.

"I shudder to think what you were like before you lost your energy," Charlie said with real feeling. "What brings on this fit of depression?"

"Oh, it's the opera. Mr. Kendrie was always very involved with it, and heaven knows I've tried to live up to his wishes, but I can't keep up." She sighed a small, neat sigh.

"What?" Charlie said in mock alarm. "You mean that you're letting the Harrowleigh Foundation, the United Crusade, the Leyton-Kendrie Fellowship, the McIntyre Hospital in Redding and the Cramer School keep you from taking care of the opera? I'm shocked."

"It's all very well for you to laugh," Elizabeth Kendrie said in a voice that tried to sound wounded and failed.

"Here you are, young, vigorous, doing exciting things with your life. . . ."

"While you sit home with your knitting?" Charlie suggested. "Don't try that on me, Elizabeth."

"Oh, very well." She turned to him with a smile that transformed her plump face, revealing the ghost of the pretty young woman she had been once. "I'm blue-deviled."

"What you need, Elizabeth," said Charlie as he sat behind his desk, "is a good fight."

"You mean that you want me to take on this fight," she corrected. "I heard from your doctor this morning. She sounds like a sensible girl. How does she come to be mixed up in this?"

"That's what I'm trying to find out," Charlie said, warming to his subject. "Assuming that she's telling the truth—and there's no reason to suppose she's not—then there is something very wrong at that precious clinic."

Elizabeth Kendrie scowled. "I don't like that."

"No. Neither do I," Charlie agreed. "It would be very bad for the Harrowleigh Foundation if there is something wrong. That's why I want you to look into this matter."

"Nonsense," she snapped. "You want me to take the pressure off that doctor, and you know it. Don't try to fool me, Charlie. I don't like it."

"Okay," Charlie said, leaning forward. "Here's the truth. Miranda is accused of malpractice, and Bjornsson wants to get rid of her. He's tried to fire her twice, but he can't because of her contract. She wants to find out what happened to her patient, and so do I. The parents of the boy are suing her. And they very likely will sue the clinic as well."

Elizabeth Kendrie pursed her lips and clucked her disapproval.

"Exactly," Charlie said.

"And this matter of the drug salesman?" Elizabeth

Kendrie's ice-colored eyes snapped. "I heard the report on the news. What does that have to do with it?"

"On the surface, nothing. There doesn't seem to be a connection." As he said it, he distrusted it.

"My, my. I hear a very large 'but,' Charlie."

"Yes," he admitted. "I don't like coincidences, Elizabeth, particularly this sort. It reflects badly on my case, it makes for lousy publicity, and I don't like the feel of it. It bothers me, like an itch I can't scratch." Suddenly he sneezed. "Excuse me."

"What's the matter?" Elizabeth asked in a tone that would do well in cross-examination.

"I've got a damn cold," he said as he pulled a Kleenex from his desk drawer. "I've been trying to get rid of it all week."

"Why aren't you home in bed?"

"Because I've got too much to do," Charlie said impatiently.

"Young fool," she chided affectionately.

Finished with the Kleenex, Charlie went back to the matter at hand. "You know, that drug salesman couldn't have picked a worse time or place to die."

"No one dies in a good time and place," Elizabeth said, her hands gripping the strap of her purse.

"Some times are better than others," Charlie maintained. Then, knowing he was being led off the point, he said, "Look, Elizabeth, I need your help. You're in a good position to know what's happening in the Harrowleigh Clinic. You can ask questions I'd have to ask on the stand. You don't want that, and I don't want that. You can make Bjornsson lay off Miranda. She's taking enough crap without his intervention. I want you to meet Miranda, talk to her. If you don't want to, you don't have to help her or me. But I hope you will want to. Promise me you'll think it over, Elizabeth."

Elizabeth Kendrie studied him. "I tell you what, Charlie," she said after a moment. "I'll pass the word to Bjornsson right now. That much I will do no matter what. And I'll see that girl. If she's a right one, I'll back her up. If she isn't, then you'll have to do it on your own. Fair?"

"I can't ask for fairer," Charlie said, feeling a deep sense of relief.

"Nonsense. You'll ask for everything you can get, and a little bit more. That is why you are my attorney, young man, and not one of your partners. And don't think I'll be fobbed off with that gorgeous nincompoop in the next office," she went on, not allowing Charlie to interrupt her. "Oh, I know. You wanted me out of your hair the other night, and I can't say I blame you. You had more important matters on your mind than my contractual questions. But remember you represent me because you're worth more than the other two put together." She shifted in her chair, lining her spine up with her feet.

"Come now, Elizabeth . . ." Charlie began, acutely embarrassed.

"No. Now you listen to me, Charlie Moon," she said, her eyes growing stern. "Willis Ogilvie is too busy being a political kingmaker to care about anything but expediency. I've known him for years, and I've watched him. He loves political power the way a junkie loves the needle—he's ruthless. And that Alex Tallant is overbred. Too pretty and too arrogant by half. He's never been hungry a day in his life, and he's never been really scared. But you're different. You've had to scratch, and you know how to stay in a fight. And you have been scared, so you're hard to frighten. Now you can tell me I'm making this up, but there's something else about you. You have a power, Charlie, and you don't think like the rest of us. If you don't choose to tell me about it, that's your affair. But don't think you can fool me because you can't."

Charlie was unable to speak.

"There. I've said it," she announced when the silence

had become oppressive. "Now I'm going to leave. I will see you tomorrow. You may have Lydia call me when you want me." She went to the door, her determined, stiff-legged walk making Charlie think that if she ran into you, she would not so much knock you down as drive you straight into the ground. At the door she turned. "And you should be home taking care of that cold." The door closed firmly behind her.

Charlie breathed in the steam as it rose from the gushing taps in his bathtub. It billowed in hot clouds around the room, fogging the windows and mirror. With a cough Charlie drew more steam deep into his lungs, feeling the sweat break out at last along his back. He knew the efficient heater had driven the temperature of the bathroom into the nineties, and he found his next breath easier, some of the deep tightness breaking up under this onslaught.

After smearing a vile-smelling ointment on his hairless chest, he tossed a handful of herbs into the tub, their pungent aroma mixing with the steam. He gagged once on the rush of aromatics, then adjusted to their penetrating scent.

At last he hoisted himself to the top of the towel closet, the highest, hottest perch in the room, and let the healing sink into him. For good measure he began to chant, listing each characteristic and symptom of the cold and ordering them one by one to depart.

He was wrapped in a long terry-cloth robe, sipping bouillon in the kitchen when the phone rang. A quick glance at the wall clock told him it was after eleven, and he frowned, wondering who would be calling him this late.

He picked it up on the fourth ring. "Charles Moon," he said, pleased that the cold-fostered thickness was gone from his voice.

"Sorry to call you this late, Charlie," said Frank Shirer,

"but do you think you can make it in early in the morning rather than tomorrow afternoon?"

"Why?" Charlie asked as he put down his mug.

"Oh, Elgin's widow is putting pressure on us. She wants the case wound up, and the whole question of suicide dropped. Good Christians don't kill themselves."

"So? How can a widow from the Peninsula put pressure on you? They aren't a powerful family. And they stay away from the press in cases like this."

"You know that feisty old Florentine on the Board of Supervisors? The one who owns the hotels?" Frank Shirer's tone indicated he knew Supervisor Rocco Lemmini only too well.

"Who doesn't?"

Shirer gave a diplomatic cough before saying, "He's her uncle."

"Oh," said Charlie, thinking of all the power the Lemminis could wield in San Francisco. "I see. Okay. What time do you want me there?"

Frank Shirer sighed in relief. "Can you make it seven thirty? I know that's early, but we're getting our butts chewed. David Lemmini was down this evening, mighty upset. The sooner we can get this taken care of—"

"I understand. I'll be there." Charlie bet himself that if the Lemminis had leaned on the police, they had also called Willis Ogilvie.

"Thanks. I owe you one."

Privately, Charlie doubted it, but he said, "I'll keep that in mind. Good night."

When he had hung up, he wandered into the dining room and stared unseeing at the work spread out on the table. Sensing Charlie's worry, Rufus came to his side, whining anxiously.

"I don't like being rushed," Charlie said, absentmindedly scratching his dog's head. "Rushing makes me sloppy." He fingered one of the file folders lying open on the table. His fingers beat a tattoo against the heavy paper. "I don't like it, Rufus. Something's rotten."

Rufus cocked his head to one side.

"If it wasn't suicide, it was murder. I can feel it, smell it. Murder's Frank's worry. It's not my case anyway." But he didn't believe it.

Friday

Fog lay in pockets around the city, trapping drivers and snarling traffic from the Great Highway at the beach to the commuter congestion on the Bay Bridge and Peninsula freeways. Where the fog was light, it changed to glare, bright and blinding.

Coming in on Geary, Charlie found himself damning the fog as stoplights became lost in the mists. The cars around him were great looming shapes materializing out of the soft whiteness that swathed his windows like gauze. When he finally pulled into the parking lot at the Hall of Justice, his nerves felt ragged and he was ten minutes late.

Frank Shirer, his eyes bleary and his tie askew, sat in his office fidgeting with an unfinished report. Beside him, elegant, Italian, sleek with success, was David Lemmini.

"Morning," Frank said brusquely, casting an annoyed glance at his unwelcome guest. "Mr. Lemmini dropped by," he explained with more than a hint that Mr. Lemmini should leave.

"Sorry I'm late," Charlie said quickly, sizing up the lieutenant's predicament. "I almost got sideswiped at the Japanese Cultural and Trade Center. The fog is terrible."

"Traffic's had its hands full," Frank agreed, somewhat mollified. "Sit down, Charlie. We'll get this over as soon as possible. I know how busy you are," he added pointedly.

Charlie nodded but offered his hand to David Lemmini. "Good morning, David. I didn't expect to see you here," he said, which was no more than the truth.

"Good morning, Charlie," David Lemmini responded with a smile. "So long as I was down here, I thought I'd drop in. I've got a client being sentenced today. Sad business."

Charlie made a neutral reply, remembering the one time he had faced David Lemmini in court. The urbane attorney carried the added weight of his family name, a name that meant wealth, elegance, and, of course, employment to several hundred San Franciscans.

"Oh," Lemmini said, as if the thought had just come to him. "I understand you're representing that family with sewer trouble. It backed up into their basement or something of that nature."

"More or less. Yes, I represent the Guttierrez family."

"You know, just the other evening my father mentioned that the Board of Supervisors might look into the problem; straighten it out, you know. The Public Works department has certainly been remiss in their actions. And my father thinks it's a shame that a low-income family like that should be put to all the expense of a court case. When I said I might see you today, he asked me to mention the case to you. He thought you might ask the Board of Supervisors to review it. It would be a lot faster than taking the mess to court, and of course, the settlement would be an equitable one." His delivery was as smooth as a TV anchorman recapping headlines.

"I had no idea you were so concerned about this case," Charlie said, concealing his dislike.

"You know my father—he's a busy man, but when he hears of an injustice like this one, he's anxious to do what he can to help."

And, Charlie thought, Rocco Lemmini would not object

to the publicity his altruism would bring. "I'll tell them of his interest."

"Do that. I know he wants to hear from you." Lemmini flashed him his famous smile. Then, with a perfunctory nod to Frank Shirer, he left.

"That bastard's going to be a judge someday," Frank said as soon as David Lemmini was out of earshot.

"What would San Francisco be without the Lemminis?" Charlie wondered dryly. "How would we get along without them? Any idea, Frank?"

Frank Shirer glared at the tape cassette in his hand. "Charlie, it would take too long to tell you. The Lemminis! Descendants of humble grocers. There're too damn many of them." He fitted the cassette clumsily into the tape recorder on his desk.

Charlie had sat down in the uncomfortable chair opposite Frank. "Well, let's get this over with. What do you want to know?"

"If it's okay with you, Charlie," Frank began awkwardly as he toyed with the machine, "I'm going to record this. If you like, a transcription can be brought to you for your signature, and you can have the tape then, too, in case of errors, or if you want to make corrections."

"What for?" Charlie asked, surprised. "Why this departure from normal? You're supposed to take my statement with notes, Frank. And this transcription bit is bullshit."

"In a case like this. . . ." Frank was obviously miserable. "Charlie, the coroner might want to hear this."

"Pete Coners can call me and I'll give him a statement. What's going on?" Angered, Charlie leaned forward. "You're not being straight with me. Are the Lemminis ordering this? Is that it? They want to know what I said and if they approve?"

"Not exactly." He busied himself with checking the tape, avoiding Charlie's eyes. "Anytime we get cases like this, well, you know, Charlie, they're ticklish. They might turn out badly. . . ."

"Then they should go to court."

Frank held out the microphone. "Charlie, it isn't that important. Really."

"There are parts of my library that say it is important." He stared into Frank's face, his eyes slits and his mouth a severe line. Then he sat back, as if satisfied with what he saw. "Okay. Do this any way you want. If you go beyond the law, I'll let you know." Charlie knew that somewhere in the congenial clutter of Frank's office there lurked other recording devices, and he thought it foolish to balk at one more. If the case were that much of a hot potato, he knew Frank would need his cooperation, and to the limit of the law, he was willing to help. But he couldn't resist a last gibe. "Who else will hear the tape?"

Frank Shirer was visibly flustered. "Just the stenographer who transcribes it. And me and you. That's all. This isn't public record, you know."

"Not the coroner?" It was a deliberate jibe.

"Oh, the coroner, too, if he wants to hear it. You won't object to that, will you? I mean since you're making allowances for this case?"

Charlie let him off the hook. "You have my permission to let anyone who has the legal right to hear it hear it."

Frank jabbed at the buttons and muttered into a small hand-held microphone. "Statement of Charles S. Moon regarding his finding of the body of Sam Elgin." He looked up at Charlie. "We'll have this in more formal terms in the report. This is for my convenience, you understand."

"Okay," Charlie said, pretending this whole irregular procedure was normal. He laced his fingers together over his crossed knee. "Carry on."

"For the record, please identify yourself, full name, citizenship, place of birth, all that."

"I'm not a suspect, am I?"

"No, of course not. . . ."

"My full name is Charles Spotted Moon. I am an attorney practicing law with the firm of Ogilvie, Tallant and Moon, offices at Clay and Bush. I live at 257B Twenty-seventh Avenue. Would you like my phone number, or will you fill that in later, too?"

"555-0751," Frank muttered to the microphone. "What's the business number? I don't remember it offhand."

"It's 555-0066. As you well know. Come on, Frank. Let's get down to the case. You're stalling," he challenged.

"I have to have this information in the report."

"Okay. Sure." Charlie sighed. "Take your time."

Pretending to make some last adjustments, Frank waited long enough to be certain Charlie saw these adjustments; then he asked, "Now, about that body you discovered last . . . Tuesday evening."

"What do you want to know about it?"

"Describe how you found the body." Frank was exasperated now. He found Charlie's attitude irritating and the pressure from the Lemminis intolerable.

"The whole thing?" Seeing Frank's nod, he said, "I arrived at the Harrowleigh Clinic just before eight P.M. and parked in the lot adjoining the building on the west side. Is that what you want to have on the record, Frank?"

Frank motioned him to go on.

"When I got out of my car, I caught sight of a handkerchief on the ground. It had"—with a distasteful effort Charlie brought all his attention to that handkerchief—"pine needles in it. It was bloody."

"Handkerchief?" Frank interrupted. "You didn't mention this before. What the hell happened to it? It's evidence."

"I know that." Charlie stopped, a scowl settling between his eyes. "I can't remember. I know I had it when I found him. . . . I don't recall having it later. I must have dropped it when I examined him."

"You don't remember?" There was derision in his tone.

"No," said Charlie bluntly. "I don't remember. You know what that man looked like. You saw what I saw. Would you remember a handkerchief?"

Frank let that go for the time being. "About the body," he prompted.

"The body. It was a few feet away in the park under the trees. The branches masked him pretty well in the dark. In the day he would have been easy to see. Even the kids playing in the park would have seen him."

"Thank God they didn't," Frank interjected.

"That would have been messy, wouldn't it?" Charlie asked pleasantly.

"Why did you see him? Your headlights show him?"

"No." Charlie shook his head. "I said I found the handkerchief. I picked it up. I remember thinking something was wrong. I guess. . . . I guess the pine needles made me look in the park." He was damned if he'd tell Frank Shirer that he sensed the death from the handkerchief. "It's not a big park. It didn't take long to find him."

"Describe what you found."

Charlie's expression grew remote as he thought back. "I found a man, I'd say late thirties or early forties lying on his back in the trees. His suit was stained and torn at the knees, as I remember. His body was badly bruised. He'd had a nose bleed. His bowels had relaxed."

"Would you say there were signs of violence?"

"The man looked beaten, if that's what you mean, but there were no signs of violence around him. The ground was relatively undisturbed, and there were no broken branches on the nearby trees that I can remember."

"What did you do when you found the body?"

"I looked it over perfunctorily and then called the police. I called you, Frank." He looked straight at Shirer.

"Yes. We have the call on file."

"Then you know what I found. You already have a record."

Frank wriggled in his chair, then had to untangle the phone cord from his microphone cord. "Well, yes, but we need your statement. You might have left something out."

"Come on, Frank. You can do better than that."

"Charlie, you know we have to have these statements in order to investigate the case." He was aggravated now.

"And what has your investigation shown so far? You said yourself that the autopsy was inconclusive. Have you any idea what happened to the man? Or why?"

"Well, we know he took a great many anticoagulants. . . ."

"Oh, for Christ's sake!" He struck the desk with the flat of his hand.

Frank Shirer beetled his brow. "It's not easy, a case like this."

"Of course. The Lemminis don't want a suicide in their family. The disgrace for a Catholic family is still pretty overwhelming. Particularly such a conspicuous family as theirs is."

"Well, I'm glad you understand my position."

"How did he get the anticoagulants? Have you got a theory about that?" Charlie asked, a small part of his mind amused—Frank was the one who ought to ask the questions.

"We're not sure quite how. But we found out he had a cold. He was taking Actifeds, you know, they're common prescription pills for colds." He pretended to consult his notes, though he knew the material by heart. "Well, the Actifeds are small white pressed pills, and so is Coumadin, which is a very common anticoagulant and a drug which Elgin had in his case."

"You're saying he got the two mixed up?" He thought the idea was preposterous.

"Not exactly. We think he might have taken the pills while driving and didn't check the packages."

Charlie shook his head. "How many Coumadin cause death? How many do they think he took?"

Frank lost some of his calm. "We think he took about a dozen anticoagulants. Maybe as many as fifteen. It can take that much to kill, sometimes."

"What do you mean, sometimes?"

Now Frank was looking miserable. "Most of the time they'd have to be taken all at once."

"How many of those Actifed things do you take at once?"

"One; on rare occasions, two."

Charlie gestured a dismissal. "Two ain't twelve, Frank. Not even on a bet."

"I know." Frank switched the tape recorder off. "But we can't be sure it's suicide . . . not really. There's no real proof. And he was going back to the clinic when he died. Maybe he realized something was wrong, or he'd taken the Coumadin instead of the Actifeds—"

"Pretty weak," Charlie said. "I could tear that to shreds in court in five minutes."

"So could I," Frank admitted. "But there's no reason to think he was murdered, and that's the only other likely explanation."

"How do you know he wasn't murdered?" Charlie liked the feel of this, for in some part of himself, he was sure it was murder, and he had a growing certainty that Elgin's murder was part of what was happening at the clinic.

"By whom? Why? When? How?" Frank ticked off the questions on his fingers. "Tell me. Who would want to murder him? An addict? His sample case was locked in his car safe and sound. When? While he was driving? He was starting on his round of his inner territory. Napa, Sonoma, Santa Rosa, up to Ukiah, over to Fort Bragg, and down the coast. We know he turned back somewhere around Santa Rosa. He made his usual stop in the Valley of the Moon, but didn't stop at the Rohnert Park Medical Co-op on his list." Frank consulted a sheet of paper, which he handed to Charlie. "See? That's the record of his movements as we reconstruct them. He had to have been given the Coumadin, if he was murdered, before he left Vallejo. There's no way."

Charlie took the paper, glanced through it, and handed it back to Frank. "What about getting the drug at home, before he started on his rounds?"

"That means he'd have to get it at the clinic. But that doesn't make sense either." Frank shook his head. "I know; I know. There were witnesses. There were five or six other salesmen there, and they would have noticed if anything was wrong."

"Would they have noticed?" Charlie asked, brows up.

"We talked to Ed Shelly. He mentioned they were all giving Elgin a bad time because he was drinking orange juice instead of coffee. Apparently he was one of those ten-cups-a-day men. But since he had a cold, he told them he was swearing off coffee."

"I see," Charlie said, putting his hand for a moment over his eyes. He knew something was not adding up. He sensed Elgin had been murdered. He knew it now as he had known it when he had first seen the body. There was too much violence in that dead man for his death to have been accidental. He remembered his grandfather saying, "Only the living can be still; the dead are stopped." What had stopped Sam Elgin was murder.

"What is it, Charlie?" Frank saw the expression on Charlie's face.

But Charlie shook his head. "Oh, nothing. I can understand your problem. What are you going to do?" He knew this would change Frank's direction, turn his attention away to other things.

Frank shrugged elaborately. "What can we do? We can't demonstrate suicide, not clearly, anyway. We can't show reasonable proof of murder. The coroner's hearing will probably find death by misadventure and let it go at that. We have no reason to disagree with that finding, not with what we have now. I don't see anything else it can do."

"The Lemminis will be pleased. It's too embarrassing for a family like theirs to have one of their clan refused Catholic burial, if that still happens."

"Shit," Frank said wearily.

"Precisely." Getting to his feet, Charlie asked, "Do you have any more questions for me? Or may I go?"

Frank set his jaw, and asked, "Why were you at the clinic? For the record."

Charlie waited until the tape recorder had been switched back on and the question repeated. Then he answered, "I was there to see a client."

"Why?"

"Ah-ah-ah," Charlie warned.

"All right, then. Who?"

"For the record?" Charlie waited for Frank to confirm it. "My client is Dr. Miranda Trobridge. She practices at the clinic. And that, Frank, is all you will get for the record." He extended his hand. "I'm glad it's you and not me," he said as they shook.

"Yeah," Frank agreed morosely. "All you have to do is walk out of here and it's behind you."

"Well, you'll wrap this one up quickly and then you can get on to other cases."

"Don't remind me." Frank took the little tape recorder and hid it away in one of his drawers. "Thanks for coming down."

"Any time," Charlie said with false enthusiasm.

Frank Shirer waved him out the door.

Yet Charlie knew as he left the office that he was not rid of the ghost of Sam Elgin.

"There you are, Charlie," Willis Ogilvie boomed at him as he came into the office fifteen minutes after he left the Hall of Justice.

"Good morning, Willis. You're in early."

"I have to be in court today." He came across the hall and put a familiar arm around Charlie's shoulder. "You were in giving a statement on that Elgin death, weren't you? That's a sad business."

Charlie knew Willis wanted something, and he waited for it, knowing it would come after such preparation.

"I saw David Lemmini yesterday, you know."

Although Charlie didn't know, he knew he should have guessed it. "I saw him this morning."

"Oh?" Willis said with feigned surprise.

"He was in Lieutenant Shirer's office when I arrived."

"He probably had to be in court and dropped by," Willis improvised with a knowing nod. "The Lemminis certainly are a busy family. Rocco on the Board of Supervisors, David and his law practice, William with his hotel, Carter moving up to chief administrator at French Hospital. . . . They're really quite remarkable. And I don't suppose you've heard: William's daughter, Luisa, has been accepted at Juilliard. He's thrilled."

"No doubt," Charlie said dryly.

Willis beamed broadly at Charlie. "I wonder, did David mention his father's interest in the Guttierrez case? He wanted to be sure you knew about it. It's like him to want to help a family like that."

Charlie knew the Lemminis were Democrats and swung a lot of power in the party, as did Willis Ogilvie. Perhaps Elizabeth Kendrie was right after all. Charlie moved away from Willis. "It's an interesting proposition, and I know the Guttierrezes will be anxious to know the details of what the board might be able to do for them." He did not add that he had made good on his end of the bargain and had not insisted that the Elgin death was a suicide.

"That'll get you off the hook on part of the salary raise, won't it?" Willis made jovial gestures with his broad hands. "Now all you have to do is win that malpractice suit, and Lydia and the girls will get their raise. You're a lucky son of a bitch, Charlie, no doubt about it."

As always, Willis's ebullience made Charlie suspicious. He wanted to get away from his senior partner to think through their encounter. "I've got a client coming in, Willis. It's been good to talk to you."

"Oh, you aren't going to be rid of me quite yet. Oh, no," he said as he steered Charlie inexorably toward the inner sanctum of his office.

This room was the most amazing of the partners' offices in their suite. It was large with a thick high-price carpet on the floor. Three tall windows were draped in dull gold silk, and the furniture was seventeenth-century rosewood. Dominating the office was Willis' desk, an impressive structure of Victorian inlaid mahogany. Framed photographs showed Willis at various stages of his career shaking hands with political superstars and one or two major artists.

"Sit down, Charles, my boy. I want to be sure you understand this offer of the Lemminis." He guided Charlie to one of the rosewood chairs and very nearly pushed him into it.

"Believe me, I understand, Willis."

"Now, you do recognize that there are a few things expected of you in return for this aid to your clients—"

"I know, Willis," Charlie said with exaggerated patience. "And believe me, I did not insist that Sam Elgin killed himself. I agreed with Frank Shirer that there's not enough evidence for that. We agreed that the coroner's jury will probably find death by misadventure and let it go at that."

Willis sighed a ponderous sigh. "Yes. Well, it's probably for the best. You don't think it was suicide, do you?" This last was asked acutely, with none of the flamboyance which Charlie found so annoying.

"Do you really want to know what I think, or is this to salve my conscience?" He waited for Willis to answer.

"I'm not lost to politics completely, you know. I don't want you to lie or to bend your principles too far." He gave his next question careful reflection. "Do you think Elgin killed himself?"

"No, I don't," Charlie said, keeping his eyes firmly on Willis'. "I believe he was murdered."

Willis let out a long whistle. "Murder. God, I hope not. Not with the Lemminis mixing in." He looked out the window, then back at Charlie. "You couldn't be wrong, could you?"

"Sure. It's only a hunch, after all. But you wanted to know what I thought happened, and that's it. I can't tell you why except that it feels like murder." He opened his hands helplessly. "I'm not going to pursue it, Willis, if that's what's bothering you. It's not my case."

"No. It's not." He gave a single nod.

"At the same time," Charlie went on, frowning, "if it's related in any way to Dr. Trobridge's case, I'll have to go after it. You understand that, don't you, Willis? I can't let even the Lemminis interfere with my defense."

"You don't have to push the issue," Willis rumbled. "Remember we deal in realities. We must make certain allowances. You know that as well as I do."

"Allowances are one thing, and sellouts are another." Charlie's voice was quiet, but the words were loud in the luxurious office.

"I'm not asking you to sell out." Indignant now, Willis flung himself out of his chair and began pacing the length of the office. "I'm asking you to use a little judgment, a little sense. You must realize, Charlie, that there is no way you can fight the Lemminis on mere feelings or beliefs. They will demand proof of the most stringent nature." He wandered to the window and toyed with one of the heavy tassels holding back the draperies. "You know that the Lemminis are sure that Nina married beneath her, but that doesn't mean they won't stand by her, particularly in a case like this. You know Rocco. He keeps all the strings of that family in his hands, and he pulls them any way he pleases. He's tried to help out because of the kid, but so far Nina's said no. She won't be able to refuse now. You can't depend on him ignoring this trouble with Nina's husband. He hasn't ignored it so far." He turned back. "Charlie, leave it alone if you can. You aren't up to Lemminis."

Charlie shook his head. "You didn't understand me, Willis," he said rising and determined to leave this office before Willis could work himself up again. "I don't intend to make a thing of this. I certainly don't want to tackle the Lemminis if I can help it. You asked what I thought happened, and I told you."

"It's unhappy coincidence," Willis admitted, the tassel still in his hand.

At the door Charlie turned. "I don't really believe in coincidence, Willis."

"But, Charlie, be reasonable . . ." Willis began.

He was talking to a closed door. Charlie was gone.

"Morning, Charlie," Alex Tallant said from Lydia's desk, where he was making himself pleasant. "Got a minute?"

"I suppose so," Charlie answered.

"Been talking with the great man? Those pep talks of his scare the hell out of me."

"What is it?" Charlie asked, not wanting to get into personalities, and not wanting to face both his partners on the same morning.

Alex turned back to Lydia with a wide, practiced smile; Charlie, watching the two of them, wondered if Alex were aware of the effect he had on the lovely Chinese woman. It was a trick of her eyes, Charlie decided, a softening in Lydia's face that happened for Alex and no one else.

"That was nice of you anyway," Alex was saying. "You're a good girl, Lydia. What would we do without you?" He grinned easily, then turned to Charlie. "My office or yours?" he asked, his manner now more brisk, his stride lengthening.

"Whatever you want," Charlie said as he opened the door to his office before Alex could lead the way to the other door. "I'm closer."

Alex nodded graciously and ducked through the door, going to the window to look out at the thinning fog. When Charlie had closed the door, he asked, "How's it going for Lydia's raise?"

"I'm working on it." Charlie tried to keep his voice light, but he did not succeed. "What is it, Alex?" He was growing tired of his two partners.

"I'm making some headway in the Mayling estate," he announced. "It's not as bad as I thought. Figured you'd like to know, so you can ease off on your checking. There's a set of records the family didn't know about."

"Who did know about them?" Charlie asked, fascinated.

"Oh, the staff at the pharmacy. Talked to the men there. Haupter's in charge and apparently Jared Mayling trusted him as much as he trusted anyone. Gave him a small safe to keep. We opened it by court order, and there were the books. Good news, huh?" He rocked on his heels, satisfaction thick as cream in his face. "Not that I don't appreciate your help, but it wasn't necessary. Haupter had the goods, and Shelly explained the system."

At the name Shelly, Charlie felt an alarm triggered in his mind. He was careful to keep his voice even as he asked, "Who are they?"

"Haupter's the chief of the pharmaceutical house, and Shelly is in distributing. Very helpful, both of them. Well, just wanted to let you know where we stand now. Thanks for your help, Charlie." He extended his hand.

"I'm glad to hear you've straightened the problem out," Charlie said as he took the hand, all the while wondering what Alex was really after. He motioned to a chair. "Sit down for a moment, why don't you?"

"Oh, that's not necessary," Alex replied. "I've got to get back to work. Got to be in court this afternoon on that damned strikebreaking suit. Talk about a mess."

"Oh, yes. That's been dragging on for months now, hasn't it? Do you think you'll wrap it up before the year is out?" Charlie leaned his shoulders back against his bookshelves and crossed his arms on his chest. He knew Alex was leading up to something.

"Hope so. It's a pain in the ass." He looked up, smiling winningly. "Say, Charlie, that copyright infringement suit you're handling, that's over printing, isn't it?"

Charlie knew what was coming next. "Yes, in part. Why?" As he asked he felt like a *de jure* straight man. He wondered if there was a legal equivalent of Mr. Bones.

"So long as you're doing that, if you run across anything about the printers who were in on the strikebreaking . . . not out of your way, of course, but just in case you run across something, you might make a note of it for me. I'd appreciate it." His smiles were never forced; this one was so easy it seemed almost genuine. "Nothing too drastic, you know, but if you hear something. It would be valuable in court. Good to know anything you can find."

Keeping his face blank, Charlie assured him. "If I find anything you can use, I'll let you know about it."

"Good man," Alex said, favoring Charlie with a comradely cuff on the sleeve. "Well, won't keep you any longer. Just wanted you to know the Mayling case is winding up. It was good of you to help."

Charlie wanted to challenge him, to say he knew that the Mayling estate was a blind that allowed Alex to ask for free legwork again. "I didn't do that much," Charlie told him. "I hardly helped at all."

"You helped." Alex pointed a reassuring finger at him as he moved to the door. "You know, that's the remarkable thing about minorities: give them a chance to prove how determined they are, and it's amazing how they succeed. Look at you. Plains Wars probably just two, three generations away. . . ."

"It wasn't the same in Canada," Charlie said, hoping to shut Alex up.

"Canada, the USA, Indians got a raw deal. Anyone who reads history knows that. Tribes relocated, decimated . . . it's a blot. What happened to your people?"

Charlie gritted his teeth. "We moved north and west." Almost a thousand miles north and west in the space of a hundred years.

"Terrible. Ruined your way of life. No white man can be proud of that record. But look at you. You're doing fine in the WASP world . . . certainly a lot better than I'd do in the Indian world." Pleased with this liberal revelation, Alex made his satisfied exit.

Charlie resisted the urge to heave his heaviest lawbook after him.

Lewis Coventry was late. Charlie stood in front of Paoli's, squinting in the sunny glare. Silver and stone gleamed at him when he looked at his watch for the fifth time. The noontime crowd on Montgomery Street surged around him, jostling, rushing, so that Charlie paid little attention when a tall, thin man shoved against his shoulder. The thin man shoved him again.

Charlie looked up. "I beg your pardon?" he said, carefully neutral.

"Moon!" the man accused him. His voice was penetrating, and several people in the street stared.

"Yes?" Charlie said, annoyed.

"You don't know who I am, sir?" The voice rose, challenging him, and Charlie recognized the fierce outburst.

"You're Professor Weed," he said, resigned.

The thin man trembled, his long, unhealthy face pasty with anger. "I am, sir. I suppose you know why I am here?"

"I can guess," Charlie said under his breath, then sighed, saying in his most reasonable tone, "Look, Professor Weed, I know you're upset, but the place for this discussion is in court. Believe me, you only hurt yourself by scenes like this." He looked again for Lewis Coventry and did not find him, though several startled eyes were on him.

"This won't do, sir. This won't do. I won't be put off by your legalistic maneuvering. You can't have the temerity to expect it of me." The professor's angry voice rose in pitch and volume.

"I realize you're upset . . ." Charlie began.

"Upset. Upset! First my boy dies, then a corpse is found in the parking lot! It's criminal, sir. If you had one jot of decency in you, you would denounce that woman as the charlatan she is and investigate that clinic, or whatever it calls itself!" There was a flat shine to his eyes as his rage fed on itself.

Charlie regarded these signs with alarm. "Professor, think of where you are," he said sharply, hoping to bring the man to his senses, but to no avail.

"That's a slaughterhouse, not a clinic. Mark my words, sir, mark my words. They do murder there."

This time Charlie raised his voice, too. "Professor Weed, unless you are prepared to be sued for slander, you'd better get hold of yourself and shut up."

The man looked at him, startled into silence.

"That's better," Charlie went on evenly. "Now, listen to me. Miranda Trobridge will answer you in court and nowhere else. Certainly not here."

"She is a lying, murdering—"

"Remember what I said about slander," Charlie warned him, all his attention on Professor Weed. "The death of Mr. Elgin is being investigated by the police; you have no part in that."

"But it's a death," Professor Weed objected, his arms jerking like a puppet's.

"It is not your concern." Charlie wished that he could put Sam Elgin out of his mind. He did not want to listen to Professor Weed.

"You're a savage!" the man spat. "You're no better than the rest of your kind. You can't understand decency, sir—"

Charlie, still smarting from Alex's words, found this almost more than he could bear. He lowered his voice and said in French, "If you make another remark about my race, son of a camel, I will hurt you very badly."

Professor Weed stared, his wrath diverted. "What did you say?"

When Charlie had repeated it, he added, speaking in English once again, "My tribe is Canadian, Professor. And Canada is bilingual."

Some of the crowd around them dispersed, which brought on another of the professor's outbursts. "You can say it in any language you like, sir, but it does not excuse that woman from her guilt. She is a criminal, and I will see she is punished to the full extent of the law."

Charlie now had his own temper under better control. "If you insist on taking this to the district attorney instead of handling it in civil court, I promise you we will file countersuit, and we will win. Professor Weed, let me warn you now to leave Miranda Trobridge alone. If I hear of any threat being made to her, I will bring a charge of assault against you."

"Assault? It is she, sir, not I who—"

"Threat of bodily harm is technically assault. Remember that. Leave your case to Mr. Malton. And leave the Elgin matter to the police." He issued this last warning in a tone that was almost conversational.

Professor Weed's pallid face took on a livid hue, and his long, nervous hands clenched.

"I don't advise it," Charlie said, stepping back from the man.

"Charlie," said a man at his elbow, "when you're through here, I have a table for us."

Charlie turned and looked into the canny, saturnine face of Lewis Coventry. He nodded. "I'm just finishing up here."

"Good." Lewis clamped a friendly arm around his shoulder, and Charlie, who would normally have flinched at the familiarity, welcomed it. Over his shoulder, Lewis said to Professor Weed, "You'd better leave, man, unless you want to attract the police."

The professor's strangled objection was lost as Lewis Coventry steered Charlie into Paoli's pleasant interior. "What was that all about?"

"Another case," Charlie said, freeing himself from Lewis' grip. "It's a sticky one."

"So I gathered." Coventry nodded to the headwaiter and went to his table. "I don't suppose you can discuss it?"

He shook his head. "No. You know I can't. But I wish to God that just once there'd be a change in the case for the better."

"Bad?"

"And keeps getting worse. Every development goes against us." He looked up as the waiter handed him a menu. "Never mind about that, Lewis. You say you want changes made in your will?"

But Lewis Coventry wasn't quite ready to let the other pass. "Talking French really got to him."

"I speak German and Italian, too. The teacher at the reservation school was a refugee from Belgium and didn't have full credentials for most Canadian schools. We lucked out." He hoped that would be enough.

"The case he was talking about—are you going to win it?"

Charlie studied the menu, not seeing the elegant script. "I don't know. It depends on what else goes wrong."

"That's negative of you," Lewis Coventry said, dismissing the case.

Charlie shut the menu with a snap. "It's honest."

Miranda looked exhausted. Her short brown hair was lank, her face pinched, too pale except for the dark stains under her eyes. She had dressed in incompatible slacks and blouse, and her glasses, Charlie saw, were in need of cleaning. He knew he should tell her about his run-in with Professor Weed, but seeing her sitting so listlessly in the larger of his two client's chairs, he found he could not.

"That's no way to behave," Elizabeth Kendrie told her severely. "Look at yourself. You're a walking confession of guilt."

"I don't know what you mean," she said sullenly.

"All that's lacking is a hairshirt and flail," Elizabeth announced.

"I'm not guilty!" Miranda shouted, coming out of the chair to face her inexorable adversary. "I didn't kill Sparky, no matter what Dr. Bjornsson has told you. I didn't help his dying along. I didn't neglect him. . . ."

"That's better." Elizabeth beamed. "Keep that up, and you'll be fine. Don't do the opposition's work for them." She swiveled in her chair. "Now, what do you want me to do, Charlie?"

"Call off Bjornsson first of all."

"I've already had a little chat with Fritz this morning," she declared, and Charlie imagined for a moment the urbane Dr. Bjornsson put to flight by the determination of Elizabeth

Kendrie. "I think you'll find he'll be more reasonable now," Elizabeth said to Miranda.

"Thanks," was the uncertain answer.

"That's a good start, Elizabeth," Charlie told her. "But it's only a start. Dr. Weed is making himself very unpleasant."

Miranda covered her face with her hands. "He's such a bastard," she muttered to the floor. "If I'd done half of what he accuses me of, I'd be ashamed to be a doctor."

"Don't worry," Charlie said. "I'll have a talk with his attorney and straighten this out." He wasn't sure that James Malton of Hammil and Ward would listen to reason, but he knew he would have to give it a try. Perhaps a gentle reminder about slander would do it.

"That's stopgap measures only," Elizabeth said scornfully. "We're not solving anything, just delaying. What about those contracts Dr. Trobridge has with the clinic? Is it true she can be dismissed if she should lose this case?"

"Yes," Charlie said.

"What can stop that?"

"Not losing." Charlie turned. "Miranda, stop feeling sorry for yourself and listen."

Quixotically Elizabeth took her side. "*Someone* has to feel sorry for her, Charlie. Be a little more tolerant. She needs to let down."

"No, I don't," Miranda said, pulling herself straight and combing her hair back with her fingers. "You're right, both of you. I should do better. I'll try." She set her jaw in a firm line.

Elizabeth gave Charlie a speaking look. "I'm pleased you're taking this attitude," she told Miranda. "I like you better for it. These moping airs really put me off."

Charlie intervened before Miranda and Elizabeth could be at odds again. "Let's not waste time on this. We need to get a strategy. If Professor Weed has his heart set on turning this into a public fracas, we have to be ready for him. That means you, Elizabeth, are going to have to defang Miranda's coworkers so that she is not shown to disadvantage if we get press on this."

"Oh, we'll get press. After Sam Elgin died, there were reporters all over the place, and some of the clinic staff thought it was because of my case. They're interested, and if Herr Professor makes noise, they'll listen." Miranda slumped again.

"If it gets too out of hand, it might be in your favor in court, if we can demonstrate bias or prejudice."

"Where does that get me with my patients, Charlie?" Miranda stared at him, her eyes clear.

"Good girl!" Elizabeth beamed her approval. "Answer her that one, Charlie. It's a legitimate question."

For a moment Charlie studied his long, nervous fingers; then he returned her steady gaze. "I don't know. I hadn't considered that, and it is important."

But Elizabeth bustled in with an answer. "Now, listen here. I'm connected with the McIntyre Hospital in Redding. If worse comes to worse, I can arrange to get you on the staff up there. They need a few more good doctors, and the money is much better than what the clinic pays. You'd start at fifteen thousand more than you're making now. Think it over."

"I'm not running out on my patients. I won't." Miranda glared at Elizabeth, her hands working in her lap.

Elizabeth made a tense little smile. "No, my dear, I know you're not. Neither Charlie nor I expects that of you. But your patients read the papers and watch television, and they might have other ideas. You must consider that."

The office was still as the implications of Elizabeth's words sunk in. It was an unpleasant silence, one built of many tensions. At last Miranda opened her hands and sighed. "I'll think about it."

Charlie was relieved. "Okay, we've considered the possibility that Miranda's patients might not want to continue with her after this, and we know we have an alternative if we need it."

"We won't need it," Miranda interrupted.

"It's good to know it's there, just in case," Charlie said gently. "Now this is the way we're going to work for the time being. You, Miranda, are going back to the clinic to do your work. Let me remind you again not to discuss the case in any way with anyone. I'll drop you off on my way to the coroner's. You can get me those L-dopa samples I asked you for then. Elizabeth will exert some of her pressure where it will do the most good—on your board of directors and some of the higher-ups at the clinic, to make sure the case doesn't become public property. And we'll leave the next move to Messrs. Malton and Weed."

"You mean we have to wait?" Miranda was distressed. "I thought we could *do* something."

"We have done something," Charlie said. "We're ready to counter almost any move they make. And at the moment that is all we can do."

"It sounds like you're on the defensive," Elizabeth said, and her tone was critical.

"Of course," Charlie agreed. "That is what you do when you're defending a client. That's the way the system works. It's the name of the game."

Traffic was heavy and building up to the stop-and-go crawl of rush hour when Charlie let Miranda off at the Harrowleigh Clinic. There were no parking places available in the lot, and the on-street parking had made its four o'clock metamorphosis into towaway zones. Charlie circled the block twice, then said, "Look, why don't you run in, grab a couple of samples for me, and I'll make the circuit a few more times. You can run the samples out to me, and I'll take off. Okay?"

"Fine," she said as he pulled over to the edge of the parking lot.

"I'll be around every three minutes or so. Just wave when you get out, and I'll spot you," he assured her as he opened the door.

"It won't take long." She flashed him a tired smile as she slammed the door.

But it turned out to be more than ten minutes before Miranda returned, empty-handed. In response to her wave Charlie pulled to the curb and rolled down the window.

"I can't find any," she said without preamble.

"Can't find any?" Charlie repeated. "Why? Where is it?"

"I don't know. I checked the dispensary cabinet, and there wasn't any in it." She wrinkled her brow as she went on. "I didn't think any of our other Parkinson's patients had been in . . . I don't understand it." With a shake of her head she looked questioningly at Charlie. "What do you want me to do?"

Ignoring the determined honking behind him, Charlie said, "Is there any place else they might be? Maybe at the front desk?"

"I asked our chief nurse if she'd seen packets anywhere, and she didn't remember any." Miranda shot an anxious look at the angry driver of the Buick behind Charlie. "Hadn't you better move?"

"In a minute," he said and made an unmistakable sign at the Buick driver. There was renewed and furious honking, then a squeal of protesting tires as the car shot around Charlie's Volvo and into traffic. "See?" he explained. Laughingly he reached for her hand. "You don't have to worry, Miranda. I can take care of myself. Now, what about that L-dopa? Is there any way you might have overlooked some?"

"I doubt it." Her frown deepened. "We've never been out of it before. Low, a couple of times. I don't understand."

Neither did Charlie, but he said, "Well, you might ask around, and if you come up with some, drop it by the office.

No new delivery, just some that would have been around when you were giving those extra packs out to Sparky."

"I'll do what I can," she said dubiously.

"Good." He knew that she was losing some of her confidence. "Look, Miranda, if there turns out to be something wrong with the drugs, that makes our case stronger and gives the Weeds another whipping boy, but it does not mean that without them we're lost. For all we know, the drugs were okay and the mix-up was on another level altogether. It's way too early to get frightened. We've got lots of tricks up our sleeves yet."

"Whatever you say," she said, nibbling delicately at her lower lip.

"Miranda, you've got to keep going."

She nodded. "I will. But it isn't easy, Charlie. Everything, everyone is telling me I'm wrong. That's the real curse of the male-female thing, you know. That all their lives, women know they are wrong."

"This time you're right." He knew she could not believe him now.

"Sure," she said as she slammed the door.

Charlie gave her a friendly wave, but his manner changed grimly as he pulled back into traffic. His face darkened and his eyes narrowed for reasons other than the returning fog. Resolutely he shut these concerns away and concentrated instead on the cars around him.

Pete Coners was sitting in bearlike rumpled comfort in his office, carbon copies of years-old reports drifting around him like autumn leaves. As Charlie came into the room, he greeted him with: "Ready to admit you're whipped, Charlie?"

"No," Charlie said, finding a clear space on one corner of the large desk and sitting down. "What's going on? Are you destroying your files, or what?"

"Computers," Pete said comprehensively. "Now that

we've got one they can't resist playing with it. All our records are going onto magnetic tape, for posterity and the confusion of programmers." He held up a fistful of onionskin. "Look at that. These are from 1961. First it was five years, then a decade; next thing we'll be back to the Quake and Fire. It's ridiculous. But it's all the rage." Chuckling, he put the papers back down with the others on his desk. "Sometimes I want to mix them up, put the wrong papers together just to see what would happen. But I don't think anyone would notice."

"Probably not." As always, when he was with Pete, Charlie got the feeling that this sardonically jovial man was hiding from him, refusing to reveal a deep-seated melancholy, for he was a man whose life was devoted to the codification of death and disaster, of accident, misfortune, and personal violence.

"We got another one of those dead drunks this morning." He sighed. "They'll drink anything. As bad as the cocaine addicts: they'll put anything up their noses—anything!" Shaking his head, he looked up. "You aren't here to talk about my daily routine. What do you want?"

"I need some more information on the Weed case, Pete."

"Weed. The kid." He rummaged through the stack of papers. "I've got the report for you somewhere. . . . You know, it all points to that Trobridge woman."

"What points?" Charlie asked, keeping his voice even.

"The circumstances of the kid's death. And that Margolis death. I know." He held up his hand, a hint of smugness in his manner. "Circumstantial evidence only. But it's strong, Charlie, and civil cases, I don't need to remind you, don't require the same degree of proof as criminal. Not that she couldn't get manslaughter—kidslaughter, at least—for this." He made another chuckling sound. "And criminal responsibility for medical mistakes is one can of worms the AMA doesn't want opened."

"What on earth do you have against Dr. Trobridge?"

Charlie noticed that Pete was shying away from this question. He pressed harder. "Are you telling me you think she's incompetent or what?"

Pete stirred his big hands in the loose papers. "Crap. Lady doctors!" He paused to examine an envelope containing a parking ticket, sighed, then threw it away. "Now," he went on, "I got nothing against women, Charlie. It's not like that at all. You know me. I like women. But you've got to admit there are some things they aren't good at. Call it training or anything you want, they don't do certain kinds of things as well as men do. Medicine's one of those things—they just don't have the right kinds of brains for medicine. Well, what do you expect? I mean, their job is making life and taking care of it. It stands to reason they'd have trouble doing things that cause injury or pain."

"You know better than that, Pete," Charlie said, the warning clear in his face. "And if you do think this way, you'll be in trouble when I get you on the stand in court. Half your testimony would be worthless."

"Thanks for the warning. I'll keep my opinions to myself." He held up both hands in mock terror. "Chauvinism! How ghastly! At least when you're looking for a loophole in a case to find a defense."

"That is not what I meant," Charlie said, his body stiff.

"Look, Charlie, I'm not saying she's dumb. I admit she's got brains. There are lots of bright women. Lots of them. I'm the first one to say it. Lucile, my wife, now there's a bright woman for you. After fifteen years of marriage and three kids, she went out and got a job. It's a good job. She's an assistant buyer at Rossiter's. Now, that's a big store. You gotta be good to work for them. Her boss thinks she's great. You know," he confided, "I wasn't sure about her working at first, but she likes it, and that extra paycheck sure comes in handy these days."

"Will she ever be a buyer?" Charlie asked in spite of himself. He didn't want to antagonize Pete, but he thought of Morgan Studevant and knew she would have asked this question herself.

"Buyer?" He shook his head. "Nope. Why take on all that hassle? Her boss takes all of that." Pete ran his stubby fingers through his grizzled hair. "So I think there are better things for women to do than be doctors, does that make me some kind of criminal?" He laughed easily, tolerantly. "I told you you shouldn't touch this case. Now look at you, grasping at straws."

"I think she's innocent."

"You're her lawyer," he said, as if that explained everything.

"That has nothing to do with it. That's why I wanted that full report on the Weed boy. I want to study it over the weekend."

"Lots of luck."

Charlie's eyes narrowed, and his voice dropped a couple of notes. "There might be something we've overlooked. All along it's felt like that. It's probably obvious as hell and staring us all in the face, and we're too dumb to see it. So I'm going looking for it. That report is part of the search."

Pete nodded and reached once more into the bewildering mass of papers. In a moment he came up with a file of several Xerox sheets in it. "There you are," he said, some of his cordiality lost now. "Chisholm Harris Weed deceased. Dead of Parkinson's disease, poor little bastard. I'd hate to see a kid of mine die of that stuff. Or anybody."

"Thanks," Charlie said with an effort. He flipped the file open long enough to glance over it. "How is it going with Sam Elgin, or aren't you handling that case now?"

"I was. Nee's taken it over. Lucky thing that autopsy was inconclusive. We'll find for misadventure, and then the Lemmini tribe can relax."

"Just like that?" Charlie's eyebrow went up in punctuation.

"Just like that." Pete sighed ponderously as he reached for an abandoned cup of coffee across his desk. "I tell you, that family sure is determined. As soon as the case got transferred to Nee, they called him up and talked with him for over half an hour. And you know how persuasive Rocco Lemmini can be."

"That is not entirely within the law," Charlie said as he tapped the file folder against his open palm. "Particularly if they were trying to influence him. What does Nee say about it?"

Pete gave an eloquent shrug. "That they wanted Nee to know that Sam Elgin wouldn't commit suicide, coming as he did from a Catholic family, and that certainly the case could not be murder since Elgin's drug case wasn't stolen. As if all drug salesmen get killed for is their drugs. They really laid it on."

"Lucky Dr. Nee." Charlie rose and stood looking down at Pete as he sipped his cold coffee.

"What is it, Charlie?" Pete glanced up at him over the rim, his bright eyes shining. He reminded Charlie of some rare nocturnal animal, lazy and intelligent. And cunning. He made Charlie proceed warily.

"Nothing," said Charlie, not meaning it.

"Well, I'll find out later," Pete said with calm certainty. "Good luck." This wish was obviously sarcastic.

Charlie stowed the file in his zipper case before leaving Pete's office. "I appreciate this," he said when he was ready to go and sure that Pete would volunteer no more information.

Pete shook his head and waved him away before turning his attention once more to the welter of reports set out on his desk.

Yuri Lanoff's grocery was closed, a hand-lettered sign informing the public that Yuri's wife was ill. Charlie stood with Rufus, feeling slightly at loose ends. He had made such a long habit of buying the makings of a light supper there that having the store closed made him uneasy, like a sensation of clothes that did not quite fit.

Rufus squeaked and gave a questioning wave to his tail. He turned his head toward Charlie expectantly, as if he were sure Charlie would open the door. When this did not happen, he lifted his front paw and halfheartedly scratched at the wood.

"Don't," Charlie said softly. "Illness. What's wrong with her?" he asked of the dark, shut grocery. Only an emergency would have made old Yuri close early, for he lived over the store and would be near at hand if his wife were at home.

After a moment Charlie pulled his wallet from his pocket, and drawing a business card from it, scribbled "Is there anything I can do for you?" on the back, then stuck the card through the mail slot. "Technically speaking," he told Rufus, "this isn't legal, but I don't give a damn."

A few minutes later Charlie set off at a brisk pace for Geary Avenue, where he knew he would find stores still open. He had not known how hungry he was until he had found Yuri's grocery closed. Other thoughts crowded his mind, competing with his hunger for attention. His air was preoccupied as he turned down Geary.

Rufus trotted at his side obediently, making no demands, leaving Charlie alone with his thoughts, sensing his master's withdrawal.

Three blocks farther on, Charlie crossed the street and headed into the large bright supermarket.

Charlie ate supper in front of the television watching an old movie. He loved old movies, particularly mystery and horror flicks; the worse they were, the more he loved them.

While watching Larry Talbot's dawning horror as his palms grew fur, Charlie thought of his work, untouched on the dining-room table. But the full movie moon was working its evil on poor old Larry, and Charlie knew that the werewolf was about to put in a conscience-stricken appearance. For once, thought Charlie, the law could wait. On the screen Lon Chaney, Jr., was becoming hairier with every clumsily edited cut; horror and anguish vied with crepe hair for the domination of his face. Charlie gave in and settled back to watch.

Saturday

CHARLIE WAS STILL half asleep when his doorbell rang at eight thirty. The noise cut into his scanty rest, making his head hurt. He grumbled, wishing he had resisted the last bad movie on Channel 44 and gone to bed at two.

The doorbell rang again, this time longer, more insistent. In response to the sound Rufus began to bark.

Knowing now that he would get no peace until the door was answered, Charlie hauled himself out of bed, pulling on his terry-cloth robe as he stumbled to the top of his stairs, arriving as the bell went off a third time. More from reflex than anything else he jabbed at the buzzer to open the door before he considered that he might not want to see his tormentor.

A figure stood in the door, tall, neat, slender. "Good morning, Mr. Moon. I hope I didn't wake you," Morgan Studevant said, a slight hesitation in her formality.

"Good morning, Ms. Studevant. I had to get up to answer the bell in any case," he said, and let her think about it. "Would you like a cup of coffee?"

"Don't go to any trouble for me," she said coolly as she came up the stairs, giving his attire one withering look after which she ignored it.

"It's no trouble to make some for you since I'm going to

be making it for myself." He waved her in the general direction of the living room.

She did not move. "Mr. Moon, I have some questions to ask you, and then I'll let you get back to whatever you were doing . . ."

"I was sleeping, Ms. Studevant," he said, adding, "By myself, if you were afraid you might be intruding." His rare smile took the sting from his words just as her flush confirmed her suspicions. "It's time I was up." He didn't really think so, but his curiosity was piqued. Again he pointed toward the living room.

Reluctantly she went through the door, saying automatically, "This is a very nice apartment . . . or is it a flat?"

"A flat," Charlie confirmed. "I've got the whole floor to myself. Would you like a tour of the place?"

Morgan ignored this gambit, masking it with a quick study of the various prints on the walls. As she glanced around the room, she saw Rufus standing in the archway to the dining room. Her gaze faltered. "Your dog?" she asked, tension making her voice high.

"That's Rufus," he said, slapping his thigh as a signal. When Rufus came up to him, Charlie rubbed his head and went on, "You'll find he's well mannered, Ms. Studevant. He won't jump or fawn all over you or do any of those other things dogs do which you don't like."

She pulled herself upright, becoming almost haughty. "I haven't said I don't like dogs."

"You didn't have to." Charlie pointed to the basket in the dining room. "Go to your bed," he told Rufus, "and stay there." As he watched his dog obey him, Charlie ran through his mind for other delaying tactics.

"Really, Mr. Moon," Morgan began as she turned to him. "I have a very full day. Those contracts you left for me are finished, and now I have to read up on copyright infringement for you. So, please, I want to get this over with."

"If you'll give me five minutes, I'll be dressed and you can join me at breakfast." Charlie watched her, a glint in his dark eyes. "Believe me, I'll be much more attentive to what you have to tell me if you'll let me get some food first. Okay?"

Now Morgan looked at him uncertainly, her confusion making her appear much younger and less prickly than she was. "It's just that this is important, Mr. Moon . . . I don't want to impose on you or . . ."

"Let me impose on you?" Charlie suggested gently. "I never seduce the women I work with. And if I did, I wouldn't attempt it in an old bathrobe after five hours' sleep. I think I can safely promise you I won't take advantage of you, Ms. Studevant."

"That is not what I meant," she said, her voice becoming sharper.

"Yes, it is what you meant," Charlie corrected her, rather more harshly than he had intended. "You're so determined not to be a sex object it's all you can think of. You told me when we first met that you finished top in your class at Boalt. Well, let's see some of that precious education at work instead of all these defensive postures." He realized he had raised his voice more than he had intended. He shook his head ruefully. "I told you I'm no good for anything before breakfast. Now I've proved it."

Her face was set, the muscles in her jaw standing out against the fine bones. "That wasn't necessary."

"Of course not. I'll apologize after breakfast." He half turned from her, taking stock of his living room. "The chair by the window is the most comfortable. And the sofa isn't too bad."

It was a truce. "Don't be too long," she said as she sank awkwardly into the overstuffed chair nearest the door. One anxious glance at Rufus reassured her that he was keeping to his place.

"Five minutes," Charlie said. Then he strode off to the

bedroom, realizing as he went that he still did not know what had brought her.

He was as good as his word, returning to the living room in slightly less than five minutes, dressed in dark slacks and a heavy ski sweater of russet and chocolate wool. Lois had liked to see him in earth colors, and he still found himself buying those shades.

Morgan was standing by the bay window, blindly watching the street, when he said from the door, "I'm under the wire."

"Yes," she said after checking her watch. "I didn't mean to be uncivil, Mr. Moon. But you had no right—"

"I haven't had breakfast yet," Charlie interrupted her. "Let's wait until after. Please." He crossed through the dining room toward the kitchen. Then he stopped. "I was going to make something here, but if you'd rather, we can eat out."

"Eat out?"

"If you feel uncomfortable here, we'll go out. If you'd rather eat here, fine. Either way, you can tell me what's on your mind, and I'll be able to make sense of it."

"You can make sense of this right now," she said, opening her large shoulder-strap purse and pulling a newspaper page from it. "This is what I wanted to talk over with you." She thrust the paper at him.

It was the morning *Chronicle*. Charlie took it, saying, "I don't see what—"

"Lower right-hand corner. 'Experts Discuss the Right to Die.' Read it. The fourth and fifth paragraphs."

After a cursory look at the rest of the page, Charlie followed her instructions. As he read his face took on lines of worry. It was bad.

> . . . Among those present were the families of patients who had been given the choice of prolonged

life. Mr. Eugene Margolis, spokesman for the group, recalled his wife's death which occurred last year with these words "She had been very ill and in terrible pain. It was possible for her life to be prolonged with ever-increasing amounts of drugs, which terrified her. I'll always be grateful to her doctor, Miranda Trobridge, who left her sufficient medication to let her make her choice. The compassion of this courageous doctor fills me with gratitude and respect . . ."

Charlie wadded the paper into a ball and threw it across the room. "Shit!"

Alarmed at this outburst, Rufus jumped up from his bed and stood, barking tentatively in the dining room.

"Quiet, Rufus!" He waited a moment until he was obeyed. "Mrs. Margolis!" he spat as if it were profanity. "I knew that would come back to haunt us. From the first I heard about it, I knew it." He flung himself into a chair, one hand covering his eyes.

"I thought you should know," Morgan said, suddenly diffident.

"You're right, Studevant. I'm not mad at you, you know. I appreciate it. Christ, I was afraid of this."

"Then she did do it?" Morgan asked, not moving. "She did help that woman die?"

"Sure. I heard about it last week. Miranda herself gave me the story. The Margolis woman was terminally ill, and Miranda left her enough drugs to kill herself if she wanted to." He drummed his lean fingers on the arm of the chair.

"Did you approve of that?" she asked him.

"What does my approval have to do with it?"

More firmly now, she asked, "Do you support her actions?"

"If you mean do I think the woman had a right to die, certainly I do. But that doesn't help Miranda in a malpractice defense. And that's what I have to worry about right now." In one urgent motion he rose. "I'm still hungry. Do we eat here or out?"

"I don't want you to pay for my breakfast. That's not what I came here for." She sat straighter in the chair.

"That statement is going to be hell to deal with. I wouldn't be surprised if the DA's office got into the act now." He frowned. "They'll try for manslaughter, if they get a case off the ground. They might get away with it."

"Manslaughter?" Morgan went a little pale. "They wouldn't do that to her, would they? They couldn't. It isn't right."

He gave her a penetrating look. "If the world were fair and right, Ms. Studevant, there would be no need for the law. And you and I would be out of a job." He cast aside his bleak mood. "Well, where do we eat?"

"I don't care." Which meant she left the choice to him; she wanted no possible obligation attached to breakfast.

Suddenly he made up his mind. "Let's get out of here. I want to think without having those"—he pointed to the file folders on the dining-room table—"reproaching me every time I let my thoughts wander."

"We go dutch," she informed him.

"Anything you like. Where'd you like to go? There's a good place on California that does a nice breakfast for under five bucks."

She shrugged, then said impulsively, "Or we can go to that crepe place on Union. They do wonderful breakfasts." As she spoke she wondered why she changed.

"Union Street is okay with me." He gave Rufus a pat, then sent him back to bed. "I'll be back in a couple of hours. You look after the place."

"Your car or mine?" Morgan asked.

"What do you drive?"

"MGB," she said, perilously close to a grin.

"We'll take your car."

* * *

The small Union Street restaurant was not the terribly artsy sort of place that dominated that part of San Francisco. It was small, bright, and sunny with large windows in its north wall giving an excellent view of the Golden Gate Bridge, still hugging a mantle of fog around its twin towers, while sailboats slid over the water near the pilings.

"Do you sail?" Charlie asked Morgan once they had been seated and the silence between then had become oppressive.

"I used to," she said stiffly. "I don't anymore. I gave it up when I started law school. I can't afford it now, and I don't have the time."

"Too bad. I imagine you're good at sailing; you're a great driver."

She ignored the compliment. "We ought to have menus."

But Charlie would not be put off. "I'm not patronizing you."

"What do you call that driving remark?"

"A compliment." He watched her, wondering if she would accept this. At least she did not give an angry answer. He took a chance. "I admire competent women just as I admire competent men. I can't put it any simpler or plainer than that, Studevant."

She moved her knife and fork and realigned her napkin. "I hope the waiter won't be long," she muttered.

"Okay, forget I said it. You're harder to make friends with than a porcupine, Studevant, and that is the truth." He leaned back in his chair. "Tell me, if you're so down on me, why'd you bring that paper by this morning?"

She turned to him, startled. "But that affects your client. It could ruin your case. You had to know about it."

"Sure," he agreed. "I'm grateful that you told me. It's going to mean a lot to my case to have a jump on Malton and the Weeds. But that doesn't tell me why you did it."

"It's not important," she said, signaling for a waiter.

"Why?" he repeated as the slender young man approached their table.

"Yeah?" the waiter asked, a cynical curl to his smile.

Charlie tapped the table twice as he straightened. "We'd like two menus right now, and you may take our order in five minutes."

An odd expression crossed the waiter's face. "Anything else?" he asked, as if he really cared.

"That's all for the moment," Charlie dismissed him, and watched the waiter go for the menus.

"How'd you do that?" Morgan demanded as the young man left. "What did you do to him?"

"Magic," Charlie answered.

"Come on. What did you do?"

"I told you: magic." He took the menus from the waiter. Handing one of the beautifully calligraphed sheets to Morgan, he asked her, "You've eaten here before. What do you recommend?"

"Um . . . Well, most of the items are pretty good. Number Four, the crepes and sausage, is nice."

Charlie studied the menu, trying to think of a way to find out why she had helped him. Plainly she didn't want to talk about it. Then he hit on the answer. "One minority to another, is that it?" he asked her.

"Is what it?" She did not look up.

"Is that why you've helped me?"

"It doesn't matter. I'd like tea with mine."

"I thought this was separate checks."

"Separate checks are fine with me. I prefer it that way," she said, once more becoming flustered.

"You'll want to order for yourself?" Charlie found he was enjoying himself and felt a twinge of guilt. Studevant didn't really deserve the treatment he was giving her. He sat back and waited.

In a moment the cynical young man was back, looking

somewhat bewildered as he stood by their table. "What do you want?" he asked, some of the old sneer gone.

"Morgan," Charlie said, indicating she should order first.

"Number Four," she said, "and a pot of English Breakfast tea."

"Lemon or milk?"

"No."

"Please put these on separate checks," Charlie said and was pleased to find the young man nonplussed. "I'll have the Number Six breakfast and a lot of hot black coffee." As soon as the waiter had scribbled, Charlie said, "That will be all for now. I'll signal if we need anything."

Once more the young man withdrew.

"That is spooky," Morgan said.

"Now," Charlie said, turning toward Morgan. "I want to know if you helped me because I'm an Indian."

She studied the table. "Not entirely," she said at last in a small voice.

"I see." Suddenly his fatigue was heavy on him.

"No, you don't. Willis Ogilvie made that rotten deal with you about Lydia and the secretaries. That wasn't fair. And Alex Tallant won't lift a finger to help. So I did. Maybe partly because you're an Indian. But the other's the real reason." She lifted her chin defiantly. "Besides, you're a real Uncle Tonto. I mean, look at you, working in a real WASP firm. You aren't doing anything to help your people. Why? You shouldn't be ashamed of being an Indian. Indians have a very proud heritage, and it's the whites' fault that so much of your life-style has been destroyed."

Charlie felt himself grow cold. "First, I am not ashamed of being Ojibwa. But I don't think you appreciate my situation. My people, as you call them, are Canadian Indians. They live fairly far north on the Alberta-and-Saskatchewan border. That's a long way from Wounded Knee, Morgan, and not even the right Indian nation."

"But you could do *something*. They need your help, even if you are Canadian."

"Yes," he said meditatively. "But you see, they don't want it. I have offered and been refused. And there are very capable attorneys in the Sioux nation and among the other tribes and nations. And those men and women have shared their experience which I have not."

"Then why not practice in Canada?"

Charlie looked for the waiter, wishing that he could bring this uncomfortably personal discussion to an end. But the slender young man was nowhere in sight. Reluctantly he explained. "I was born in California, away from the tribe. We didn't go back to Iron River until I was six. My roots are there, but my home is here."

"Oh, come off it," she said, distrust in her eyes.

"What's so unusual about that? Think of the Lemminis," he went on, taking a perverse delight in comparing himself to them. "They're Florentines to the core, wholly Italian. But it would take more force than anyone's got to get them out of San Francisco because this is their home. I'm no different. I'm just on another level."

"Do you have any contact with your tribe? Do you ever see them?" She could not conceal her fascination.

"Certainly. I go back once a year for the council meeting. Why? Did you think I'd shut all that behind me?" He raised his brows, waiting for her answer.

She frowned, her face taking on the clear, studious expression Charlie had often seen in Lois' eyes. He dreaded her next question. "I didn't realize . . . You never said anything, did you?"

"We haven't been going in for confidences, Morgan. Were you expecting me to tell you this because you were curious or because you wanted to inspect my credentials, or what?" He looked straight into her eyes. "Well?"

"Oh, no, it's not like that," she said, flustered. "But when I heard your wife was white, and you didn't take an active part in the Indian community . . . what could I think?" This last was blurted out as if it were a terrible confession.

"I didn't consider you might be judging . . ." He was glad to see the waiter coming with their meals. He could at last turn the subject. He inhaled the aroma as the plates were set down in front of them. "Smells wonderful. And I am hungry."

Morgan kept the car idling in front of Charlie's place while she took notes on her instructions. "And the cases you want checked? Do you have anything in particular in mind, or a scatter-gun search?"

"Oh, Christ, anything you can find on malpractice. We're going to have to flood this case with information. This damn comment of Mr. Margolis' is distinguishable. Mrs. Margolis was terminally ill, an older woman, completely bedridden. All Miranda did was leave the choice up to her patient. That's been said consistently, thank God. It's not like the Weed case at all. But it is going to take some doing to convince the average citizen of that." Then he remembered something else. "There was a case in Florida a couple of years back. A woman sued a hospital for the right to die. They kept pumping her full of drugs and cutting down for a vein, and she knew that it was only prolonging the agony. I believe she approached the matter under 'cruel and unusual punishment' or possibly the cruelty to animals acts. See if you can get the dope on that."

"That's Florida. Isn't there anything in California jurisdiction? It would carry more weight closer to home."

"If you can find it, I'll use it." He reached into his pocket for his keys.

"I don't care if the case was in Tierra del Fuego, if it'll help, I'll find it." Then she frowned. "Besides, the Margolis case might never come up. Technically it can't be offered in evidence, can it?"

"To all intents and purposes it was entered in evidence the moment the *Chron* printed it. It's public information now, and we're going to have to live with it as best we can. I wish that man had kept his mouth shut a month or two longer. Malton is going to have a field day with it." He rubbed his hand across his eyes. "I'll call you tomorrow afternoon if I think of anything else."

"Is that all on the Trobridge defense then?"

"For the time being." He opened the door and slung one leg onto the sidewalk.

She stopped him from getting out of the car with: "And the copyright infringement case? What do you want me to do about that? You wanted that immediately, too."

"I want you to spend your time on both." He turned to her. "You know what the pressures are. You've heard what I have to handle in this Trobridge case; you know about the copyright infringement; you should have read up on Elizabeth Kendrie's contracts by now. What I want is everything you can give me on all of them. I'll be spending my time on Miranda's case right now because it's an emergency. But you know what the situation is. You set your priorities the way you see fit, and I'll accept that."

She had stiffened as he spoke. "Are you testing me?"

"What?"

"Is this some kind of exam, to find out if I'm capable?"

"No. No, it's not."

"Are you indulging me, then? You know, giving the kid a chance to prove herself?" The challenge was back in her face.

Charlie got his temper under control as he pulled his leg into the car again and carefully closed the door so that they would be private. "You're going to have to learn to order your priorities at your own discretion. And the sooner you learn how, the better. That's for your own protection. You've got me and Willis and Alex to deal with, and we're all going to assume you have no one else making demands on you . . . All three of us. Remember that. Last year we had two associates working for us, but they've gone into partnership together, and you, Ms. Studevant, are going to be expected to take up the slack on all levels. That is one hell of a load for anyone, and I don't care how high you finished in your class. Just because you've passed the bar, it doesn't mean you'll be doing much more than clerking for the first six months. Willis won't let you start doing case work until he knows how well you clerk. He's that way with everyone. So you're going to have to get used to establishing your priorities and keeping to them, no matter what the pressure or who's doing the pushing."

She sat still through this and now turned on a terribly sweet smile, which she displayed for Charlie's benefit, as she said, "But of course, this doesn't apply to you, does it?"

"Damn right it applies to me." Again he opened the door. "I'm not going to fight with you, Morgan. I need your help too much." He got out of the car and stood for a long moment looking down at her. "It was a nice breakfast. And I do appreciate the warning. I'm glad you were willing to come by with the paper. And before you decide that was a put-down," he added impishly, "I'm going in."

She almost smiled. "I'll talk to you tomorrow, Charlie." Then the door was slammed, the engine revved, the gears clicked, and she was gone.

"I suppose you've seen the nonsense in the *Chronicle*?" Elizabeth Kendrie demanded as soon as Charlie had picked up the receiver and before Charlie could say a word.

"Good morning, Elizabeth. Yes, I have seen the *Chron*, and I am as upset as you are about it."

"No doubt," she snapped. "Is it true?"

"Yes." Charlie waited, knowing that without Elizabeth's support Miranda could not hold out at the clinic. The muscles in his neck grew tight as the seconds lengthened.

"Was the woman's condition as the husband stated it?

Was she terminally ill? Was this an ethical decision?" The questions rapped out like gunfire.

"One at a time," Charlie cut in. "First, yes, apparently Mrs. Margolis was in bad shape. Miranda tells me her kidneys had quit, and she was unable to eliminate the poisons building up in her body. She might have lived quite a while longer with constant machine assistance, but there was no chance of recovery. From what I gather Miranda made no decision but to leave the woman enough medication to kill herself if that was what she wanted."

Elizabeth grunted. "But this destroys your case, doesn't it, Charlie?"

"Oh, not entirely," he answered, hoping it were so. "I think we can still present a good defense. It'll be a lot harder, but I think I can do it."

"Very good," Elizabeth said, warm approval coloring her words. "Then I'll keep the board of directors of the clinic tied up a little longer. I thought you should know that Fritz Bjornsson was on the phone to all of us this morning trying to get our permission for the termination of Miranda's contract. I can hold out a couple of days, but you'll have to go into action there early in the week. Bjornsson wants Miranda out of there."

"I know," Charlie said bleakly.

"What has Miranda said to all this?"

"I haven't talked to her. I'm planning to go by the clinic later today. She and I will have to make plans. But there are some other things that must be done now. I've got Studevant working on part of it, and I'm working on the rest." He did not mention that part of what he was working on was an answer if the district attorney started to take an interest in the case.

"Charlie," Elizabeth said sternly, "tell me honestly, do you think you can save her?"

Charlie paused. "That depends on what you mean by save her, Elizabeth. I think I can keep her from losing too much to the Weeds if I can delay the case in court for a couple of months, so that this furor about Mrs. Margolis can die down. She might not win, but I think we can reduce the Weeds' demands to a reasonable level. I'm reasonably certain we can work a deal, if it comes to that; if we can arrange a reasonable settlement, I'll support it. Whatever the issue in court, I don't think that will be her main concern. There will be repercussions. There's almost nothing I can do about that. She'll have to weather them as best she can."

"What about the clinic? How badly will this affect her position there?"

"I don't know. You're closer to the situation than I am, Elizabeth. What do you think the chances are for her dismissal?" He let the question hang.

Elizabeth was silent. Then she said, "Then it's very bad, isn't it?"

"Yes," said Charlie slowly. "Yes."

As he drew into the lot at the Harrowleigh Clinic, Charlie glanced nervously toward the park and the shadow of the trees there, remembering the terrible discovery he had made. It was calm now, the sunlight filtering through the branches and dappling the earth. Beyond on the grass two boys were playing an abbreviated but intense game of football. Charlie was tempted to linger, watching them wrestle with the football as the sun slid behind the buildings and into the ocean. But there wasn't time for it. Abruptly he turned and walked away from the lot, into the clinic.

The waiting room was jammed, several mothers hanging onto complaining children. Charlie saw that three of the children wore heavy braces on withered legs and supported themselves doggedly on shiny lightweight aluminum crutches. The women's faces all had the same shadow across them, the shadow of hopelessness and despair.

"Yes?" the receptionist hooted at him when he rang the buzzer.

"Charles Moon to see Dr. Trobridge."

The woman looked down at the log on her desk. "I'm sorry, Mr. Moon, I don't have an appointment here for you—"

"I'm not a patient—"

"We aren't allowed to take social messages—"

Ruthlessly Charlie overrode her. "I am Dr. Trobridge's attorney. Now I've gone through this kind of nonsense with this desk before, and I am not going to go through it again. Please have Dr. Trobridge notified that I'm here and tell her that I must speak with her immediately. I am sure she knows why. If you think you haven't the authority to do this, I'll arrange authorization with Dr. Bjornsson."

"Really, you don't have to take this tone . . ." the woman began, her eyes widening. Unlike the previous receptionist, this one was rather pretty in a cold, plastic, unreal way, like a grown-up Barbie doll.

"I certainly had to take this tone before. Please do as I ask. I'll wait for five minutes; then I'm coming in unless Dr. Trobridge has been told I'm here." He did not want to be polite at all with this woman, and the longer she forced him to deal with her, the more offensive he became.

"Oh, very well." The woman pouted. The window between her desk and the waiting room closed with a snap.

Charlie turned away from the window and found himself faced with the difficult problem of dealing with the other people in the waiting room. He felt the curious, slightly hostile eyes on him and did not want to return the looks. He was helpless in the face of their fear, their hurt, which touched him as deeply as their probing looks. Those keen eyes reminded him of his grandfather who would still turn his sightless eyes with piercing accuracy on those near him. For that reason Charlie had felt awkward around him, far more awkward than old William had felt with Charlie.

These marked children, in his tribe they would be singled out, and some would die, and those that lived be venerated for the special knowledge their private torment gave them. But here there was no veneration, only pity, a subtle aversion, and an invisibility. He looked down at the little girl sitting near him. She was no more than six, a quiet child, neatly dressed, her soft hair framing a face misshapen by fire. Two stricken eyes pleaded with him to see something other than the terrible scars. She did not speak.

Charlie reached out and touched her shiny hair. "Never mind," he said softly. "Never mind."

The window snapped open once more, and the receptionist peered out. "Mr. Moon? Dr. Trobridge will see you in her office now." Apparently she disapproved of this, for she shut the window with even more force after making a contemptuous sniff. The glass rattled, echoing her opinion.

Charlie entered the inner office, saying, "I know the way," to the poker-faced receptionist as he turned down the long hall that led to the offices jammed together at the back of the building behind the therapy room.

"Miranda?" he asked as he knocked on the door.

"Charlie. Oh, Charlie!" There was so much relief in her voice that it startled him, and he hesitated as the door was flung open. "Charlie!"

"What's the matter?" The force of her emotion struck him like a blow. He stepped inside the office quickly, closing the door as he looked at her.

Her face was distraught, mottled from crying, and her mouth trembled. Her brown hair, usually neat, was in disarray, and her blouse was rumpled. She looked at him, her hands turned up, and her eyes filling with tears. "Shit, Charlie," she choked. "Shit, shit, shit."

"What is it?" He had reached out to take her hand, worried now. What had happened to her to bring this on? Had Bjornsson fired her? Had Weed read the article and confronted her with it? Had one of her patients castigated her or refused to be treated by her? Had there been trouble in the clinic? "What is it?" he repeated.

"The paper." She sobbed, pulling away from him. "Mr. Margolis, in the paper . . . He said . . . he said—"

"I know what he said," Charlie interrupted her. "Tell me what's happened."

"I can't bear it. *I can't!*" Suddenly she cast herself into his arms, her hands clinging to him, holding his arms in a drowner's grasp.

"Miranda, stop it," he said, shaking her to get her attention, to break the hold of her panic. She was on the verge of real hysteria, and he knew she must not lose control here, at the clinic. "Stop it. You mustn't, Miranda."

"I can't do it!" This last was almost a shriek, her voice rising with each word. "I can't, I can't, I can't."

Alarmed now and sure that a sharp slap would not suffice Charlie resorted to his other method. He seized her head between his hands, thumbs forcing the upper eyelids open, and he brought her face within an inch of his own. When he spoke, it was in a soft, rapid chanting. "Look at me, Miranda, and listen to me. You are not going to cry anymore. You are going to be calm; you are going to be able to tell me calmly what has happened to you. You are going to keep control of yourself while you do it. You will tell me clearly and concisely what has upset you, and when you have said it, you will feel more confident, more relaxed, so that when we leave here, you will be able to relax, to get the rest you need to regain your strength and your perspective. You are not afraid now. You can give the fear to me. I will take your fear. Do you understand?"

She muttered a word.

"Do you understand me?" This time he said it more slowly, his voice nearly normal.

"I understand," she said, the wail disappearing. Her hands loosened on his arms.

Carefully, tenderly, Charlie guided Miranda to a chair.

He watched her critically as the tension faded from her face, as her mouth relaxed. Soon her breathing was better, and her hands lay softly on the arms of the chair. "Now," he said in his lowest voice, "tell me what happened to upset you."

Her eyes were dreamily fixed on the tiny window behind her desk. She stared at it as she spoke. "There was that story in the paper this morning, about the Right to Die conference up at Cal Medical. Mr. Margolis was there, and he said I helped his wife die. But that isn't what I did."

She began to grow agitated once more, and Charlie put his hand on her shoulder. "You don't have to be afraid. You gave me your fear, remember?"

"Oh, yes. Some of my patients read it." Her voice was distant.

"Did they give you a bad time?" Charlie asked, thinking that Elizabeth was right about the patients.

"It was terrible. I hated it." Her hands came together and clung to each other for comfort. "They asked me questions. Old Mr. Guden, he was the worst. He sat here and he begged me—"

"What did he beg you?" Charlie said, puzzled now, thinking that the old man must have really broken down. "What did he want?"

"He wanted to die," Miranda said, and her words caught in her throat. "They all wanted to die. They asked me to give them the drugs so they wouldn't have to go on living. Oh, Charlie," she said, looking up, her eyes wet, "I can't do it. I can't handle it. I can't bear it." She drew in a shuddering breath. "When they ask me, I hurt."

"I'm sorry." It was inadequate but all he could offer.

She shook her head, trying to keep control of her weeping. "I know I shouldn't be doing this. But I don't think I can cope. And when they beg and beg and I tell them that I can't do it, they don't believe me." She pushed her clenched fist against her teeth, scraping the knuckles.

"They don't believe me. They think I'm lying to save myself, that I don't care if they suffer. But I wouldn't let them suffer if I could stop it . . . I wouldn't. Mr. Guden swore at me. He's got degenerative heart disease. We can't do a lot for him, except buy him a little time. He's in pain . . . Maybe he should get the choice to die. Maybe that's his right, *but I can't kill him!* I can't, I can't." She started to shake, which upset her even more. "I keep doing this." She tried to hold her hands steady. "It should stop. I don't know what I'm doing wrong. I shouldn't be shaking . . ."

"Here." Charlie pulled her to her feet, drew her near him, and wrapped his arms around her. "Don't worry, Miranda. It will stop."

Another spasm shot through her. She grabbed his shoulders convulsively, gasping for air. Color mounted in her face, then receded, leaving her skin with a waxy pallor. Slowly the trembling subsided.

When she was breathing normally, Charlie stepped back from her. "Better now?" he asked, keeping her hands in his. It was too bad they had never been lovers, for then his embrace would not be strange to her, and there would be a familiar comfort in his nearness.

She withdrew her hands, putting them to her forehead. "I'm sorry. I didn't think I'd go to pieces that way. It's getting to me." She made a sound that was supposed to be a laugh. "Charlie, could you get me out of here? I've got to get away—"

"Sure." He cut her off. "Is Bjornsson around, or do I have to reach him at his home?" He didn't relish dealing with Swanhilda again.

"He's probably in the therapy room. We've got a couple of muscular dystrophy cases in today. They fascinate him. He's doing some sort of study on the rate of degeneration in the young and the psychological effects of the disease. All very scientific."

"I can imagine," Charlie murmured, thinking of Fritz's cold pale eyes. He turned his attention to Miranda. "You get your things ready. Just pack them up any old way. I'm going to arrange for you to take a leave of absence starting right now."

"A leave of absence? I don't need that long. Only a couple of days, until I get hold of myself and work this through." She reached out in protest, then drew her hand back. "Charlie, don't make a big thing of this. Please."

As gently as he could Charlie reminded her, "You told me your patients want to die. They are asking you to kill them. This isn't going to stop just because you're gone a few days. They will ask you again when you get back, and you will have to be able to answer them with a good record. The whole matter of Sparky's death is going to have to be settled before you can work here again in peace."

Miranda was shocked. "You don't think they'll keep asking me, do you?" Her hands started to shake once more. "They won't keep on, will they?"

"Get your things ready, Miranda," he said, and slipped out the door.

Charlie thought that most of the equipment in the physical therapy room looked like leftover playthings from the Spanish Inquisition, but he didn't say so. He paused in the door, watching as one of the therapists repositioned the braces on her teenaged patient's legs.

Fritz Bjornsson stood watching, a remote, appraising expression in his face. "Excellent," he told the young man whose face was twisted in agony. "You mustn't let yourself get careless. We can't help you if you don't help yourself. Now try it again, and this time, pay attention to Miss Bressin's instructions and do what she tells you to."

"But, Doctor . . ." the therapist began, and was cut off by a curt gesture from Fritz.

"Oh, Doc, it hurts," the boy said, his adolescent voice cracking.

"Yes. But that's only temporary. It will take you a while to get used to it, but you will."

Charlie caught the tight-lipped look the therapist shot Fritz Bjornsson and decided it was time to interrupt. "Dr. Bjornsson," he said as he came across the room. He held out his hand as he neared the chief of the clinic and forced a genial smile onto his face.

Fritz Bjornsson looked up at the sound of Charlie's voice, and a shadow of anger crossed his face so quickly that Charlie was not entirely sure he had seen it. "Mr. Moon," Fritz said as if he had trouble recalling the name. "I understand from our receptionists that you've been a frequent visitor here these last few days." His tone implied that Charlie was not entirely welcome.

"It certainly seems that way," Charlie agreed, noticing that while Fritz's attention was occupied, the therapist was loosening the braces on her patient's leg. Charlie adopted a more forceful attitude. "Yes, you see, this case is becoming more difficult."

Fritz made a cultured sneer. "I understand your predicament. I read the *Chronicle* this morning." His face grew pinched with disapproval. "Whatever possessed the man to make a statement like that?"

"I'm certain he didn't know that Dr. Trobridge was involved in litigation," Charlie assured him, mentally telling himself to check this out, because Malton might have talked to Mr. Margolis. It was a long shot, and it would put Malton in a bad light, but Charlie knew he had to find out one way or the other. "I'm sorry to have inconvenienced you and the clinic if my visits haven't been at the best times. But considering the gravity of the situation, I'm sure you can appreciate why I have maintained such close communication with my client." Just to make his point, he added,

"If Miranda were to lose this case, her conviction might have some unpleasant ramifications for your clinic."

"Of course. I didn't intend any criticism," he said, meaning nothing of the sort. "Is that all you wanted to tell me?" he demanded impatiently.

"No," Charlie said, watching disgust shape Fritz's features. "However unpleasant this case may be to you, Dr. Bjornsson, it is much more unpleasant for Dr. Trobridge."

"Naturally," Fritz muttered.

"I'm glad you realize this," Charlie went on, taking full advantage of Fritz's superior attitude. "Not everyone in your position would. I'm depending on you to help me in this. You see, Miranda's in an intolerable position at present, what with the adverse publicity the Elgin death had brought the clinic and the unfortunate remarks of Mr. Margolis. She feels her duty is here, and she has done her utmost to fulfill her obligations to her patients." As he spoke, Charlie thought that this was the sort of speech that Alex ought to make; he had the more convincing manner. "But her patients are also aware of her situation now, just as you and I are, and this has made her work impossibly difficult for her. That's why I'm requesting an immediate leave of absence for her until this whole matter has been satisfactorily resolved."

"In the courts?" The implication was snide.

"Quite probably," Charlie said with his best professional nod.

"You may tell her I'll accept her resignation." Fritz's long-fingered hand toyed with his tie clasp. "That will be the most reasonable solution to her problem, I would think."

"I see no reason for her resignation at this time. And I can see a great many other reasons for her not to resign. You'd like her to settle with the Weed family and be done with it. But that settlement would affect the clinic because your insurance would have to pay it. If you read through Dr.

Trobridge's contract, you'll see that I'm right." Charlie had the advantage now; he could tell it from the restless way Fritz Bjornsson's hands moved. Resolving to keep this advantage, he went on: "You want Dr. Trobridge to accept a tacit guilt, if not an actual one, but she will not do this. I will not allow her to do this because it would follow her all her life. Believe me, you had much better accept the leave of absence."

Fritz pursed his lips, his eyes focused on some point about three feet behind Charlie's head. "I don't see how she can win. The evidence is against her—"

"Not evidence, Dr. Bjornsson," Charlie corrected him. "Opinion. As yet no evidence has been presented, only requested; it hasn't been accepted. The effect of that opinion can be reversed in court if I can demonstrate—and I can, believe it—that Dr. Trobridge has been a victim of prejudice."

"Mere posturing," Fritz said, waving this away. "It has no bearing on the issues."

"But suppose there are new elements in this case that throw the whole matter of Sparky Weed's death into an entirely different light." Charlie wished desperately that this were true. It would take so little to save Miranda, but he had not found it. "Surely you don't want it to come out in court that you forced Dr. Trobridge to resign on faulty assumptions and very shaky circumstantial evidence? You might then face legal consequences yourself."

Behind Fritz's back the therapist Bressin gave Charlie a wide grin and a closed-fist salute. Charlie's eyebrows flickered in response.

"What makes you think this evidence you claim to have will exonerate Dr. Trobridge?"

He was hedging his bets now, and Charlie sensed it. He said, "I'm sorry, Dr. Bjornsson, but I'm not at liberty to discuss that. I haven't got the final confirmation I've requested on the new evidence"—he thought that was certainly being honest, considering he didn't have any more to go on than a hunch—"and until I do, I'm sure you can understand why I am very reluctant even to mention the matter. But in a case like this, where so much is at stake, I think it might be best if you know how things stand. It will save you a certain amount of embarrassment in the future." And if there were much more said, Charlie could do the traditional snowshoe dance of his people.

"I see. Of course, you must do as you think best." Dr. Bjornsson was very plainly withholding judgment until he could get more out of Charlie.

"Good, I knew you'd realize the importance of new developments in the case."

Fritz did not answer, but turned and looked back toward the teenaged boy in braces and the therapist. "Miss Bressin," he said in his best professional hauteur, "I think you may as well take Danny back to the examination room now. I will join you there presently."

"Don't go yet, Miss Bressin," Charlie said as the young woman rose. "I do need a witness for this agreement, Dr. Bjornsson, and having Miss Bressin here will save you the trouble of sending for your secretary."

Fritz's face had frozen. "Naturally," he said after a moment. "I didn't think of that." He glanced poisonously at the therapist. "You may stay, Miss Bressin. I am sure this won't take long."

"I'll be very brief." He nodded to Miss Bressin. "What I need from you, Miss Bressin," he said, "is your willingness to listen and remember. Now, I have been talking to Dr. Bjornsson about Dr. Trobridge, who, as you may know, is involved in litigation which is potentially damaging to this clinic."

Fritz put one elegant hand to his eyes.

"I've heard some of the others talking about the case," Miss Bressin admitted, giving Charlie an outrageous wink.

"Then," Charlie went on, forcing himself to keep his

expression grave, "you see why Dr. Trobridge is taking a leave of absence. Of course, she will not expect to be paid for the time she does not actually work here."

"Oh, you needn't go that far," Fritz objected mildly, obviously relieved that Charlie had not insisted on half pay.

"As you are in doubt as to the possible outcome of her suit, this is quite reasonable. And there is a good chance you will be called as a witness when the case is tried."

Too late Fritz saw the trap. His mouth set in a hard line. "I see."

"I was sure you would." He turned back to Miss Bressin. "At the conclusion of her case Dr. Trobridge will resume her duties here with full pay and with no blot on her record. During that time the clinic may need to hire another doctor to take care of Dr. Trobridge's duties, but that will be with the understanding that the position is temporary."

Miss Bressin nodded brightly. "That's clear."

Charlie raised his brows, wondering why the therapist disliked Fritz Bjornsson so much. He was sure it went beyond mere dislike to intoxicating, fermenting hatred. "Good. I'll send along a confirming letter, stating what we've outlined here. There will be a copy for both of you, and I'll have a copy which both of you will sign and return to me. That way we can be sure we all agree about this discussion."

"An excellent precaution," Fritz said, his urbane manner badly out of trim. "How thorough you are, Mr. Moon."

"I try," Charlie said. He stretched out his hand to Miss Bressin. "Well, I'm sure you're as busy as I am. Thank you for your help, Miss Bressin." He turned his attention to Fritz. "I'll be leaving shortly, Dr. Bjornsson. And I do trust you have no objections if I take Dr. Trobridge with me now? She is due at a conference this evening, and this will save me a second trip."

"Oh." Fritz sounded very out of patience now. "You must do whatever you think best. If you feel she should leave, then take her with you, by all means." When Fritz took Charlie's hand in his, Charlie again felt the vague repulsion of the cool, dry skin. "Well, good afternoon, Mr. Moon. I trust you are satisfied."

"Very much so. Good afternoon, Dr. Bjornsson." With a last diplomatic nod of the head, Charlie turned for the door.

As he passed Miss Bressin, she whispered, "You got the old prick. Good for you."

Charlie almost laughed. "Miss Bressin, I certainly appreciate your help," he managed to say.

Danny, the teenager with the braces, who had been watching with a certain awe, finally got up the courage to ask Charlie, "Mister, what are you? I mean what race are you? I know you're some kind of lawyer."

"I'm an Indian," Charlie said, looking at the boy.

Danny's face lit up. "Really? A real Indian? Like Sitting Bull? And Red Cloud? And Geronimo?"

"Well"—Charlie hesitated—"maybe not quite like them, but I'm an Indian, just the same."

The boy grinned. "Far out. Far out!"

Miss Bressin's smile followed him out of the therapy room.

"Ready?" he asked Miranda a few minutes later when he returned to her office. "We can go now."

"Almost ready." She was standing with a large cardboard box in her hands, looking uncertainly around the tiny office. "I can't seem to think straight," she apologized.

Charlie came across the little space to her and looked into the box. There were books, a stack of computer printouts, another stack of file folders, and a small leather pouch—the spirit bag he had given her. "I see you've kept it," he said, touched.

"Yeah." She looked down at it, the weathered rawhide making a strange contrast with her other civilized paraphernalia. "It's friendly."

"It's supposed to be," he agreed. "Look, Miranda, how

much of this junk do you need right away? Other than what you've already packed?"

She bit her lip. "I don't know. Just the fountain pens and that stack of reports." She pointed to a sheaf of papers lying on top of her bookcase. "I guess the rest of it can wait."

"Then don't let them worry you. You can always come back if you miss something. Leave the rest of it and come on. Gather up the pens and reports, and let's get out of here."

She reached obediently across the desk, then hesitated. "It seems so final, Charlie. I feel like I'm going away forever."

"Fat chance," he said, grabbing the papers off the bookcase. "These the ones you want?"

"Yes. Yes. Just put them in the box. I'll sort them out later." She looked frantically around the office once more. "What do I do if I lose, Charlie? What happens then?"

"Worry about that if it turns out that way. But I doubt it will." The words were automatic, the bolstering goodwill that was meant to sustain her through all the difficulty. But Charlie felt the gut-cold fear of failure. And of all people to fail, it had to be Miranda. To cover his feelings, he said to her, "I don't want you moping about while I work on your case. It's the worst thing you can do. That's why I'm taking you to Elizabeth Kendrie's. She's got a small recording studio in the basement, and you can help her there."

"Recording studio?" Miranda was so surprised that a smile burst on her face. "What does she do with it?"

"Records books for the blind. She rents it out to one of those organizations for a dollar a month. Which she usually gives to them as a donation. She reads down there for one day a week. And you can do it, too."

"But, Charlie—"

Charlie had taken up the box. "No buts." He opened the door.

* * *

No words were exchanged as he put her box in the trunk of his Volvo, and as they pulled away from the clinic, Miranda sat in stony silence. The minutes stretched out. "Okay," Charlie said at last as they swung west onto Clement. "Tell me about it."

She sighed. "I've been thinking. I know you want to get this case into court. I mean, I can understand that you as a lawyer see solutions in a legal framework. But sometimes that's not the right way."

"And what is the prerecorded message leading up to?" Charlie's eyes had narrowed, and his face was set.

"It's just that I think I ought to settle with the Weeds and bring this to an end. I thought I could stand the strain, but I can't, Charlie. And there it is. Will you do whatever has to be done?"

"Then you are guilty?" Charlie asked with deliberate cruelty.

"No. No." She pulled at one tendril of hair, staring blindly at the expensive houses. "I never thought it would be this awful."

"This is awful?" The irony was thick in his voice. "Miranda, we haven't even got started yet. Awful is what happens when we get into court and take Dr. Weed apart with a trowel."

She made a complicated gesture, saying, "Charlie, don't."

"Don't what? Don't defend you? Don't save your job? I'm supposed to defend you. It's *my* job to do that. I thought you wanted to work at the clinic. I thought you wanted to clear yourself? Well?" The car jerked as he braked for a stop sign.

"Yes, yes, I want to, but not this way, Charlie." She turned miserable eyes to him. "You don't understand."

"No. It's you who doesn't understand, Miranda. You say you don't want to do it this way. Well, my girl, there are no other ways, not now. Your options were exhausted when Dr. Weed filed suit. We can negotiate to a point, but any capitulation now would be an automatic confession. I can't let you do it."

She sat straighter. "Look, it's my case."

Charlie gave an irritated snort and pulled to the curb. "Now," he said when he had turned off the engine, "suppose I had a broken leg and I came to you to have you set it. Then, before you had done more than taken a couple of X rays, suppose I changed my mind and said that I didn't want it set because it would hurt too much, so I thought I'd let it heal the way it was?"

"But that's stupid," she said in a rush. Then, realizing what he was saying, she flushed. "It's not like that at all."

"Isn't it? What would happen to me if I let that leg heal improperly?"

She fiddled with her glasses.

"What would happen?"

"All right, you'd be lame. Probably." She was petulant.

"And what would you be with no place to practice and the possibility of losing your license?"

"They wouldn't do that." She was shocked. "Come on, Charlie. That's not fair. They aren't going to take away my license." But from the tone she was no longer certain of it.

"It has happened before. And, Miranda, you have to admit you're a target. Please," he said, touching her shoulder, "please think about what you're doing to yourself. I know you hate this. I know you feel some responsibility for Sparky's death. I know you don't want to turn this into a wide-open court fight, which could happen. But if you don't—Christ, Miranda, you can't let it all go just like that."

She looked into the dark slits of his eyes. "Charlie," she began, "I don't know if I can go through with it."

Slowly he let out his breath. "Okay. Maybe you're right. But promise me this. Give me a couple of weeks to do the right groundwork before you insist on anything. You hired me to represent you; let me try. That's all I ask of you. Let me make the effort." He saw her doubt in her face and went on. "If it turns out that we're really in a corner, then I'll drop the defense and try to work out a settlement with the Weeds and the clinic. You have my word on that."

She nodded. "Mrs. Kendrie is expecting us," she said.

Henry Tsukamato, Elizabeth Kendrie's very dignified houseman, took Miranda's box from the trunk with profound disapproval. But his voice was propriety itself as he told Miranda, "Mrs. Kendrie is waiting for you in the tea nook. Go to your left as you enter, and through the second archway." He turned to Charlie. "Will you be joining the doctor and Mrs. Kendrie, Mr. Moon?"

"No, Henry, not today. Please give Mrs. Kendrie my regrets. I'm certain she and Miranda will have things to discuss that will go on better without me. Perhaps another day." But as he turned down the invitation, he felt a twinge at the thought of missing the buttery currant scones and flaky shortbread that were standard fare for tea in the Kendrie household.

"Very good, Mr. Moon. I'll give Mrs. Kendrie your message. If you'll come with me, Doctor." He stopped Miranda's attempt to carry the box as he started back toward the house which sprawled over half an expensive acre of choice San Francisco real estate. A rhododendron hedge masked the house from the street, and as Miranda walked through the redwood gate Henry held open for her, Charlie heard her remark with delight, "Why, it's just like a Tudor manor house. How lovely."

"It *is* a Tudor manor house," Henry informed her grandly, unbending a bit to retell the story of Mr. Kendrie's extravagant present to his wife on their silver anniversary fifteen years before.

Charlie got back into his Volvo and drove off.

Half an hour later, back home, Charlie was wolfing down the remains of a late and uninteresting lunch. The file folders on the Weed boy waited for him on the dining-room table. As he drank the last of his tomato soup, Charlie felt suddenly reluctant to tackle them. He had been so sure that Miranda was right, that he would find the answer in those records, but now he was not sure. What if the autopsy revealed nothing? What if he could find no defense? He had given Miranda his word he would not carry on the case unless he knew they had a chance, but at the time he had assumed that they would be able to build a defense from the evidence hidden in those files. Now he wondered if there was anything to find, if he had a chance at all.

There was so little he could do. He put down the empty mug and stared at the files and felt their very presence accusing him. His fingers drummed restlessly on the table. He didn't want to read them. He didn't want to know. He considered taking Rufus out for his walk early. But that would buy him only an hour or so. Then he would have the files to face once more. "Oh, shit," he said, dropping into the cane-backed chair.

He greeted the abrupt ringing of the phone with relief. Gratefully he rushed to answer it, glad for the delay it meant. He lifted the receiver. "Hello. Charlie Moon."

"Charlie," Willis Ogilvie boomed at him, "get your ass over here right now!"

Charlie realized too late that the call was not a reprieve.

The Ogilvie house on upper Broadway was three stories of tradition and solidarity. It had once belonged to a U.S. Senator, as Willis Ogilvie never tired of telling people. It was famous for the enviable view it commanded of the Bay, particularly in the living room, where the water and the hills of Marin County were framed in high, arched windows and Italian brocade.

Charlie trod up the steps reluctantly. Usually he stopped

to admire the beautifully preserved gingerbread façade, but today he did not notice it.

It was Shannon Ogilvie who let Charlie into the house, her lovely artificial smile perfectly adjusted, a blend of rancor and deference. "Hello, Charlie," she said sweetly.

Charlie looked down at Willis' third wife. She was a tiny woman, no more than five feet tall, and slender. At twenty-eight she looked sixteen. Her long amber hair was parted in the middle and fell sleekly over her shoulders. Charlie knew that a portrait of her hung in the formal dining room. The painting showed her on her big gelding, Capriole, whose shiny coat exactly matched her hair. At the moment she was wearing a long housedress of red and gold iridescent silk. "Hello, Shannon," Charlie said as she stepped back to let him into the house. "Willis asked me to drop by." He would not tell Willis' wife that her husband had ordered him to come over.

"Willis is very upset," she announced. Her smile had disappeared.

Charlie decided not to take up this conversational gauntlet. "Shall I wait in the living room?"

"I'll tell him you're here. He's on the phone." The implication was plain: If Willis had not been on the phone, she would not have been forced to deal with Charlie. She closed the door, then went off, very straight and stiff.

Charlie looked after her, shaking his head. He stood in the foyer for some time, jangling his keys in his pocket for amusement. Then he strolled into the living room. He made the rounds of the paintings, inspecting them with care and attention as if he had never seen them before. But in fifteen minutes the paintings, even a mildly erotic Picasso, were exhausted, and he had to turn his attention elsewhere. He toyed with the idea of leaving but gave it up. Today, tomorrow, Willis would have to be faced. At last he flung himself onto one of the sofas and pulled a coffee-table edition of the paintings of Andrew Wyeth onto his lap. He thumbed through the book, not really looking at it.

He was still turning the pages when Willis surged into the room, resplendent in a lavishly embroidered Western shirt and heavy twill riding pants which he always wore when he went to watch Shannon ride. His rough-hewn features were set in severe lines, and his hazel eyes were as cold as gun-metal.

Charlie closed the book. "Hello, Willis. You wanted to see me?"

Willis stared down at him. "There is just a chance that I might have saved your case," he told Charlie.

Charlie became guarded. "What do you mean, saved my case? Which case?" He hoped Willis had made a deal with the Lemminis about the Guttierrez suit, but he knew with dreadful certainty that it was Miranda's case Willis meant.

Willis opened a large walnut cabinet against the wall, revealing glasses and bottles. He took a tumbler and filled it with bourbon, splashing a little soda into it for effect. He made a point of not offering Charlie any. "You know what I mean. I mean that the Weed family wants to file criminal charges against your precious Dr. Trobridge. I heard from Murphy at the DA's office last night."

"He called you and not me?" Charlie was stunned.

"Certainly. Now, I think we've got a workable deal going—"

"Wait a minute." Charlie interrupted him, his voice lowering. "You made a deal with Murphy about my client? What's going on here?"

Willis turned to him. "Weed wants your client arrested on a charge of manslaughter because of the death of that child. Do you understand that?"

Charlie glared at Willis. "Okay. And?"

"And Murphy called me about it. I've been on the phone with him and with Horatio Cronin most of the afternoon. Now, this isn't quite official, but they've agreed that if

Trobridge will settle with the family on this malpractice, they'll drop the criminal charges."

"You and they have agreed? Where do I come in? What the fuck is going on?" Charlie was on his feet now. He felt his anger turn cold. He all but crackled when he moved. "This is my case, Willis. And I'm not going to sell Miranda Trobridge out."

Now Willis was furious. "You don't seem to understand, Charlie. I am not asking you about this. I am telling you. As your senior partner." He took a generous sip of the bourbon. "You have made one holy mess of that case. I've talked to Bjornsson, I've talked to the Weed family, and there is no defense. The woman is responsible. That's that."

"Where do you get off talking about my clients behind my back? What kind of treatment is this?" Charlie felt his hands close into fists and willed them to relax. "You're out of your territory on this one, Willis."

Willis spread his hands, the picture of wounded innocence. "I told you not to take on the case unless you could win. I warned you what would happen. Now we've got to get you out any way we can. And that means settling with the Weeds right now, before it gets any worse." He put down the glass on the coffee table as he sank onto the sofa. "Let's not get excited. We're reasonable men, Charlie. You've let yourself believe that you're on some kind of crusade with that woman. Well, I don't blame you. She's damned attractive."

Although Charlie knew it was useless to object, he said, "It's not that kind of relationship."

"I know," Willis said with a leer. "You're just good friends."

"Okay," Charlie said, making no further protest. "Tell me the details."

Willis began to smile. "That's better." He motioned to the other sofa. "Sit down, Charlie. We've got a lot to talk about." Obediently Charlie sat. "Now, Cronin has told me that if Dr. Trobridge settles—and before you object, hear me out. Part of the deal is rough, but give it a chance." He caught up his cadence again. "If Trobridge settles, and, *and*"—he raised his finger to be sure Charlie paid attention—"she agrees not to contest the lifting of her license, criminal charges for manslaughter will not be pressed. Under the circumstances, Charlie, you'd do well to consider this." Again, Willis took a pull at the bourbon.

"So they're planning to take her license away already?" Charlie asked woodenly.

"That's what Cronin's really concerned about. He doesn't want to hound her, you understand." He said this with his usual political smoothness.

"Oh, of course not," Charlie said sardonically.

"But," Willis overrode him, "he doesn't want Dr. Trobridge to continue in practice. Besides, she can go into research work, if she wants. There's lots of things a doctor can do besides practice medicine."

"What's she supposed to do, just blithely chuck her career? She wants to practice medicine."

Willis chuckled, a great, rumbling sound. "She'll find other ways to keep herself busy. Now, I want you to get hold of Hammil and Ward on Monday and get the settlement under way. I imagine you should have it cleared up in a month or so."

"Where the bloody hell are your ethics, Willis?" Charlie said, his words bitter.

"Oh, come, Charlie, this has nothing to do with ethics. This is a matter of pragmatism. Look, maybe she is telling the truth. Maybe she didn't do anything deliberately. But that doesn't matter. What matters is that she cannot prove it in court. Can she?" He gave Charlie a disturbingly canny look. "No. I see you haven't found a defense. And her word against Bjornsson's and the Weeds' isn't worth sour owl's shit."

Charlie looked across the immense gulf of the coffee

table at Willis. What did it matter, he thought, now that it's all sewed up. Miranda wanted to drop the case, and Willis had given him a way out. Why didn't he take it? He felt tired, a fatigue that had nothing to do with his lack of sleep. It would be so easy to let it all go, to accept the terms. "No. I haven't found a defense," he admitted.

"So you see." Willis smiled expansively now. "Well, talk to that man—is it Malton?—on Monday. Everything's all set up."

Charlie sat very still. He stared hard at the carpet and noticed that it was three different shades of bronze. "No."

"What?" Willis sounded as if he did not believe what he had heard.

"No. N-O. I am not going to talk to Malton on Monday. I am not going to sell Miranda out. I am going to do what she hired me to do: defend her."

Charlie," Willis began, his face darkening.

"No, now it's my turn." He pushed himself off the sofa and began to pace. "You say that it's all fixed up, no criminal charges, just a little civil suit and everything is fine. All Miranda has to give up is her integrity and her career. Great. Really great. She loses her license, and then what? Just where do you think she'll find a job? And don't give me that crap about research. She's thirty-one years old. What's she supposed to do for the rest of her life? Well? So you're offering me a way out. Me, not her. That's about the shittiest thing you have ever done, Willis. It's blackmail. I am not buying. And if you say one word about expediency, I will ram your upper plate down your throat." Charlie was speaking softly, but each word was a shout.

"And when do I applaud this heroic little speech?" Willis asked with heavy sarcasm.

"You don't. You stop mucking with my cases."

"I see."

Charlie leaned over the back of the sofa. "Now that you've told me what you're going to do, I will tell you what

I am going to do. I am going to find out what really happened when Sparky Weed died, and why. I am going to see that Miranda is exonerated. And I am going to find out who is responsible and make sure they are prosecuted to the full extent of the law. Believe me."

Willis watched Charlie with careful eyes, calculating. He took a reflective pull on his bourbon. "All right. If that is the way you want it, you have until Friday."

"Have what until Friday?" Charlie had stopped leaning on the sofa.

"You have until Friday to prove your little theory that Trobridge is not responsible for that child's death. And I do mean prove. I will not accept hunches or vague possibilities. I mean you will produce hard, factual evidence that will hold up in court."

"Generous," Charlie said it dryly, but was secretly surprised. "What's the catch, then?" For there had to be one.

"Oh, yes. The catch, Charles, my boy, is that if you do not have this proof, by Friday, if you have made me throw a bargain out the window needlessly, then you too are out."

Charlie frowned. "Out of what?"

Willis lifted his eyebrows. "Out of Ogilvie, Tallant and Moon. And you had better believe *me*. Because it is the absolute truth." Raising his glass, he drank to that certainty.

III

April

Saturday Night

WHAT HE WANTED to do was get gloriously drunk, to throw the whole case, all his cases, to the wind and forget it. Forget the variety of San Francisco and go back to Canada, to Iron River, to be the medicine man there now that his grandfather was blind, to touch the powers of nature and the soul and be free of the burden of rationality and the law. That is what he wanted to do. What he did do was drive thoughtfully back to his flat and start the percolator going—it would be a long night.

The files lay on the table where he had left them. This time, when he sat down, he opened them with a resigned sigh. He glanced over the various pages and selected Miranda's file first. He might as well get the beginning before he got the end. He pulled his pad of legal-sized foolscap nearer.

At his feet Rufus yawned once, then rearranged his compact body for sleep. There would be no walk for the time being. He sensed that his master was alone with himself. He thumped his tail once, then slept.

Charlie rubbed his eyes and then began with the form the boy's parents had filled out when he was first brought to the Harrowleigh Clinic.

"WEED, Chisholm Harris (Sparky)," the typed tab on

the folder read. There followed a cautionary list for all the doctors at the clinic.

> Parkinson's. Do not administer any drugs except L-dopa. Do not prescribe antihistamines. Do not give muscle relaxants or tranquilizers. Do not administer aspirin. Do not prescribe cortisone or its derivatives. All vaccines must be given in half doses. No milk products. If milk products are inadvertently given, induce vomiting. Do not treat poor breathing with adrenaline or adrenaline substitutes. Do not prescribe thyroid or its substitutes. L-dopa only. Laser surgery inadvisable at present.

Charlie copied out all the warnings, thinking it was useless. But there had to be some answer. He turned the page and read the results of the boy's first series of tests and Miranda's first notes on the case. He noticed that even then, at the first visit, Miranda's long-term view of Sparky's case was pessimistic. "Moderately advanced Parkinson's," she had written. "It may be too late. Priority 1: stabilize condition." That would not look good in court. He made a note of it and read on.

It was after eleven when Charlie took a break. He pulled on a light jacket over his sweater and clipped the leash to Rufus' collar. "Come on," he said. "Let's get out of here."

When he opened the door at the foot of the stairs, the wind hit him as it blew in from the north. Charlie paused to zip up the jacket; then he and Rufus went out into the cold wind.

The sky was clear, with stars standing out in sharp relief against the darkness. With Rufus tugging at the leash, Charlie amused himself by locating the familiar stars and planets overhead. The wind made his face sting.

A few blocks beyond his place Charlie turned into Sea

Cliff, the rich district located between the green swath of Fort Mason and the Russian district of the city. All the houses here were large, imposing buildings, some three stories, all of them burnished with the fine sheen of wealth and care. Rufus led the way down the sleeping streets, sniffing eagerly at lawns and lampposts and barking once when a magnificent Burmese tom crossed his path and condescended to hiss at him.

The last time Charlie had walked this way he had encountered Lois and her new husband leaving a party. For a moment he had stared at her, not believing he was seeing her after two years. But she had turned her wonderful golden eyes on him then, saying, "Good evening, Charlie. How are you?" He had mumbled some reply. Then she added, "I don't believe you've met Janos. Janos, love, this is Charles Moon." Charlie recalled how the man had glared as they shook hands. Janos Zylis was not tall, but made up for it in the powerful breadth of his body. The grip of his hand was painful, and under his gray brows his eyes burned.

Charlie realized he had stopped now in front of the house where he had had that last meeting with Lois. But the house was dark. And Lois was with her aging Hungarian physicist at Stanford or Irvine or MIT. Or on Mars, for all it could mean to Charlie.

"Come on, Rufus," he said gruffly as he tugged on the leash, leaving Sea Cliff and heading toward the golden onion domes of the Russian Orthodox Cathedral.

Obediently the dog trotted at Charlie's side, his pink tongue lolling, his ears erect.

On the walk back Charlie did not look at the stars.

By two o'clock Charlie was on his second pot of coffee and had turned his attention to the coroner's report Pete Coners had given him. It was easier to read, more organized, impersonal. But Charlie was also sleepy and had to force his attention on the report. It would be so easy to drowse off, to drift into sleep there at the table, he thought as he made his first notes, not really reading what he had written. But this had to be done, he reminded himself sternly. This was Miranda's case. And his. He had until Friday.

Shortly after three he finished his second set of notes and toyed with the idea of comparing them with his first set, which he would have to do eventually. But sleep was heavy to him, and not even nine cups of coffee could counteract it. The day unraveled back from him to his wakening. Breakfast with Morgan seemed years ago, centuries ago.

He put books on the two separate stacks of notes to keep them from getting out of order. He made one last attempt at tackling the folders but gave it up as the cobwebs gathered in his mind. With a deep yawn he wandered off to bed.

Sunday

HE WOKE WITH a start from a dream which faded almost as fast as his eyes opened. He had a confused impression of Fritz Bjornsson turning into Janos Zylis as the result of a bargain made by Willis Ogilvie. There had been other things too, shadowy figures of uncertain identity waiting like armies out of sight. He felt uneasy.

Charlie pushed this from his mind, sitting up slowly, the ache of fatigue still in his body. He stretched out his arms, making small circles with them, rowing the knots out of them. He began to feel better. The dream blurred and was gone. He swung out of bed and stood naked by the window, looking down at the small yard he shared with his upstairs neighbor. It was a beautiful day, but the nodding trees told him that the wind was still there. He felt the gooseflesh rise on his body in confirmation. Tentatively he did a few stretches and was satisfied as he felt the tension in his back diminish. A twinge from his bladder reminded him of all the coffee he had drunk the night before, and he trudged off to the bathroom.

He had bathed and eaten by the time he returned to the dining-room table to study his notes. The room was awash with brilliant sunlight which made the colors seem unnaturally vivid. As Charlie took his seat again, he knew he would be distracted by the shimmering beauty of the morning, so he gave himself fifteen minutes to sit, staring bemusedly at the dining room. It was a rare time. How beautiful it was, he thought, and wished he could lose himself in the beauty. He turned his mind to work.

Rufus stretched and shook himself, then enjoyed a good scratch that made the tags on his collar jingle merrily. He came and sat by Charlie, head to one side, waiting.

Charlie looked down at him. "You want to go out, huh, Rufus?" He gave the dog an affectionate tug. "Okay." He got up, walked through the kitchen to the back porch, and opened the door. "There you go." He stood aside as the dog bounded by, heading down the stairs to the backyard. Charlie watched him for a moment, sad that all that Rufus had was a small backyard to run in. Then he closed the door, reminding himself that he could not take the day to play with Rufus. There were other, more pressing matters to attend to. He went back into the dining room.

The job ahead of him was long, tedious, and boring. From all his notes, he would have to take out meticulously all the information which was corroborated in both reports. He hoped what was left—if anything—would tell him what had killed the Weed boy. He took up his red felt-tip pen, pulled his notes from under their books, and lined up the first two pages.

The sun had long since passed overhead, and the dining room was now in shadow, like the street outside. Charlie had turned on the overhead light a few minutes before and now set about the task of looking for loose ends, those critical variables that would make the difference in court for Miranda. And, he reminded himself, for him.

He quickly set aside the differences in description of the boy's appearance. Death had altered Sparky Weed, as it altered everyone. Charlie ruled out those discrepancies impatiently; they had no bearing on Miranda's case. The next difference he came upon were family reactions, which he set aside. Fritz Bjornsson, he noticed, had not found the family concerned about the boy's condition which he had followed up with the observation "Mother overreactive." Although these things had little bearing on the boy's cause of death, they might prove useful in court. There were a few other inconsequential variables which he knew Miranda would class under medical style.

And then he found it.

No milk products. If milk products are inadvertently given, induce vomiting.

Milk traces in the matter of the lower bowels, the stomach and vomitus present in the esophagus.

Sparky Weed had been allergic to milk, yet there was milk in his body. And his parents knew he was allergic to milk; they had instructions to keep him away from it. There, in the autopsy report, was the key to Miranda's case. Charlie sat back, made almost dizzy by the wash of relief that went through him. He was close to giggling as he looked down at the two sheets of foolscap. Somehow the boy had had milk just before he died. The milk could have been the final trigger. Sparky's death was not Miranda's fault. It was not Miranda's fault. He beat on the table with the palms of his hands. It was not Miranda's fault.

In a moment his euphoria was gone. He examined the records once more, being as critical as Malton would be, as critical as Willis Ogilvie would be, and his optimism faded. Charlie knew this question of milk would cast doubt on Miranda's role in the boy's death, but it might not be enough. Certainly it wasn't solid proof of her innocence, or lack of responsibility. Malton could still insist that Miranda had discontinued or switched drugs. There were too many ways that Sparky might have taken the milk, too many accidents that might have occurred. The coroner's report said traces; that would mean conflicting debate on its effect. How much milk did the boy have to have to trigger his allergy? Had he ingested enough or was his tolerance level high enough to allow him a little milk without reaction? Charlie rubbed his forehead, imagining endless debate on the witness stand.

He got up from the table, stumbling a little because one of his feet was asleep. He resolved to take a walk as soon as he had talked to Miranda.

Henry Tsukamato's measured tones rang in Charlie's ear. "This is the Kendrie residence. May I help you?"

"Henry," Charlie said, keeping the urgency out of his voice, "is Dr. Trobridge there? This is Charles Moon speaking."

"I recognized your voice," Henry informed him grandly. "Yes, Dr. Trobridge is in. She and Mrs. Kendrie are playing croquet. If you will be kind enough to wait a moment while I call her?"

"Of course." Charlie drummed his fingers as he waited, wondering how Miranda would take the news. In a few minutes he heard the click of footsteps on the other end of the line.

"Hello, Charlie. What is it?" There was a distance in her words, as if she had disassociated herself from him.

"Miranda, I need the answers to a few questions."

"Go ahead." Still remote but not so disinterested.

Her coolness put him off, and he stuttered as he began, "Now . . . now, about the milk. You said the boy was allergic. . . ."

"It's all in the folder I gave you."

Charlie held back his temper. "Look, Miranda, I think I've found something that's going to make a difference. Will you help me?" He waited while she thought about it.

"Make a difference?" she repeated in a small voice.

"I can't promise anything yet. That's why I need your answers. But it could be we've found a way out. At least it will offset some of the damage of Mr. Margolis' statement."

"I see," she said, her words carefully neutral. "You're telling me not to get my hopes up too far, but maybe it won't be too bad."

Charlie's jaw tightened in exasperation. "No, damn it, that is not what I'm telling you. I'm trying to get enough information to know what to tell you, if you'll help me. I don't know how much good this will do until I get some answers." He let his breath out slowly, then said, "Now, please, Miranda. Tell me what you can about Sparky's allergy to milk?"

That surprised her. "Milk?"

"Yeah, the white stuff that comes from cows," he said, and immediately regretted it. "Forget I said that. Just tell me about the allergy."

Her coolness returned. "Why?"

"Because there was milk in the kid when he died, that's why."

There was a pause. "There couldn't be."

"The coroner says there was." Charlie wished he could stop the tingling in his foot. He wiggled his toes experimentally. The tingle got worse.

"He didn't drink it. It made him sick," she insisted.

"How much milk made him sick? Did he have any tolerance for it at all?"

Again Miranda paused, and when she spoke, her manner was seriously professional. "He wasn't able to take milk in any form. Even a couple teaspoons of it was enough to upset him. He'd vomit violently if he drank half a cup of it. He stayed away from it in all forms; he didn't eat most candies, for example, and he couldn't tolerate puddings or ice cream in any form. He didn't eat cheese or sauces with milk or anything derived from milk. I'd guess that if he'd taken one good swallow of it, he would react pretty violently."

"Then the early vomiting he experienced after he saw you could have been from milk allergy, not from Parkinson's?"

It was a long shot, and he hoped it might give him the answer.

"There's a chance of it." She thought. "The Weeds were very careful about his diet, though."

Another thought came to Charlie, and this one was less welcome than the other. "You said he took calcium lactate. Would this be mistaken for milk in the autopsy? Is there any reason to believe that he'd only been taking his calcium?" He knew with stark certainty that no matter what he decided, Malton would insist that the trace matter was from that supplement.

"It isn't too likely," she said. "If there's enough to test it, it should indicate whether the traces are milk or just plain calcium."

"Suppose," Charlie suggested, venturing onto speculative thin ice, "suppose Sparky ate something at school, something he didn't realize contained milk. Maybe some kind of dessert. Or a candy bar. Candy bars have milk in them, don't they?" Charlie had his pen poised to write on his phone pad.

"He brought his own lunch to school to avoid that sort of problem. The school insisted on it. And I will say this for Kirsten: she kept an eye on Sparky and made sure he ate the right things."

"Good for her," Charlie said dryly.

On the other end of the line Miranda hesitated, and Charlie was sure she had bit her lip. "Maybe he did get something, though. He was an active boy, and he disliked the restrictions he lived with. You can't blame him for that," she added quickly. "It's hard to watch yourself all the time, even for adults. For a kid it's almost impossible. Maybe you're right, Charlie. He might have got a snack with the other kids, and that set his allergy off."

Her enthusiasm dampened his. "Well, it's a thought," he said, feeling his case slip away once more. "I'm going to check it out, and I'll call you back if I need any more information." He wondered why he was doing this, why he would reject his own discovery.

"Charlie," she said, sounding very vulnerable now, "I'm going to lose, aren't I?" There was silence between them.

"Oh, I don't think so," Charlie said, hating the phony confidence in his voice.

"I see," she said, and hung up.

He was disgusted with himself. He sat with his head in his hands, glaring down at the table. He'd been a complete fool to go off half-cocked like that, building up Miranda's hopes and then having to let her down. Damn it, she'd taken enough. He was wrong to have called her. But he had wanted to hope as well. He had been the one who had insisted on grasping at straws. "Am I really so callow?" he asked the foolscap in front of him.

When the phone rang twenty minutes later, he had done nothing but stare at the folders. He was in a deep funk and felt helpless to snap out of it.

"Hello?" he answered. "Charles Moon here."

"Charlie, this is Morgan. I have some of the information you want."

"Information?" he repeated stupidly.

"Yes," she said, sounding impatient. "You know, about L-dopa and how it's made and who makes it and what it does and how effective it is and its statistical rate of failure. . . ." Her voice trailed off. "Are you okay?"

"I remember." Then in a rush, he added, "I'm sorry, Morgan, I'm tired and grouchy. You've got a knack for catching me when I'm like this. I know what we talked about yesterday, so go on."

She accepted this with reservations. "If you're ready? I also got some FDA publications on drug-control laws and packaging regulations. They've got warnings about everything you can think of." She shuffled papers, and the sound came through the phone as a crackling. "I'm going over them now, and then I'll start on the brief for you."

"Great," Charlie said, trying to suffuse some encouragement into his voice.

"I also found out where Max Wannermahn is, if you want to see him."

Charlie drew a blank on the name, then remembered him as the expert who had helped Miranda with Sparky Weed. "Okay," he said. "Where is he?"

"He's at the University of California Hospital on Parnassus. In the entertainment lounge."

"Working on Sunday?" Charlie pondered aloud. "An emergency or what?"

"He's not working; he's rehearsing. He's expecting you at five thirty."

The entertainment lounge was really a large dining room with a tiny stage at one end. Men and women in white and green bustled about, taking orders roared by an elderly, ferocious white-haired man in a badly fitting Italian suit. Charlie watched from the door, bemused, as the old man bellowed once more.

A few minutes later a well-scrubbed intern came up to Charlie, an apologetic smile spread over his shiny face. "I'm sorry, sir, this is off limits to everyone but the *Razz* cast and crew."

"I'm here to see Dr. Wannermahn," Charlie said, and handed the intern his card. "He's expecting me."

The intern was dubious but trotted off to find Dr. Wannermahn while Charlie lounged in the door, waiting, amusing himself by trying to figure out which one was Max Wannermahn. He had a good mental picture built up around the name, a man of solid, sturdy competence, and was surprised when a rangy, loose-limbed fellow of about forty detached himself from the confusion and strode his way.

"Mr. Moon?" he asked in a radio announcer's voice extending a long, gangly arm. "I'm Max Wannermahn."

Charlie returned the strong grip. "I'm glad to meet you," he said, and hoped it would be so. With a significant glance at the chaos around them, he added, "Isn't there someplace a little more—"

"Private?" Wannermahn finished for him. "This way." He pushed open a door next to the one Charlie was standing in. "Box office," he explained as he flipped on the lights in the small room. "This private enough?"

"It's fine," Charlie said, settling onto one of the tall, hard-backed chairs. "How much did Studevant tell you when she called?"

"Your secretary?"

"My associate. What did she say?"

"You're representing Miranda Trobridge in the suit the Weeds have brought against her. That's right, isn't it?" Wannermahn leaned back, shoulders against the wall, his arms crossed over his chest.

"Yes."

"How does it look for her?" Wannermahn kept a strict neutrality in his tone. "What do you think, honestly?"

"Honestly, it doesn't look too good. That's why I'm talking to you, Doctor. You followed her treatment of the child, you're one of the experts on Parkinson's, or so the AMA *Journal* seems to think. What's your opinion on her handling of the boy's case? Honestly." Charlie felt his neck knot as he waited for the answer.

"Well." Wannermahn rubbed his chin, a distant look in his eye. "For the most part she did as much for the boy as anyone could have. I'm frankly surprised that he lasted as long as he did."

Charlie's eyebrows raised. "Why is that? And what do you mean, for the most part?"

He looked down as if his answer was on the toes of his shoes. "It was the family. I would have moved heaven and earth to get that boy out of there, to find him a foster home with people prepared to deal realistically with his disease. The Weeds were not. The father in particular. And his behavior had a very bad effect on the boy."

"How?" Charlie felt his shoulders ease. This might be the answer. He might have found an out.

"Dr. Weed is a very critical, perfectionist sort of man. Parkinson's in chronically tense environments tends to degenerate more quickly. Keeping Sparky in that situation materially affected his health and sped his death."

Charlie watched the doctor narrowly. "Would you be willing to say that on the stand?"

Dr. Wannermahn did not respond at once. "Is Fritz Bjornsson testifying for the Weeds?"

"I don't know," Charlie answered truthfully. "But probably. It looks like it's going that way."

"I see." Wannermahn pushed himself away from the wall. "It would be difficult. And it would be open to question."

"Fritz is Miranda's boss; his testimony against her will be damning."

"I understand that." He turned away from Charlie. "I don't like to appear in court against a colleague."

"Hell, man, Miranda's your colleague." Charlie felt his frustrations building up again. "Maybe you don't know what can happen to her if she doesn't get your support. First, she'll be dismissed from the clinic, no recommendations, no contacts. Their version of a dishonorable discharge. Then she'll have the agony of trying to find a place to practice, which isn't bloody likely in this area."

Wannermahn paced, taking very few steps each way in the little box office. "Isn't there some other defense you can come up with?"

"Such as?" Charlie requested.

"Well, I'd heard that the boy had rejected the L-dopa. She couldn't do anything about that. Perhaps the drug companies could be held accountable, but not Miranda. She shouldn't be working at the clinic, you know. She's not built for that kind of work, where all you can do is slow down the rate at which your patient dies. She should be working with patients who live."

Charlie's dark eyes grew darker. "That may be. But she is working at the clinic, and she is in trouble. Now, will you testify?"

Max Wannermahn examined the backs of his hands, as if the answer were hidden there in code. "There's a great deal of professional ambivalence about women doctors, Mr. Moon. I'm sure you're aware of this."

"I'm learning more about it by the minute," Charlie assured him sweetly.

"I don't want to turn this into a fight between Fritz Bjornsson and me. That wouldn't prove anything. But if the situation is as bad for Miranda as you say it is. . . ."

"You'll testify, is that it?"

"If you have no other way to defend her case, yes. But I would much rather you found a way to exonerate her without my testimony." He studied Charlie, an appraising expression on his face. "You know, if I were you, I'd see if the coroner's report has any significant information."

"I've already seen it. Unfortunately, it shows no trace of L-dopa in the body, which supports Fritz's contention that Miranda was consenting in the boy's death because the case had deteriorated." Charlie rose to leave, the sinking feeling back in his gut.

"Wait a moment, Mr. Moon. You said there was no sign of L-dopa in Sparky's body? Is that what the autopsy said?" The tone of his voice had changed, and it held Charlie where he was.

"I had the report from Pete Coners. That's what it said," Charlie said, curiosity piqued.

"Anything else?"

"There were traces of milk products in the bowel. But

that could be from the calcium. I haven't found anything else."

Max Wannermahn was interested now. "Mr. Moon, if I were you, I'd check out the drugs the boy took. It sounds to me as if that's where the problem was. Make the drug company responsible, and that'll get Miranda off."

"I could get her off, of course, but unfortunately for Miranda there aren't any of the drug samples left," Charlie said, feeling a terrible fatigue creep over him. "I already thought of that. We've drawn a blank so far." The other blank was that he would have no help from Dr. Max Wannermahn. Charlie rose and held out his hand. "You see the spot we're in. Well, thanks for the time, Dr. Wannermahn. I won't call you unless I have no other choice."

"Don't leave quite yet, Mr. Moon," Wannermahn said, blocking the way to the door. "I wonder if you've considered this: what if the autopsy shows for sure that the boy had got anything he was allergic to or any of the things on his restricted list, aspirin, for example? Or if the parents allowed Sparky to have drugs or food he shouldn't have, then the responsibility is theirs, not Miranda's."

"Swell," Charlie said dryly. "Even if this was so, how am I going to get them to admit it?"

"That's not important, is it? What matters is that Miranda must not be convicted."

Charlie considered this, thinking for a moment that this might be the only way he could build a case. "I see what you mean," he said at last. "But I don't like it, and Miranda will hate it."

"Worry about that later," he recommended. "Some of my patients don't like the scars they've got, but it's a hell of a lot better than having cancer." He stood aside and smiled. "You may not believe this, but I wish you luck, Mr. Moon. And I am very pleased you came to see me."

Charlie shook hands mechanically. "Perhaps I'll see you in court."

"Try the other first." It was difficult to tell if this were a request or an order. Charlie waited for the rest. "If you come up with anything that might show lack of care on someone else's part, I'll be happy to testify. I know you can subpoena me, but I'd rather you didn't. I'm not anxious to referee in a medical feud. It's too messy."

Just as Charlie left the box office, he asked, "By the way, what are you rehearsing?"

"The *Razz*? Oh, it's a tradition here. The interns make up a bunch of skits about the hospital and their training, and the staff performs them. It's a painless revenge. See the director?" He pointed to the strange man in the ill-fitting suit Charlie had noticed earlier. "That's Dr. Hartog. He's chief of orthopedic surgery here. He's directed the *Razz* for twenty years. A great doctor, a great surgeon. But somewhere deep inside he really wants to be Richard Lester. And who knows," he went on to Charlie's surprise, "if the Hindus are right, maybe he was or will be." After giving Charlie a friendly pat on the arm, he strode back into the entertainment lounge.

Charlie watched him go, thinking that Dr. Hartog wasn't the only surgeon with greasepaint in his blood.

The plate of scones dripped butter, and the shortbread cookies crumbled when you looked at them. Henry Tsukamato was wheeling in a second cart with a fresh pot of tea.

"That doesn't sound very promising," Elizabeth Kendrie said when Charlie finished telling her of his reading and his meeting with Dr. Wannermahn.

"It's better than nothing."

From her chair, Miranda said, "Oh, Charlie, what's the use. Let's settle it and forget it."

Charlie turned, knowing how much Miranda wanted to disappear. She had sat in her chair as if she were invisible, making no comment while Charlie told Elizabeth about his progress so far. "Look, Miranda, you've given me a week to see what I can do. We can always settle, even after we go to court. But I don't want you to admit responsibility if it isn't yours." He was getting tired of protesting. He had had his fill of it with Miranda, with Willis Ogilvie. For a moment he considered bringing the whole case to an end. But he shut the thought away. "Okay, we've got a real fight on our hands, but that doesn't mean we're going to lose. It means that we have to do more, to search more. And that is what I'm doing, Miranda. And even if I find twenty, fifty dead ends, that doesn't excuse me if I miss the one that isn't a dead end. So help me, okay?"

She nodded, saying nothing.

"I'll remove the first pot, Mrs. Kendrie," Henry said with immense dignity. And in a manner suggesting he was carrying several of the better king's ransoms, he did.

When Henry had gone, Elizabeth rose and stalked, stiff-legged, about the room. "Charlie, I think you're going to do it. But for the life of me I don't know how."

"No," Charlie agreed miserably. "Neither do I."

Miranda rose. "I'm going up to change, Elizabeth. I'll be down in twenty minutes." She did not even glance in Charlie's direction.

"You know, Charlie," Elizabeth said as she came back across the room, "I didn't want to say this in front of Miranda, because she doesn't understand just now, but I think what Dr. Wannermahn said about her is right: She should be working with the living, not the dying."

"You're making progress, are you? When does she leave for the McIntyre Hospital in Redding? I imagine that's where you're sending her." Charlie put down his heirloom teacup and helped himself to another scone.

"When she's ready. I think she'll need a little vacation before she takes up her duties there. I thought she might go back East for a month or so to visit her brother and his wife. That ought to get the megrims out of her. Then she'll be fresh when she starts work there." Elizabeth's well-planned manipulations might have amused Charlie if he were not so sure they would work.

"Elizabeth," he told her, "you are the most ruthless woman I have ever known."

"Nonsense," she said, making a moue of distaste. "I'm not at all ruthless. You should know that. You defended that Abbington woman, and she killed three people. I've never killed anyone."

"My dear," Charlie said, "if she had been you, she wouldn't have had to kill them. She would have dealt with the whole situation in your incomparable manner, and there would have been no conflict, no violence at all."

Elizabeth eyed him suspiciously. "You are trying to get me off the point, Spotted Moon. Oh, yes," she went on as he started. "I know about that. I know all about your grandfather and the Iron River tribe. I told you once that I knew you had a different sort of power. I like to know about the people who handle my affairs." She smiled widely. "I enjoy having a medicine man for my attorney."

Charlie all but squirmed. "For Christ's sake, Elizabeth, don't go around saying that. It's bad enough as it is."

"I wouldn't dream of it. It would ruin all my fun if everyone knew." She poured herself a cup of tea and held out the pot to him. "You're Canadian, so you're used to tea."

Damn, had the old woman run a complete check on him? "Just how much do you know about me, Elizabeth?"

"Well," she said seriously, "I don't know your blood type."

He held out his cup, laughing a little in spite of himself. "I should be furious with you. It isn't right that you know so much."

She filled the cup and put down the heavy earthenware pot. "Perhaps. But because of what I know, I can give you some advice. You're carrying too large a load, Charlie. You've got Miranda to deal with, the pressure from Willis, and no doubt from others as well. It's getting to you, Charlie. You aren't thinking; you're going from crisis to crisis. Well, if you'd stop, if you'd take the pressures one at a time and really think, you'd find a way out, I'm confident of that. You must let your mind work, or you're lost. Take tomorrow off and indulge your hunches, Charlie. Otherwise you'll be in real trouble." She offered Charlie the plate of buttery scones.

As he took one, Charlie said somberly, "My blood, Elizabeth, is type B."

It had been raining since eight, a gentle persistency that had at last triumphed over the bright morning that had begun the day. The drops tapped at the windows and ran races in the downspouts.

Charlie had let Rufus in from the yard and done a perfunctory job of drying him. Now the big dog lay stretched in front of the dying fire while Charlie stared at his notes for what felt like the millionth time.

"Assuming that Miranda isn't lying," Charlie said to his sleeping pet, "and assuming that the Weeds are telling the truth, too, the only thing that's left is the drugs. There had to be something the matter with the drugs." He shuffled the notes. "There's the milk in the bowel, but that's chancy. And there is another thing I overlooked this morning."

Rufus' tail flopped on the floor once or twice to assure Charlie he was listening.

"This is the only other lead, and it points to drugs, too. Listen, in Miranda's records it says that he must not have aspirin. But in the coroner's report there's some aspirin in the urine left in the bladder. He got aspirin from somewhere. Sparky was allergic to milk and was not allowed to have aspirin: was it enough?" Charlie rubbed his eyes. If he didn't have a hearing in the morning, he would have been tempted to take the day off. But he knew he would be in court most of the day, and there would be no chance on

Tuesday. Tuesday was the day he and the Guttierrez family would be working out their presentation for the Board of Supervisors.

He pushed away from the table and wandered into the kitchen. A cursory glance told him that there was no more coffee in the pot, and he stood for some minutes trying to decide if he should make more. "It's got to be the drugs." He beat an irregular rhythm with his long fingers on the empty coffeepot. Too many things pointed to drugs. There was Sam Elgin's death, and Charlie knew that it had not been an accident. He had felt Elgin's dying when he touched his blood. The man was murdered. He hated unnecessary death, and it seemed to haunt him. First Sparky Weed, then Sam Elgin. . . . There was a connection, he was certain. If he had the time to look deeper. . . .

Well, it would have to wait. He had other clients besides Miranda Trobridge, and they needed his services as much as she did. Maybe after the hearing he could spend more time on the drug side of her case; maybe he could get a lead on what happened to the Weed child. But now he needed his sleep, needed the silence and the dreams.

He filled the coffee pot with water and drowned the fire in the living room before he went to bed.

Monday

HE HAD FORGOTTEN to take his suits to the cleaners. Charlie gave a disgusted sneer to the clothes hanging in front of him. He had to wear a proper suit, with Judge Landau sitting on the case. There was his other suit, which he had only worn once since its last cleaning, hanging in Lois' closet . . . the suit he had been wearing when he found Sam Elgin.

Charlie pulled open the closet door and peered at the suit. It still had the fetid presence of death clinging to it. But it was clean, and its blue-on-gray plaid would be appropriate for Judge Landau's courtroom.

Reluctantly he pulled it from the closet and chose a dark-gray tie and pale-blue shirt to wear with it. He told himself, without too much conviction, that wearing it would take the ugliness from it.

They had been waiting in the courtroom for more than an hour when the bailiff brought in the news that Judge Landau was still sitting on a case and would not instruct the jury until that afternoon or the following day. This case would therefore be continued.

"For ten days," Charlie said, turning to his client and his terrified wife. "Well, let's have a meeting in my office on Friday. We can work out a few extra angles then and be ready for the hearing next week."

The young man laughed with false bravado. "You'll get me off," he said, making it a threat, then added, to his wife, "You do just like he says, you hear? If he tells me you aren't cooperating, you know what'll happen."

"You don't have to tell me, Larry. I know." She was perilously close to tears as the officer came and took her husband from the courtroom. "Mr. Moon," she whispered once Larry was gone, "I don't know what's happened to him. He wasn't like this before. . . . He was gentle and nice. . . ." Her voice trailed off.

Charlie had a pretty good idea that Larry Sutherland had always been the bully he was now, but he held his tongue. There was no point in upsetting this woman any more. "I'll call you on Thursday, Mrs. Sutherland, and we'll set up the time for the meeting then."

"Yes. Thursday." She nodded, grateful, then scurried away.

Across the courtroom the assistant DA looked angry as he stuffed his material back into his briefcase. He looked over at Charlie when Mrs. Sutherland was out of the room. "It won't do you any good, Moon. That kid has been lifting car engines all over the Upper Mission. We'll get him, sure as shit."

"Probably," Charlie said. "But let's go through the motions of law anyway, Nat. For the exercise."

Nat Beecham relented, grinned and started for the door. "That's what the law's for. Exercise." He held the door and waited for Charlie to catch up. "Sorry to hear you're having trouble with that malpractice thing. Malpractice is a bitch, if you ask me."

"That it is." Charlie sighed. "What particular trouble are you talking about?"

"I thought you knew. Those Weeds were down at the DA's office on Friday. They want your doctor tried for manslaughter."

Although he had known this was coming, Charlie still felt disappointment and frustration. "Okay. What more?"

Nat Beecham let the door swing closed behind them. "Oh, you know, the usual. They want the full glare of publicity, and Cronin isn't buying that. But that attorney of theirs. . . ."

"Malton," Charlie supplied.

"Yeah, Malton, that's the one. What a little bastard he is. He's really playing this for all he's worth. I think he's been watching too many *Perry Mason* re-runs, and now he wants to be a legal eagle. Cronin is waiting to see what happens with your suit before proceeding himself. But I thought you ought to know that he's keeping his watchful eye on your case." Nat gave Charlie his angelic smile, his round face slightly pink now.

"Sure. Well, thanks, Nat." Charlie stood with him at the entrance to the Hall of Justice. The breezeway under the overhang was more like a wind tunnel. Charlie turned to Nat. "Are you going back to your office?"

"After I get a cup of coffee."

"Then thanks again."

Nat waved him away, watching as Charlie fought with the buffeting wind. Then he opened the door himself. "Hey, Charlie. Chris and I saw Lois a couple nights ago. She looked great. The baby should be here the middle of May."

"Oh?" Charlie stopped. He hadn't even known that she was pregnant. "In May? Tell her I wish her a safe delivery and a healthy child." This was said automatically; he did not realize how harsh his tone was. The shock in Nat's face told him, and he added, "Pay no attention, Nat. I've had a hellish weekend. My regards to Chris."

"Right." Nat looked relieved. "See you in court." Then he pulled the door closed.

Charlie watched him go, conflicting emotions holding him glued to the breezeway. So Lois was pregnant, Lois who had not wanted children. Not his children anyway. Gloom, as lowering as the sky, settled on him. He tucked his zipper case under his arm and felt something push against his waist. Curious, irritated, Charlie patted the pocket and felt a small, soft lump there. Frowning, he reached into the pocket and pulled the object from where he had placed it six days before. He held it up to see it more clearly.

It was a bloody handkerchief with a few pine needles caught in the blood.

He told himself, as he sat in his car, that the sensible thing to do was to turn the handkerchief over to Frank Shirer. But Frank had as much as told him the case was closed. He would not welcome a new wrinkle, if the handkerchief was indeed of any importance. And how would Charlie explain having the thing now when he had already told Frank he had lost it? Frank could claim he had withheld material evidence, and then he would be in the soup.

The parking-lot attendant made a point of walking past Charlie's car, a forbidding frown on his face. Charlie quickly opened his zipper case, as if looking for something. The attendant went back to his booth.

Once more Charlie touched the handkerchief, feeling the aura of Sam Elgin's death. He could hear his grandfather again, hear the old man telling him of the gifts of the spirit which must not be ignored. If Charlie had the handkerchief, his grandfather would say, it was because Sam Elgin meant for Charlie to use it, to reveal the crime and criminal that had killed him.

Charlie had one day free. One day. He had something of Sam Elgin, some of his blood, which was a thing of the spirit. Sitting in the parking lot, alone with himself and that potent token, he was tempted. It would take him a little more than an hour to perform the ritual which began the spirit walk, and surely in the space of that one day he could make the walk. Or drive. He would have to drive if he were to follow Sam Elgin on his last day. A spirit drive was something new in the world. Charlie felt dangerously close to laughter.

"Oh, come off it," he said aloud, but the words rang false. If there was a connection between Elgin and the clinic, between Elgin's death and Sparky's death, he could find it out. Spirit walks, he reminded himself sternly, were not admissible evidence. But . . . but if he made the walk, he would know what had happened to Sam Elgin the day he died. He would know it because he would share it. And with that knowledge, he would be able at last to find the evidence he so desperately needed.

Eyes narrowed, he looked out the window, seeing not the parking lot, but his own alternatives. He had until Friday to convince Willis Ogilvie. He had until Friday to convince Miranda. Only until Friday. With this chance he was dead certain he would have the material Willis and Miranda required. He had spoken the truth when he told Miranda that spirit walks were the remedy of last resort, not to be undertaken except in extreme need. But this was his last resort. Without the information he could get on the spirit walk, he would have no chance to save Miranda. Or himself.

He picked up the handkerchief.

"Out of town?" Lydia Wong repeated, faintly surprised. "For how long?"

"Only for today," Charlie assured her. "Here," he said, handing her a few handwritten sheets. "Have Annie type these up for me and send them over to Dr. Bjornsson at the Harrowleigh Clinic. I'll need four copies."

But Lydia wasn't being put off so easily. "Why are you going out of town? I thought you had that hearing today."

"Judge Landau is still sitting on another trial. We've been continued for ten days." He wanted to leave.

"I see." She gave him a cool stare, and Charlie knew that Willis Ogilvie had let the office in on his ultimatum.

"Sorry, Lydia," he said ruefully. "You might not get that raise. But I have until Friday. There's still a chance."

Lydia did not deign to comment. "I'll give this to Annie. Any other instructions?"

"No," Charlie said, then changed his mind. "Wait a minute. Will you ask Studevant to meet me at the Harrowleigh Clinic about eight tonight? I might be a little late, so tell her to stick around if I don't show up quite on time."

Lydia made a complicated gesture composed of equal parts of resignation and disgust. "Oh, all right. Anything else, Charlie?"

"I don't think so," he said, making a quick mental check on the rest of his day.

She studied him for a moment. "What about your calls? Lieutenant Shirer phoned earlier. And I should imagine Mr. Guttierrez will call later on. What do you want me to tell them?" This was a challenge; her almond eyes were bright with it.

Farther down the hall a door slammed, but neither of them paid attention.

"Take down the names and numbers, and tell anyone who wants to reach me that I will return their calls tomorrow. If the message is urgent, give it to Studevant tonight before she leaves, and she can give it to me when I see her at the clinic." He looked down at Lydia, feeling a strange compassion for her. "I'll try not to let you down. Remember that." Before he gave in to the need to explain his plan to someone, he bolted for the door.

Charlie's flat was strangely quiet at midmorning. Rufus was in the yard, the flat above him was empty for the day, and the traffic on this residential street was light. No children shouted, for they were in school. No sirens wailed; no trucks lumbered down the street. He was glad of that, for the silence, the stillness, for it would make his concentration easier.

It took him half an hour to assemble his supplies and another ten minutes to lay them out in the prescribed manner on the carpet before the fireplace. When he had kindled the fire, he drew heavy draperies across the bay window. Then, in the muted light, he stripped, setting his clothes aside neatly for the time he would don them again. He removed his watch last, putting it down so that the stones shone up at him, and the silver gleamed palely in the flickering light.

Naked, his face blank, he knelt before the fire and fed it the particular things from the materials set out on the carpet. There was an order to this, and he took great care to observe it, for it was a harrowing business willingly to replay another's death in his own body. He would have to be prepared and protected from the force that killed Sam Elgin.

He had made spirit walks only twice before: once when his grandfather had finished training him as a medicine man, as a kind of final test; the second time when one of his uncles had disappeared without a trace into the forests of Alberta. The first walk had been a revelation, but not dangerous, for he walked in the spirit places many others knew. But the second was dangerous, though not as dangerous as this walk would be. Charlie thought of himself like a stereo system, playing out the record of a man's death. Just as the record was not the performance, so the spirit walk was not the death. But he would know the suffering of Sam Elgin as surely as the speakers knew the sound of trumpets.

Soon the air was redolent with disturbing scents as smoke rose in the fireplace. Charlie felt his senses begin to slip, to shift as if making room for someone else. He breathed deeply, with almost the slowness of sleep. A sound rose in his throat. He picked up a clapper and began to tap out the monotonous beat, the rhythm echoed in the swaying of his body. Gradually the summons grew stronger, and he felt a hidden part of himself wake and open.

Much later, when the call to the dead was made and answered, he rubbed his sweat-soaked body with Sam Elgin's handkerchief. And then, with somnambulistic precision, he got dressed.

Sam Elgin's throat was scratchy and his chest tight, as much from worry as from the flu, as he crossed the Bay Bridge and drove north toward Richmond. His hands were clenched white on the steering wheel, and he fought to keep his mind on his job.

Anxiety crept through Charlie as he followed the right fork of the freeway between the racetrack and Albany Hill. The unfamiliar road did not seem strange, and he knew his link with Sam Elgin was strong and growing stronger. He reminded himself that he would have to pay strict attention to his driving, for as the tie grew, he might find that it was Elgin's car and Elgin's traffic he experienced, not his own. There was enough hazard in the spirit walk without adding the possibility of an accident to it.

His chest was tighter as he swung off the freeway in Richmond, turning toward the tower of Brookside Hospital and the doctors' offices on Vale Road. His stop there was quick, methodical, mere routine. But even handling the drugs made him uneasy, brought a flicker of fear to his mind. There was too great a risk. He would be found out.

Charlie circled the route and headed back to the freeway, tension growing through his shoulders and into his upper arms. For a moment there was bile in his throat, and a deep revulsion came with it, making him grimace. Quickly he mastered this; he must not let himself be overcome, not now. But he took the precaution of pulling to the side of the road to get his bearings once again. Breathing deeply, like a diver preparing for a difficult plunge, he steadied his focus before taking the freeway north out of Richmond.

He drove through Pinole without incident, his extended senses dormant. Around him the rolling hills were still a rich spring green, late rains having staved off their summer fade to khaki. At another time he might have relished the country, drunk in its vigor and its solitude, but not this day. This day he drove with murder beside him.

The first twinge came as he approached the Carquinez Strait Bridges. It was so slight that he hardly noticed it, just a minute tremor in his chest. The cough that followed it satisfied him that it was nothing more than the flu. Concern for his child soon dominated his thoughts, and he credited the next tweak to the ulcer he was convinced he was breeding in the acidic incubator of his duodenum.

Now Vallejo lay ahead, the city where Charlie had been born. It was peaceful under a tranquil sky where puffy clouds grazed like insubstantial sheep. With ever-diminishing farmland to the east and north, the town had grown on the point where Suisun Bay, the mouth of the Delta, gave way to the gray hulks in the Mare Island naval shipyards. It was there Charlie's father had come at the start of the Second World War and there he had returned, many years later, when Charlie was studying at McGeorge.

Sight of the city never failed to crowd Charlie's mind with memories, but this time they were vague, filmy, like fragments of long-forgotten movies. Charlie was always startled to see how commonplace Vallejo was, for as a young child he had found it full of adventures and strange, private beauty. That was the mystery of childhood that, once left behind, would never come again.

He drove through the downtown area, seeing that it was a little grimier, a little more old-fashioned than the last time he had seen it. There were four physicians' offices downtown. Elgin had stopped there. Beyond that was the suburban squalor of tract houses. There were three convalescent hospitals on Sam Elgin's route, as well as a doctors' cooperative. With each stop he made, Charlie felt malaise growing in him, as if the very thought of drugs made Elgin uneasy. Charlie's hands were slippery on the steering wheel as he swung west to pick up the road to Napa.

As he drove, Sam Elgin wrestled with his conscience. Guild and anger waged war in him, darkening his face as the strain worked on his body. The surge of blood alarmed him and brought his attention back to what he was doing. His chest hurt in earnest now. Panic flooded through him in icy waves. Heart attack. Heart attack! He refused to accept it. It could not happen. He would not allow it. The pain hit him with a jolt, and for a moment his chest spasmed brief agony. His arms convulsed, and he fought to hold his car on the road.

The Volvo lurched, nearly colliding with a speeding florist's van. The driver honked, swerved, and gave Charlie the finger as he accelerated.

Shaken, his body filmed with sweat, Charlie pulled off the road. He sat dumbly, letting the motor idle as he brought his racing pulse under control. The pain that was not his pain slipped off him like a garment being shed. He leaned against the steering wheel, his forehead against his hands. How he dreaded the finish, if this was a foretaste of it.

"Hey, Mac, what's the trouble?"

Charlie had not heard the Highway Patrol car come up behind him or the approach of the ruddy-faced cop who now loomed over him, tapping on the window. "What?" he said, his voice sounding rusty.

Some of the belligerence left the patrolman's face. "Fella, you don't look too good."

Charlie could imagine what his clammy skin and glazed eyes must look like to the cop. He made an effort to control himself. "I'm okay, Officer," he said, taking a deep lungful of air. "I got dizzy. I don't know what it was."

The cop's eyes narrowed, and now he scrutinized Charlie, his face hardening under the weight of his suspicions. "Awright, fella, let's see some ID. Come on. And the registration." He gestured impatiently with the flashlight which dangled from his belt.

"Certainly." Some of the terror had faded, and Charlie felt his strength returning. He reached into his vest pocket and drew out an English-style wallet. He flipped it open and offered it to the officer, reaching onto the steering wheel with the other hand to detach the registration card.

"Come on, come on. Roll down the window, fella." The cop's patience was running out. His belligerence increased, and he began casting knowing glances at the backseat.

As Charlie rolled the window down, he said, "Sorry, Officer. I guess I'm still a little shaky." He handed the wallet to the officer and waited, wishing he could spare the energy to deal with the man properly.

The cop grunted as he saw Charlie's license and his array of credit cards. Then he read the business card. "A lawyer," he said, full of disgust. "I tell you, lawyer, you guys make me sick."

"Are you through with that?" Charlie extended his hand for the wallet.

"I dunno." The cop rubbed carefully at his pugnacious chin. "Could be you're carrying something illegal."

"I could be," Charlie agreed pleasantly. "But what's your probable cause?" His hand became more insistent.

The cop spat and shoved Charlie's wallet and vehicle registration through the window. "If I catch you driving like that again, I'll have my probable cause. I could take you in for reckless driving. Maybe driving under the influence of alcohol or drugs."

"Bring on your breathalizer," Charlie invited.

The cop's heel ground in the gravel as he clumped back to his black-and-white parked behind Charlie.

Charlie waited until the Highway Patrol car was out of sight before he gingerly eased his Volvo back onto the pavement, keeping up a rigid concentration, his hands straining on the steering wheel. That had been a near thing.

He would have to hold Sam Elgin in check, or he would be in a great deal of danger. He kept his speed down as he drove toward Napa.

He recovered quickly. It wasn't a heart attack. The fear which had gripped him as much as the pain began to drain from him. The dull ache left in his chest and shoulders convinced him that his flu was turning to bronchitis. He reduced his speed and reached for his sample case. He had an open packet of Actifeds there, and one of them should take care of his flu in short order. It was reassuring to know he had the right drug with him. His hand scrabbled with the case on the seat beside him, pawing through the unseen packets and plastic cases. Then he found the open packet and expertly thumbed a pill from its nesting place. Just to be sure he held the pill up and was relieved to see the familiar round pressed form, very white against his skin. He admitted to himself that he was relieved. The way he was feeling, he could get a pretty severe reaction if he took the wrong drug by mistake.

A couple of miles down the road the Highway Patrol officer was waiting, parked under a scrub oak. He pulled in behind Charlie and tailed him, keeping a shade closer to his bumper than safety allowed, until Charlie was well into central Napa. There the traffic built up, and as Charlie followed Sam Elgin's route, the cop lost interest and gunned his engine as he raced away.

There were a number of doctors' offices on the list here, and Charlie circled around the center of town, making a last check at a fairly good-sized community hospital on the west side, near the highway that would carry him to Sonoma, the next stop on the route.

A pleasantly mild euphoria flooded him, casting out the depression which the attack had caused. He took several deep, tingly breaths of air and was pleased when this was not accompanied by coughing. The last pill must have done it. He would be fine now.

Charlie felt a return of good spirits. Here on the edge of the wine country with the trees bursting with spring, he was wistfully attracted to the sunny slopes and the sternly cropped vines that marched in strict formation over the hills. The steady incursions of condos and houses troubled him but today he paid little attention. Flexing his fingers, he convinced himself that the stiffness came from his tension which had gripped him for all those miles. Perhaps he had been wrong about Sam Elgin. Perhaps the spirit walk was a waste of time. But he didn't mind. It was too beautiful a day to waste.

His hands felt funny; maybe he had a touch of arthritis. He moved his right shoulder experimentally, testing for that grating that he dreaded. His left hand was still firmly on the wheel. For good measure he stretched his arms stiff and felt the elbow. No doubt about it. The joints were sore. He thought about it, and realized he might be getting a reaction to the Actifeds. Nothing to worry about. Only, now that he thought about it, he realized he had a headache, too. It was the kind he got with eyestrain. Damn. He couldn't afford to be ill. He'd have to shake it. He rejected the idea of another Actifed for a while. If the aches were a reaction, he'd have to give the drug a little more time to wear off before he took more. He could tell better then what had happened. There was no rush. None at all.

The headache took Charlie by surprise, locking his skull in its vise before he had prepared himself for it. And with the headache came other pains. His body ached abominably, the kind of ache that comes with more than fatigue, that comes with severe strain, with damage. The depression which had left him returned, and the hills around him that had looked so pleasant a few miles ago now appeared sinister, dangerous. He grabbed the steering wheel more firmly and increased his speed. He wanted to get away. He knew he needed help. That Sam needed help.

But the help did not occur. There had been a stop at a

small convalescent hospital about ten miles outside Sonoma, hidden in the bend of an orchard. Charlie pulled over to make a note of it before heading on. The place was old-fashioned enough to call itself a rest home. Sam Elgin had not lingered there, just made his usual delivery and left. Now Charlie was puzzled. If he was hurting, Sam was. Why didn't he talk to a doctor while he was there? Surely one of the staff physicians would have looked him over if he had asked. Why hadn't he done that? The worry rode with him as he drove toward Sonoma.

Sam Elgin was scared. The pain was increasing, he was deeply flushed, his face a much deeper pink than usual. He felt the heat in his hands—his palms were hot, as if he had a fever. It couldn't be the Actifeds, not now. There was something else. Desperately he tried to think. He ran over his day in his mind, searching. There was nothing. He'd had that confrontation at the clinic but it ended quickly and amicably. He'd been relieved. He could see the measuring look which had met his request, a look that turned that darkly handsome face older, more cynical. That was over. That was over.

Now he could feel his feet swelling. The pain distracted him, pulled him away from his thoughts. His whole body felt puffy. Were his kidneys failing? A sharp tweak from his bladder reassured him. If not the kidneys, what? Had he become diabetic? He resolved to have a snack when he reached Sonoma. If he was becoming diabetic or—and this was far more likely—hypoglycemic, a snack would do him a world of good. He chortled, shutting out his discomfort. Worry about his child was turning him into a regular hypochondriac. There wasn't anything really wrong. It wasn't possible.

Now Charlie was hungry. Sonoma wasn't far, he told himself, and he could get lunch there. His hands were slick with sweat, and his face was dark from strain and the agony of Sam Elgin. The road was not rough, but he had a great deal of trouble holding his car steady on it. Each move he made seemed magnified by the car. If he tightened his hands, the car swung erratically about the pavement so that he had to fight to keep it on the road. The pain in his body was slowly numbing his other senses, leaving him vulnerable, unprotected. He breathed deeply until his mind cleared.

He brought the car back under his control by making all his movements, every motion tiny, careful and slow. The car responded, keeping to its lane, moving now predictably toward Sonoma.

Soon he would be on the flat. Sam Elgin felt better even with the thought. He would be able to have lunch, to get out of the car. Some of his illness must be connected with motion sickness, for every bend in the road made him worse until he felt raw.

His next breath was rusty-sounding, wheezy. He coughed, cringing against the pain that shot through his chest.

Perhaps he had asthma. That would account for it. Sam was close to gagging on his own breath. Or maybe he had the disease his child did, maybe it ran in families, and the flu had set it off. The next breath was even worse, his bronchial tubes outlining themselves in fiery relief. The Actifeds should have stopped this. His breathing should be clearing up. But this was getting worse with every breath. Inhaling was a penance. A cough racked him. He hunched over the wheel and concentrated on Sonoma.

Doesn't he know? Charlie wondered. Doesn't he realize? His own breath was tearing through him raggedly. His body felt slimy, and he knew there were two rivulets of sweat down his back. He wasn't sure he'd be able to eat when he reached Sonoma. There was too much discomfort, and he was beginning to feel the first churning of nausea. What an ugly death the man had had.

He would bypass Sonoma. Santa Rosa wasn't far, and he

could take the county road instead of the freeway. He might be able to catch up to the man at Rohnert Park at the student health center at Sonoma State.

There could be another explanation to this sudden attack. Part of Sam's mind squirmed away from the idea, but he faced it, in spite of himself. He had wanted out, and the others had let him out. Perhaps they had let him out permanently, and this was their revenge. He had a sense of relief for a moment. Then it gave way to panic.

If he hurried, he would catch the leader at the Student Health Center at Rohnert Park. He always took time out at Sonoma State. Sam had met them there many times before, as they had met at the clinic. If the others had done this to him, he would make them help him. They couldn't do this to him. His anger fought down the rising tide of pain. He drove north toward Santa Rosa.

Charlie felt a wave of triumph. Others. There were others. He knew he could not get a name, but with any luck, Sam Elgin would let him *see* one of them, and then he could proceed. If Sam realized this was murder, Charlie could find the murderer and exact vengeance. The oppression in him lightened. He would not endure this torment for nothing.

At the sign promising the wonders of General Vallejo's house, Charlie turned north along the county road. There was very light traffic now, most of the through cars preferring the speed of the freeway. Charlie let up on his vigilance as he drove, opening himself more to Sam Elgin. He wanted a face. He could have one if he did not have to resist.

He had started to pray. Not the formal prayers, not the comforting ritual of the Ave Maria, *but strange, half-spoken prayers, and even Sam did not know for certain what he prayed for. He wanted to find the others. He wanted them to admit what they had done. And he wanted them to be sorry. He wanted them to be sorry. They had been wrong. They had been very wrong.*

He also wanted them caught. He realized this as the pain came back, stronger, hitting him like a hammerblow. What had he taken, he wondered. And when? What was killing him? Why had they done it? Just because he wanted out? Or had they been afraid that he would give them away? Well, they would find out. He would show them that he would not tolerate their deception. He still had a chance. He could reveal their conspiracy. He would. He would. All he had to do was get someone to listen.

His vision blurred, cleared, then blurred again. He was seeing through a mist. His head ached; his muscles were sore; his hands were swelling. Doggedly he went on. All he needed was time. Not much time. Once more he prayed.

Now Charlie was tired, the strain of the spirit walk tugging at him. He felt grief for the man he followed and sadness at his waste. He knew that Sam would not seek medical help now, that he had resigned himself. But why?

Perhaps this was enough contrition. Idly Sam wondered what was killing him. He checked the time. Something over two hours had passed since he had had his first symptom. He must have got the stuff much earlier. He wanted to know what it was. Carefully he thought about the morning. The last time he'd seen the others was in San Francisco at the clinic. They'd all been having coffee except himself.

Charlie strained with expectation.

He'd had orange juice, lots of it. There had been a second big glass. Charlie caught another blurred impression of a handsome, cynical face, dark hair and flying eyebrows whose slim line angled sharply upward. *He's been the one, Sam realized. If anyone could harm him, the dark man, the leader of the others, he would be the one. Was the orange juice it? Was that how he did it? Sam's heart labored, shutting out his thoughts. There was a wrenching in his side, and his breathing turned strident. All thoughts of orange juice left him.*

He couldn't make Rohnert Park, not now. He had to go back, back to the city to the clinic and find out what he had taken. There was too little time. At the clinic he could talk. He could tell them what the others had done. Even now his thoughts cringed at the thought of his crime. Damn it, Charlie thought, what is it? What had they done? Obviously, since they were all drug salesmen, it must concern drugs, but how? Were they selling them? Substituting them? Counterfeiting them? Peddling them on the side? Supplying them illegally? Charlie ground his teeth. There was no way he could force Sam Elgin to reveal what he had done. Frustration grated in him. If he could only ask questions. But that was not possible on a spirit walk; you could take only what was given to you.

The next road west was a narrow country lane, barely wide enough for two cars. It meandered down the hills between scrub oaks and fruit trees. The late-afternoon sun slanting through the remaining blossoms made the apple trees glow white, the spring grass at their roots taking on the preternatural clarity from the white petals. Charlie was enchanted. He longed to stop, to walk in the shimmering light, to wander in the radiant afternoon, drinking in the sun and the color. But it was not possible. Sam Elgin pulled him on.

Recklessly he plunged down the road, striving to hold his car on the badly banked curves. His pain was engulfing him now, stressing the urgency of his flight. His eyes were clouded. He had to get back to the city quickly, quickly. There was so little time. He had this one chance to save himself, one chance to be revenged. He thought of the others—Who is the guy with the eyebrows? Charlie wondered as the face swam hazily before him once again—*and felt cold dread fill him. Unless he could get back and find out what they had done to him, they would get away unscathed. He could not allow that to happen. There were things flesh could not bear. The obsession gave him strength. A couple of hours was all it would take. He could be back to the city then. Once at the clinic he would have help. He would have a chance to stop them.*

Why did he insist that he return to the clinic? Charlie hung on the wheel as his car raced dizzily around a sudden bend. The danger distracted him, and for some minutes he kept all his attention on the road, frightened by the increasing speed. He negotiated another steep curve, his right wheels digging into the soft gravel of the shoulder. He swung around the next turn, jamming on the brakes as a tractor rumbled toward him up the center of the road. Tires squealed; the laconic farmer jerked alert and pulled hard at the wheel.

With his right wheels off the pavement, riding perilously close to the ditch that gave drainage to the roadway, Charlie shot by, catching the farmer's angry consternation in his rearview mirror.

Adrenaline soared through his veins, then subsided, leaving him giddy and weak.

He'd reach the freeway soon, and then it would be a fast run into the city. He kept reassuring himself, fighting off the lethargy which came with the pain. He could rest once he reached the clinic. For now, he must stay awake, he must drive. He crossed himself as he thought how close a call he'd had. If the symptoms had hit him after Rohnert Park, between Fort Bragg and Willits or on the long haul to Eureka, then he could not have had a chance in the world. But he'd been lucky. His foot inched down on the accelerator.

Charlie fought down his enervation. He had to complete the spirit walk. A break in the trees showed him that he was almost out of the hills. Ahead the slope lessened, giving way to the Bennett Valley and the road to Santa Rosa.

The last spasm frightened Sam Elgin. The cramps were

getting worse, and his eyes did not respond well. The lids felt grainy and hurt when he moved. Light bothered him, too, and his stomach had started to distress him. He could not kid himself it was an ulcer now. Charlie sensed that Sam knew he hadn't been poisoned, so that the additional hurt was unpleasant but unimportant. *Which of the drugs would do this? Sam regretted his inadequate knowledge. He did not know what overdoses did or how to identify the characteristics of each overdose.*

A side road beckoned, leading toward the Cotati Valley and the freeway. Charlie felt Sam Elgin's pull, and he turned left, his car leaning as he went. Long golden fingers of sunlight poked between the evening shadows, making the countryside glow. Charlie shut the beauty away and pushed on the last three miles to the freeway.

He felt himself relax. He was on the freeway, and the commute traffic was coming in the other direction. He would have a clear run into the city. He pushed his car past the limit, cruising at more than sixty. There was no sign of the Highway Patrol. He shot another look into the rearview mirror and was horrified to see how bloodshot his eyes were. No wonder his head ached, no wonder his eyes felt like chopped meat.

Charlie pulled to the inside lane and drove for San Francisco.

The bottleneck at Novato had been eliminated, Sam remembered thankfully. No more slowing down, no more stoplights. He let his mind drift now, back to his family. He felt a sharp pang as he thought of his sick child. The others would manage, but not that one. And it was part of his guilt. If only he could expiate his sin, offer up his guilt to Our Lady. He prayed again, but the words were incoherent, and his thoughts were scattered.

Palsy developed in his right leg, and he felt his car shudder as the pressure on the gas varied. He didn't know how to control it. Although he knew it was foolish, he took his brake foot and put in on the accelerator. The car steadied. He would do it.

Charlie like his grandfather was sensitive to alcohol and had a lively dread of drunkenness. And now he felt drunk, as if his limbs were poorly attached to the rest of him, and his thoughts were elusive as fish. His tongue felt thick, unwieldy, crowding up his mouth. And his nose ached. After Novato, it would be easy up to San Rafael. The hands that grasped the steering wheel were as thick as boxing gloves. He shook his head to clear it and was rewarded with a new wave of nausea. He wiped his forehead on his arm and hung on grimly.

Warm stickiness welled in his throat, and he gagged. Forcing himself to swallow, he felt the heaviness in his face. He thought of his wife . . . of her softness and strength. Charlie would have known the woman anywhere, he thought, for she was so much like David Lemmini—the same sleekness, the same elegance, the same brilliant eyes. No wonder Sam Elgin was crazy about her. A woman like that would be a treasure to Sam. *He would lose her. The new terror came in a rush. He would lose her, his children, and his vengeance. He had to hurry. The stuff was back in his throat again, warm and salty.*

Traffic at Corte Madera was bunching up, even in the southbound lanes. Sam reduced his speed, grudging each moment it lost him. Over the hill and toward Mill Valley and Sausalito. The northbound traffic was hopelessly snarled, inching along in the foggy twilight. Only the Waldo Grade was left before the long descent to the bridge. His breath came in gasps now, each one more difficult than the last. He felt a bubbling in his chest.

A honk and flashed lights reminded Charlie that darkness had fallen. Sam had come this way two hours before Charlie did, and the soft light was Sam's, not his. He pulled on the lights, slightly disoriented. The Spencer Avenue turnoff reminded him he was in Sausalito. Good. There was only a little distance left. He started to cough.

He slowed for the fog-bound bridge, flipping on his lights as he came down the hill before entering the eerie length of the Golden Gate Bridge. At the toll gate he fumbled for his money, handing over his loose change and heading on before the tollman could count it. There was enough. He knew there was enough.

"Hey, mister," the tollman said as he handed Charlie the requested receipt, "you got a bloody nose. You want to take care of that."

"Thanks," Charlie muttered. He didn't dare say more as he drove toward the clinic.

The elevated roadway forked, and he drove for Lombard Street. His mind was thick, unwieldy. He was hard pressed to remember the way to the clinic. He fumbled his way through the six o'clock traffic, taking the last turn almost by accident.

There were no spaces in the lot, and the street was all towaway. Sam panicked, then recalled an alley nearby where he could leave his car. He drove there, skidding over the curb in his hurry.

Although the streets were dark and almost deserted, Charlie parked in the alley, opened the door, and almost fell as his knees wobbled under him.

It was less than two blocks. Sam resisted the languorous pull of his brain and his body. He could sink down now, be rid of his pain, but it would not give him vengeance. He would meet God with his sins on him and no compensatory acts in his favor. Hell rose up before his eyes and he plunged on.

Charlie staggered. There was blood on his upper lip now, and his eyes were smarting with unshed tears. He made the last few feet, seeing the park in front of him. Almost there.

The clinic was in sight. Sam saw it as he sank to his knees. Only a few more feet.

There was one car in the lot, Charlie saw. A low, dark car. He forced himself to go on.

Sam reached out. But his hands implored the pine boughs and the misty sky. His wife's face hung before him. He tried to talk. He wanted to explain. He sank back as the darkness came over him.

Charlie stumbled; then his knees buckled, and he pitched forward toward the dark car in the empty lot.

"What the fuck?" Morgan demanded as she bent over him. Her anger came from worry. She loosened his tie and wiped the blood from his face. Her hands were shaking, and she pressed them together to stop. She saw Charlie's eyes were open and bloodshot. "What . . . what happened?"

Charlie's arms flailed helplessly. "Up," he grunted. "I have to get up." He pulled himself to his knees. "Take me home."

"Not until—" She was white with anxiety.

"Take me home." He turned his stricken eyes on her.

"If that's what you want," she said, quelled.

It proved difficult to cram him into her car. His arms and legs moved as if they belonged to someone else. When he was in the passenger's seat, Morgan asked, "What about your car?"

"Later." He did not speak again until he was in his flat.

He built up the fire once more, and while he chanted, he pulled his clothes off. When all lay in a pile, he dropped bitter herbs on them, assigning them for destruction. He was vaguely aware that Morgan was in the kitchen making coffee, but he could not believe it was real.

When he had completed most of the ritual, he took the bloodstained handkerchief and tied it to a small wooden pipe. Then both handkerchief and pipe were burned.

It was over.

"What was that smell?" Morgan called to him when he had been silent for some minutes.

"I'm just burning something I don't need anymore," he said, knowing that the handkerchief was material evidence. It couldn't be helped. He had to close off the spirit walk. Rising, he remembered he was naked. "Morgan, will you close that hall door for a bit?"

"Sure. Why?"

"I'm going to shower and get changed. Then I promise you I'll tell you all about it." Well, not all, he thought.

"All right," she said, and he heard her close the door. "Don't be too long. The only thing I know how to make is coffee."

Charlie stopped, his hand on the bathroom door. He realized with a rush he was famished. "We'll go out, if you're hungry."

"Fine. If anything's open." She paused. "It's after ten."

"I won't be long," he assured her.

But he stayed longer in the shower than he'd planned, for the water was washing away more than the sweat which soured his body. He felt himself rid of the last vestiges of Sam Elgin. He breathed deeply. There was so much to do, so many things to check on. "It'll wait till tomorrow," he said aloud.

"Huh?" Morgan's voice came in from the kitchen. "Did you say something to me?" She opened the door to the hall.

"It's nothing!" he yelled. "I'll be out shortly."

"Right." The door closed once more. Reluctantly Charlie climbed out of the shower, wrapped himself in a towel, and went to his bedroom.

In the end they did not go out to dinner. Charlie had a couple of steaks in the fridge, as well as an assortment of vegetables. He set the steaks to broil, started chopping vegetables, saying to Morgan, "Sorry, but this is going to be a work session after all. Do you have a note pad with you?"

"I am an attorney, not a secretary," she snapped.

"Okay. You chop the vegetables, and I'll take notes."

She glared at him. "I don't know how to cook. And you know it."

He stopped, knife in one hand, green bell peppers in the other. "Look, Morgan, I've had a very rough day: You said you want to know what happened. Now tell me. Do you want to take notes or do you want to do this? I'll go along with any decision you make."

Morgan glared at him. "That's blackmail." Her eyes shone with a brittle light. "I'll take notes," she said through her teeth.

As he resumed his work on the chopping board, Charlie grinned.

"What am I taking notes about?" she demanded when he had been silent for a few minutes.

"The death of Sam Elgin."

"Death? Christ, that's a closed case." She slapped her note pad closed on her thigh. She rose, then heard a whining at the back door. "What's that? Your dog?"

Charlie turned, shamefaced. "I forgot I'd left him out." He did not explain how his pet had managed to slip his mind for so long. He went to the back porch and opened the door. Rufus gave a shrill bark and launched himself into the kitchen, romping for joy. "That's enough of that," Charlie said sternly before he knelt to hug the dog. "Hey, I'm sorry, old fella. I should have remembered."

Rufus licked him enthusiastically, then investigated Morgan. "Go to your bed," Charlie said, motioning the dog away.

"What a fine master you are. Two seconds of affection, and you banish him to the living room. That isn't very kind." Morgan was satisfied to have this opportunity to strike back at Charlie.

But it didn't work. "You're right. I'll have to spend more time with him before I go to bed. And that might be very late."

The guarded look came over her once more, and a retort hung on her lips.

"Come off it, Morgan. I didn't mean anything by that except that I am very tired. Okay?"

She studied him for a moment, then opened her note pad once more. "You get back to the vegetables, and I'll start on the notes."

Much later they had their supper. The steaks were overdone, but neither of them noticed.

Tuesday

THE DOOR TO the offices of Ogilvie, Tallant & Moon burst open as Charlie hurried in, late. He had a sheaf of loose-leaf paper in one hand and his zipper case in the other. "Morning, Lydia. Is Annie free?"

Lydia answered with gelid civility, "Good morning, Mr. Moon. I am afraid that Mr. Tallant—" She broke off as she looked up. "Good lord, what happened to you?"

Charlie had seen his haggard face in the mirror, and he knew how his bloodshot eyes and swollen hands must look to the receptionist. "It's not as bad as you think," he said to reassure her, which only convinced her that it was much worse.

She gulped elegantly. "Annie is in with Alex, Charlie. She'll be free in about half an hour."

He was touched. "Don't give up yet, Lydia," he said cheerfully. "There's still a chance you'll get that raise."

She smiled wanly as he strode toward his office.

It took him ten minutes to organize his plans; then he called Elizabeth Kendrie's, saying to Henry Tsukamato when he answered, "This is Charlie Moon, Henry. I have to speak to Dr. Trobridge. It's important."

"She's in the recording studio, Mr. Moon." His tone made it obvious that he was loath to interrupt her.

"I see. Look, Henry, I know that's important work, but this concerns Dr. Trobridge's suit very closely. I think she'll be willing to talk to me if you'll be kind enough to tell her I'm calling." He kept his growing impatience in check.

Henry sniffed. "Very good, Mr. Moon."

Three minutes later Charlie heard Miranda's tired voice say, "What is it now?"

"It's new information."

"Like the milk in the autopsy—or was it calcium lactate?" She paused, stifling her anger. "Tell me what it is."

"That's a good martyr," Charlie cajoled her. "Don't be so glum, Miranda. I've got some new information, and I think it will exonerate you. And if it won't get you completely off, it will certainly mitigate your responsibility in the case."

She sighed. "Whatever you want. But I'd rather we let the whole thing go. I'm leaving the clinic anyway."

Silently Charlie congratulated Elizabeth for a successful campaign. "You're going to Redding, I take it?"

"Starting in July."

"Well, that's good. But let's get this out of the way first, okay?" He made his voice confident and hearty.

"Can't we just end it?"

Stung, Charlie answered, "You know that wouldn't be right. Look, Miranda, there's more at stake here than your trouble with the Weeds. But I need your help. Now, will you answer some questions?"

"Ask them," she said in resignation.

He felt put off by her reception, but he set up his notes and began. "First, that drug that killed Sam Elgin—"

"Oh, for Christ's sake—"

"Are you going to answer or not?" he demanded, some of his calm leaving him.

"I'll answer," she sulked.

"The drug that killed Sam Elgin. Cou . . . something like that."

"Coumadin," she supplied.

"That's it. What does it taste like?"

"You're kidding." She hesitated, his silence telling her that he was not. "It's kind of acidic, sharp-tasting."

"Citric? Like orange juice?"

"No, not like orange juice. It's not that kind of acid—"

"Could it be disguised in orange juice?"

Miranda hesitated, then said rather slowly, "I suppose so. There's a sharp odor to it, and I don't imagine most people would ignore that."

"And if that person had a cold?"

"Perhaps; it would depend—" She broke off. "Is *that* how it happened? Oh, shit."

Charlie did not let her distract him. "Tell me," he said, "is there a drug salesman who fits this description? He's about medium height, possibly slight or perhaps only slender. His hair is dark and I think a little wavy. He has a rather sardonic face with upslanted eyebrows. I'd guess his age about mid-thirties."

"That's Ed Shelly. He's the head salesman for the Mayling company." In spite of herself, she was curious.

"One last thing, Miranda. And this you have to be certain about, because you may have to testify to it in court. How much orange juice did Sam Elgin drink that morning?"

"Well, he was finishing a glass when I came in. It was a big glass, too, one of those ten-ouncers." She searched her memory. "A little later he had another big one. They were all kidding him about his cold."

He checked off his impression from the night before, and then asked, "Did he get the orange juice himself, or did someone give it to him?"

"I don't know: I wasn't paying attention."

"Think, Miranda." Charlie waited, almost holding his breath, as she went over that morning in her mind.

"Paxton was joking with him, I remember. Then one of the others got up to get a refill of coffee. Paxton suggested that Sam get a refill too."

"And did he?" This was the most crucial.

"Well, he had another glass. . . ." Again she retreated into her mind. "Wait a minute. He didn't get up. Now I remember. He and Paxton got into a bit of an argument. Something trivial. One of the salesmen came back in with the orange juice. That's right. He brought it to him and gave him an Actifed. They all made some joke about prescriptions."

"Who brought him the orange juice?"

Her pause was longer. "I'm not sure. I didn't really look, you know, Charlie? I just glanced in a couple of times."

She didn't want to accuse anyone, Charlie realized. Unless she had run smack into the man, she would not commit herself. But she had triggered another crucial question. "About the Actifeds—how do you know that's what it was?"

"Well, Actifeds are small white pressed pills, about the size of a birth-control pill. That's what he got."

"And what does Coumadin look like?" Charlie's fingers beat a restless rhythm on the arm of his chair.

"It's. . . ." Her tone altered completely. "It's a small white pressed pill. About the size of a birth-control pill. I didn't think of that."

Charlie let his breath out slowly. "Good for you, Miranda."

"Is that what happened? Really?" There was horror just below the surface of her voice. "They killed him right under our noses?"

"What better way?" Charlie asked. "The symptoms hit him when he was a long way from here. There was no reason to think that anyone would associate his death with his morning orange juice."

"I don't see what that has to do with my case." Petulance

was creeping into her words. Charlie knew that she still felt vulnerable.

He offered her a very simplified explanation. "Look, Miranda, if the salesmen were messing with the drugs, then you aren't responsible for Sparky Weed's death. And why else would they kill Elgin?"

"I see," she said dubiously.

"Think about it," he urged her. "Do you have any of the drugs you prescribed around the time of Sparky's death. Samples, I mean, not regular prescription."

"No. I left them all at the clinic. And you know we were out of the L-dopa."

Charlie kicked his wastebasket. "We're stuck without them."

"I could call a couple of my patients and ask them if they have any left over. There might be a couple of them who do."

"We've got to have them. We've got to demonstrate tampering, if there's been any. And I bet you my job that there has been." He knew he had already bet his job, but it didn't matter to him, not when he was so close to a solution.

"Most of our patients use their samples. Chronic diseases take a fair amount of maintenance."

"It's a damn shame," Charlie said. Then he remembered. He reached into his coat and pulled out his wallet.

"Charlie, are you still there?"

"I am." He opened the wallet and there, where he had tucked them, were the unused and useless cold pills. "Miranda, we have what we need." And he reminded her about the pills. "I'll get them analyzed today."

"But what if they're okay?"

"Then you start calling patients."

"Whatever you say, Charlie. I'll talk to you later." She hung up abruptly.

Charlie sat with the packet in his hand, reflecting that this was not the first time he had won a case and lost a friend.

Well, Miranda would be happier at the McIntyre Hospital in Redding, he knew that. She certainly wasn't prepared to deal with more patients who wanted to die. He flipped the packet onto his desk.

"Lydia, buzz Studevant and ask her to come in here, will you?" he asked of the intercom.

"I'm sorry, Mr. Moon. She's with Mr. Ogilvie in court this morning. He's helping her get her feet wet, he says." Lydia was very polite now: too polite.

"When's she expected back?" He was annoyed with himself. He should have found out what her schedule was last night.

"Noon. She's not staying for the afternoon session."

"Okay. Look, when she gets here, tell her that I have an urgent errand. And now will you call Hammil and Ward for me? I have to have a few words with Mr. Malton, bless his heart."

Lydia plainly did not approve of this. "All right, Mr. Moon. I'll buzz when I'm through." She clicked off.

"What is it, Moon? You ready to settle?"

"No, Mr. Malton," Charlie said suavely, "I am not ready to settle. I have a request to make of you, and I am sure your client will be interested."

"Request away," said the scrappy voice.

"I think you should find out from the Weeds if there are any of the sample packs of L-dopa left over from their son's illness. By my calculations there should be at least one pack left. I'd recommend you have those drugs analyzed to find out if they are L-dopa." He made his suggestion as flat as possible in the hope it would not irk Malton.

"You are clutching at straws, Moon."

"Perhaps I am, Mr. Malton, but I remind you that drug companies have a lot more money than the Harrowleigh Clinic. And suing the drug companies will be much more profitable." He wondered what effect this approach would have on James Malton.

"You're right," Malton conceded. "I tell you what, Moon. We'll have the tests done, just in case. But if you're wrong, the ante for our settlement goes up."

"You know I can't make that kind of bargain, Mr. Malton," Charlie said, sweet reason thick in his words. "But I warn you that if you neglect to make these tests, I will bring it out in court, and that will not look well for your case. You should be vigilant in pursuing the case, Mr. Malton. Any stone left unturned by you can and, I promise you, will be used by me to demolish your case in court."

Malton hesitated. "I'll check it out," he said, his manner turning surly. "But if this is just another dodge, Moon, I'm warning you. . . ."

"You are not warning me of anything. I am warning you. And you should be grateful that I did. I could have done my own checking and left you with liberal amounts of egg on your face." He knew this wasn't true, but it sounded good. Charlie was enjoying giving Malton his own back.

"I said I'd check it out."

"I knew you would. I do look forward to hearing from you shortly on this. Good hunting, Mr. Malton." He beamed pleasantly at the receiver.

"You're a bastard, Moon," Malton said before he hung up.

Charlie was on the phone to the Guttierrezes when Annie came into his office. He gestured her to sit down and went back to his conversation. "Very good, Mr. Guttierrez. But we'll need those pictures you took, too. The Board of Supervisors will want all the concrete information you can bring. Those pictures are necessary." He paused, a frown creasing his forehead. "Yes. I understand that, Mr. Guttierrez. . . . No, I don't think that would be wise. Mr. Guttierrez, please get out the documents and pictures I requested, and we'll go over them at our conference this afternoon. . . . Good. . . . Good. Thank you. Yes. I will. Good afternoon." He hung up.

"What is it, Mr. Moon?" Annie asked, her long handsome face close to smiling.

"That's the Guttierrez case. I tell you, I sometimes think they don't want their case solved. Well, never mind. I'll tell you what I need." He handed her a well-scribbled-on paper. "I need copies of this letter sent to all the institutions on this list." He handed over a second piece of paper. "And this letter is to go to the names on this list." Two more sheets joined the first two. "Read the copy and ask me if there's anything you don't understand. I hope you can read my writing. The addresses are in Ms. Studevant's hand. She's a lot neater than I am."

Annie picked up the sheets and glanced over them. "I think I can make it all out. When do you need this?"

"Tonight, if you can. Certainly all the letters to the names on the first list should go out tonight. You can sign them for me, if you like. Make sure you enclose a return envelope. Oh"—he handed her a small card—"run off a bunch of these, and put one in with each letter. That'll increase our chance of a return."

Annie studied the letters once more. "Drug failure? Laboratory analysis? This sounds pretty dire, Mr. Moon."

"Drug counterfeiting is dire, Annie." He pulled at his tie, then straightened the knot. "What I need is twenty-four hours of uninterrupted sleep."

"You do look tired." She gathered up the papers. "I'll get the first lot out tonight. The others will probably have to wait until tomorrow. I'm doing up contracts for Mr. Tallant, too."

Charlie looked up. "Is Alex here now?"

"He said something about going out to lunch shortly."

"Did he?" Charlie grinned, purest mischief in his dark eyes. "I wonder if he'd mind my tagging along."

"Why don't you ask him?" Annie said as she went to the door.

"Come," Alex called as Charlie knocked on his door a couple of minutes later.

"Hello, Alex." Charlie beamed as he came in the door. "You busy? Are you going to lunch?"

"I'm getting ready to leave," Alex admitted, his polished smile slightly out of plumb. "Anything I can do for you?"

"Well, join me for lunch, why don't you?" Charlie dropped into Alex's scooped-out modern chair which was near the window. "Beautiful day, isn't it? I'd forgotten how beautiful the spring is."

"Be through here in a minute," Alex said testily.

"Take your time." Charlie leaned back, resting his head against the uncompromising chrome.

Alex bustled about, making his already neat desk even neater. When he was satisfied, he rose. "I was planning on Elbert's," he said, as if he expected Charlie to take back his invitation.

"Fine with me." Charlie pulled himself out of the chair. "Elbert's it is."

They had got through the salad and were both into their entrées when Alex could stand it no longer. "What is it, Charlie? What's on your mind?"

Charlie did not answer directly. "Are you still busy on the Mayling estate?"

"Sometimes I think it'll be forever." Alex sawed at a tough bit of prime rib. "This meal's not up to their standard," he commented sadly.

"Prices must be getting to them," Charlie agreed. Then he prodded gently. "What's the trouble with Mayling?"

"Everything. The more we find out, the less we know. It's a Red Queen's world." He chewed on the prime rib, making a face as he did.

"Are you spending a lot of time with the pharmaceutical end of the business?"

"Yes. That's where the money is, of course."

Charlie toyed with his meat, relishing the moment. "Well, look, Alex, so long as you're working on the case, would you mind checking into a few things for me?" Inside, Charlie was laughing with unholy glee. "Nothing much, mind you, but there are a few things I need to know. And after all, you're already working on the estate. . . ."

This time Alex's glare was not due entirely to the tough meat. "What do you want to know?"

For the next fifteen minutes, Charlie outlined the information he needed, told Alex his suspicions about the drug counterfeit, and watched as Alex took it all in. At the conclusion, he waited while Alex strove to recover his Robert Redford charm.

"Jesus Christ," Alex said at last. "What a racket. I wonder if old Jared knew or if this was cooked up on a lower level of the company?"

"I don't know," Charlie answered honestly. "But I'd appreciate anything you can find out." He was relieved to know that Alex could not afford to refuse his request without compromising his own clients.

Alex looked disgustedly at his meat, which was now cold. "Do anything I can, Charlie. What a mess."

Charlie was delighted to pay the very expensive tab for lunch.

Morgan was in his office when he got back. She surveyed him critically, eyes slightly narrowed. "You're looking better," she told him when she was convinced of it herself.

"Thank you. You don't look too bad yourself." He sat down. "Alex is going to be checking out Mayling for me. How was your first morning in court?"

At that Morgan shook her head. "Willis Ogilvie has all the finer instincts of a pirate," she said.

"Correction: of a politician." Charlie studied her face. "He's an excellent attorney, Morgan. There's none better."

"Maybe so," she allowed. "But he's ruthless." She let it go. "Well, what's this errand you need? I didn't know associates were supposed to run errands."

"In general they don't," Charlie said affably, "but because this might be the break we talked about in the Trobridge-Elgin case, I thought you'd like to be in on it. You said so last night."

There was a confusion of emotions on her face, anger vying with the lure of victory. Victory won. Suddenly she grinned. "Tell me all about it, Charlie."

He tossed her the packet. "I had a cold last week, as you may or may not know. Miranda gave me these for it. She said they were the ultimate thing for colds. They didn't do a damn thing for me. You'll notice this is a salesman's promotional pack, not a standard prescription bottle. You'll also notice that three of the little pockets are empty, so you know I took some of the pills from the same batch."

The lawyer in her made her say, "I know you told me you did."

He laughed. "That's true. Now, considering recent new . . . well, not evidence, but information . . . I've encountered, I think it might be wise to have these pills analyzed."

She nodded as she took the packet. "I'll take them over to the lab right now. What do I do when I get back?"

Charlie sighed. "Well, I have an appointment with the Guttierrezes in about thirty minutes. You might take the time, if Willis and Alex let you have any, to study the Sutherland case. I have to find some sort of defense by the middle of next week."

"Sutherland?" She frowned. "I don't remember. . . ."

"He's the very nasty piece of work who's been stealing anything automotive that isn't tied down in the Upper Mission district. He's got a weepy wife and a terrible temper. And I've got to find a way to stop the court from throwing the book at him." Charlie toyed with his pen and went on: "I think, personally, that the kid needs a good psychiatrist. He's violent, and that violence is just waiting for a chance and a place to erupt. He's dangerous. I can feel it. But unfortunately he won't agree to plead for a reduced charge, so I'm going to have to try it."

Morgan nodded again. "I'll try to get a line on it," she said, and Charlie knew that she would.

"Good. But first things first," he reminded her as he pointed to the packet she held. "That's the most important thing right now. Get on it."

She waved the packet over her head. "Excelsior!" she said.

"Charles, my boy," Willis thundered at him as Charlie started back for his office, a cup of hot coffee in his hand. "Let me congratulate you. Yes. You've done a magnificent job."

Charlie stopped, wishing he could sink through the floor. "Thank you, Willis. I'm glad it all turned out."

"Of course you are," Willis agreed, striding out of his office to clap his arm around Charlie's shoulder. "You're a real credit to the firm. Alex and I both remarked that you handled this whole matter ideally."

"I won," Charlie said evenly. Some of the coffee spilled and burned his fingers.

"I want you to know I'm delighted and proud." Willis took in Lydia Wong with his expansive smile. "We're all delighted." He winked archly.

"Well, I'm glad you're glad, Willis. But this isn't my only case." He wanted to slug Willis now. "I'll talk to you later, okay?"

"Certainly, certainly. Shannon was just saying this morning that we ought to have you over more often. Maybe breakfast on Sunday?" His smile somehow continued to get even wider.

Shannon had said nothing of the sort, and Charlie knew it, but he said, "That would be nice, Willis. I'll talk to you about it later." And then he bolted for his office and slammed the door.

The Guttierrezes had just left when Charlie's phone rang. He rubbed his eyes, then lifted the receiver. He was very tired. "Hello. Charles Moon here."

"Charlie," Elizabeth Kendrie said in her firmest accents, "what's this farrago Miranda tells me about counterfeit drugs?"

"Well, I don't think it *is* a farrago, Elizabeth. I think that's what's been happening. And I am setting out to prove it."

"And you think this Elgin person was murdered by other salesmen?"

"Yes." Charlie didn't think Elizabeth was angry, but there was a very forthright tone about her, and that might bode ill. Elizabeth was not entirely pleased. "What's the matter, Elizabeth? Are you afraid Miranda will change her mind and go back to the Harrowleigh Clinic? You needn't worry about that."

Elizabeth dismissed this impatiently. "Of course not. She's perfectly capable of making her own decisions. I was merely curious to find out how you came to this interesting conclusion. Where did you unearth this evidence?"

Unearthed. Well, Charlie supposed that in a way, he had done just that. "It was just a hunch that paid off." He made no reference to his ordeal of the previous day. "I'm reasonably sure that Miranda will be totally in the clear when I get all my facts."

"That's good to know." She stopped, then went on awkwardly: "You mustn't feel bad about Miranda. She would have made the change sooner or later. This suit only hurried the process. You're not to brood about her, Charlie."

"I hadn't planned on it," Charlie said, mentally deploring Elizabeth's kindness. "You don't have to tell me this. It isn't necessary." Why was her blunt sympathy so hard to bear? he wondered.

"I am aware of that," she said with some asperity. "But you know as well as I do that she blames you for a great many of the things that have happened to her recently. She believes that you manipulated her for your own profit and aggrandizement. She's not being realistic."

Charlie knew that she was winding up for a lecture, and he made an effort to sidetrack her before she could get into stride. "You can understand why she feels as she does about me. Think of what I represent. She can't help associating me with the case, her trouble at the clinic and all the negative effects of her predicament. Let's leave it as it is, Elizabeth. Maybe sometime later, when she's got distance and years separating her from this, maybe then we can salvage something, but not now."

Elizabeth's humility surprised Charlie as she said, "You're more compassionate than I am, Charlie. I won't interfere."

There was an old monster movie on Channel 44, but Charlie was too tired to watch it. The fatigue went beyond mere exhaustion; it was part of his bones, tied into the clock that turned the world. He sat in front of the TV, his mind as empty as his face. He told himself he was pleased; he had found the key to the Weed boy's death. Miranda would be completely cleared. The drug counterfeiters would be apprehended and tried. Sam Elgin's murderer would not get away. He would be sure Sam Elgin was avenged. But the enumeration of these things did not elevate his mood. As he considered his accomplishments, he felt nothing but despair. The law and its working would not bring back the dead any more than an artificial leg restored a lost one. For Mrs. Elgin, for the Weeds, for Miranda, there would be deep and abiding scars, testimony to deep wounds. All the law could offer as remedy was the legal equivalent of a bandage. It could provide some value for the loss, even though there was no way to restore the lives which had been forfeited.

Rufus yapped playfully, vainly attempting to distract his master. His frolic went unnoticed.

"I'll feel better in the morning. I'm still hung over from yesterday," he told the ceiling as he studied the pattern his living-room lights made there. He pulled himself out of the chair, moving like an old man. He reminded himself that Morgan would have the lab results for him tomorrow, and if they demonstrated counterfeit, as he knew they would, he would call Frank Shirer and would let the lieutenant take it from there. He yawned, thinking that yawns were very trivial.

As he undressed for bed, he reckoned that he would have a wakeful night. He had so much on his mind he knew it would intrude. He climbed into bed, feeling a morose satisfaction that he would be tossing until morning.

He was asleep before he had time to turn out his reading light.

Wednesday

"NOW LET ME get this straight," Frank Shirer said as he organized the clutter on his desk. "You say you can prove that drug counterfeiting is going on and you've got an idea who's doing it?" His disbelief was so strong on his ordinary, ferrety face that Charlie came close to laughing.

"Well"—he handed him a small manila envelope—"here's some cold pills I was given and the lab analysis is with them. Go ahead and read it."

"Tell me what it says," Frank countered, not taking the envelope.

"It says," Charlie said patiently, "that the pills are supposed to be prescription-strength cold pills with a little codeine to take the edge off a cough. The report tells me that they're nothing more than aspirin. And here"—he took half a dozen postcards from his zipper case—"are the first responses from San Francisco on a drug failure query I sent out yesterday. Three of them were sent 'round by messengers. The others, as you can see, are special delivery. Each one of them indicates that some time in the past eighteen months one or more of their patients has had trouble with a drug sample. I've sent out letters to every hospital, clinic, private practice, and convalescent home on the standard Northern California drug salesman's run. What would you like to bet me that the results will run true for all of them?"

Frank Shirer looked furtively at the envelope, as if it might contain poisonous insects. "You're sure about this?" he said.

"Read it for yourself." With great unconcern he dropped the envelope into the confusion of Frank's desk.

"Cronin is gonna go on a tear," Frank predicted, looking more depressed than ever.

Charlie cordially despised the District Attorney and let a little of his rancor show when he said, "Cronin the Conqueror can do what he wants in the way of political hay with this. But I think you'll find the Lemminis will want to take a hand."

"The Lemminis?" Frank put his hand to his head. "First it's Cronin, and now you're bringing the Lemminis in. What did I ever do to you?" By way of dismissing Charlie, he started to roll up his shirt sleeves. "Well, I'll do what I can," he said, a little more briskly.

But Charlie wasn't quite ready to be sent on his way. "The Lemminis are going to be interested because Sam Elgin was murdered. And that gets them where they live—in the family."

"Come off it, Charlie," Frank implored him. "Have a heart. There've been two assault homicides in North Beach in the last two days. Let me take care of them, and then I'll listen to you."

Charlie's affable manner evaporated. "No, Frank, you'll listen to me now." He put his hands flat on the desk and leaned forward, deliberately looming over Lieutenant Shirer. "Sam Elgin was murdered by one of the drug salesmen. He was given an overdose of Coumadin in his second glass of orange juice. If you ask around the clinic, I'm sure someone will have seen who gave him that second glass. So we're not just talking about mislabeling of drugs, which is what most counterfeiters are guilty of when they make their unofficial placebos. We are talking about murder and, very possibly, conspiracy to do murder. And that, Frank, is your specialty."

"How do you know that?" His jaw was set.

"Privileged communication between client and attorney." Wryly Charlie thought that he had not really lied. He had had very privileged communication with Sam Elgin. "But check it out."

"The Lemminis are gonna hate this."

"No, they won't," Charlie said, standing up once more. "They will use this to crack down on the drug business, to harry the FDA, and to smite the wrongdoers. David Lemmini is a fair man. And it is in his best interests to see this case pursued. And," Charlie added as a clinching afterthought, "do you really think you could keep something like this from Rocco Lemmini? That man knows when a mouse farts."

Frank capitulated. "Awright, awright. Don't set it to music. I hear you." He picked up the manila envelope. "Aspirin, huh?"

"Aspirin. Malton is having the Weeds check the L-dopa they still have left. Weed may be a domestic martinet, but he's not going to kid around about drugs like this. You'll want to call him tomorrow and find out what the results are."

Frank Shirer was harassed. "Sure I will," he said miserably. "God, I've handled drug murders before, but nothing like this."

"Think of it as a little variety," Charlie recommended.

Frank made a terse suggestion to Charlie as to where he should go and what he should do when he got there. Then he changed his attitude. "What about that doctor you're defending? I suppose this changes her case."

"I had a call from Malton this morning before I had to appear in court. The Weeds are dropping their suit against her and are going after the pharmaceutical company involved. There's more money in it."

"Yeah." Frank looked up. "I'll keep you posted on what happens."

"I'd appreciate that," Charlie said, making a movement not unlike a bow.

"I don't know how you did it," he mused. "But, Charlie, no matter what I said just now, I'm glad you did."

Morgan was in her office going over the first two lab reports on the counterfeit drugs which had been sent over from the Harrowleigh Clinic. She didn't look up as Charlie entered, contenting herself with "I'm working" as a greeting.

Charlie let this pass. "I saw Frank Shirer after I got out of court," he said. "He'll be taking the case from here, so you can ship those over to him, along with any others that come in."

She looked up. "Well, goddamn," she said, delighted. "I was beginning to think I'd never get through these." She returned the reports to their file, wiping her hands distastefully when she was done.

"You didn't like this one, did you?" Charlie asked gently.

"It was ugly." She swiveled her chair, revealing her nervousness. "God, I hope I don't run into many cases like this one when I go into practice for myself."

"I hope so, too." He smiled. "For all our sakes."

"Do you think Shirer will get them? Really?"

Charlie leaned against the wall. "Well, I can't tell the future, but I think he'll get some of them anyway. And I think the FDA'll lend him a hand."

"The FDA can get after them too, now, can't they?"

"Yes." Neither said anything for a short while.

She fingered the top button on her jacket. "Charlie, why did they kill Sam Elgin? Do you have any idea?"

Charlie cleared his throat. "I can make an educated guess," he said, ill at ease. "Assuming he was in on the counterfeiting originally, he was too much of a risk for the others." Her expression invited him to elaborate. "Look at it from the killer's point of view. Elgin had been part of the group, right? He knew their names, and he knew what they were up to. That's bad. But add to that Elgin's own child coming down with a chronic disease, which would certainly reduce Elgin's desire to profit from counterfeit drugs, since one of those counterfeits could easily kill his kid. Also, you have to remember Elgin was Catholic and probably had a highly developed sense of guilt. If you were a counterfeiter, would you leave someone like that running around loose? Particularly when Elgin was showing marked signs of stress?"

Morgan nodded, making a point of consulting her watch. "Charlie, you've got to excuse me. Willis is going to brief me for court tomorrow morning. He's starting his defense in that airline charter fraud."

But Charlie didn't move. "Okay. But I've got a question to ask you first."

"What is it?" Her prickly suspicion had crept back into her face.

"Will you let me buy you a drink Friday night? For the extra work you've done on the case." He added the last in the hope it might persuade her.

She rose, her eyes very bright. "If this is your idea of a joke. . . ."

"Not a joke, a date." He grinned at her. "When Dick Patterson helped me with a case last year, I took him and his fiancée out to dinner. I'm not doing you any particular favor. I like to acknowledge my debts. And I think you might enjoy it. Okay?"

Her suspicions were not lessened. "Where were you planning to take me?"

"Well," he said, crossing his arms, "I'm going to the Magic Cellar to see the magic shows there. I like magic shows. I'll meet you at the door at eight."

"Live magic?" she asked, intrigued in spite of herself.

"Yep."

"The Magic Cellar. Where is it?"

"A couple of blocks farther down Clay, half a block up from the Pyramid. Come on, Morgan. You'll have fun. I'm not going to force my attentions on you in the middle of a nightclub." He stood aside and opened the door. "You can pay the cover charge yourself, if it'll make you feel better."

She flushed and then let the anger wash away with laughter. "I'll meet you there Friday at eight. Now I *do* have to go."

Charlie stepped into the hall and pulled the door closed behind him.

On his way home that evening Lydia stopped him. "I wanted to thank you," she said, not quite willing to face him.

"Oh? What for?" Charlie raised his brows and waited.

She held out a memo. "I got the raise. So did Janis and Annie."

"Great," he said, offering Lydia his hand in congratulation. He thought to himself, this round goes to Moon.

"I'm sorry I was bitchy about it," Lydia said, and it was obvious this was an effort for her.

Charlie could afford to be magnanimous. "I don't blame you. There were times I thought I'd blown it."

She turned her hand over and studied the long palm as if she had lost something there. "That's very kind of you."

"Save some of this magnanimous feeling, will you?" he said as he bent to kiss her cheek. "I might need it again some time."

The beige brocade of the sofa was stained orange by the setting sun. Charlie stood by the window, looking out into the late afternoon, waiting, as the dying day crept across the floor.

The tap of her shoes announced her. She hesitated as he looked up, then moved to one of the elegant chairs. "Henry said you were here."

"Yes." Now that he saw her he did not know what he wanted to say. "I guess you've heard. You're in the clear, Miranda."

"Elizabeth told me." She sat primly, her hands folded tightly on her lap, her face reserved.

"It was drug counterfeit all along. You were never to blame—"

She cut him short. "I know."

He let his gaze wander back to the window. "The complaints against you will be dropped, of course, and the clinic will furnish you with a full recommendation for your new job." How empty the words sounded, even to him. He breathed deeply and tried again. "Apparently Shelly, the Mayling salesman, was the organizer of the ring."

"Oh?" The sound was barely polite. She shifted in the chair.

"Look, Miranda," Charlie began, coming across the room toward her, "I realize this has been rough for you. . . ."

"Rough?" She turned incredulous eyes on him. "I almost lost my career, my whole life, and you think it's been rough?"

Charlie bit back a retort. He longed to tell her that his job had been on the line as well, that he would have failed if he had not been as desperate as he was, if he had not made the spirit walk. Instead, he said, "I'm sorry it had to be that way."

"Christ." She looked away from him and bit her lower lip.

Suddenly his anger and frustration welled up. "Cut it out, Miranda. You're acting as if you're the only one who has trouble, and you know it's not true."

Her hands tightened. "Go on," she said icily.

He studied her, the fine lines of her face, the eyes hidden behind her glasses, her short brown hair, which he now noticed she was doing in a new, becoming way. "Never mind." He sank onto the sofa. "I wanted to tell you that it was all over."

She said nothing.

"I like your hair that way," he said after a moment.

"Thank you."

He looked at his watch, wondering how long he would have to remain here, wondering what else there was to say. The smooth turquoise seemed dark in the fading light, and the silver was smoky. "I hear Redding's nice. The McIntyre Hospital has a fine reputation. I know you'll like it there."

"I'm looking forward to it," she said, with more warmth, more enthusiasm than she had shown yet.

She was so remote, Charlie thought. He remembered that he had kissed her, months ago, but could not recall what it was like. They had lost touch and would not regain it. He got to his feet. "I'm glad it all worked out. Good luck, Miranda." He held out his hand but was not surprised when she did not take it.

He was almost to the door when she said, "Thank you for all you did for me." Resentment smoldered in her voice.

Charlie looked back once. "Good-bye, Miranda."

Friday Night

THE YELLOW AND white striped awning offered Charlie a little protection from the evening drizzle. He waited, his hands deep in the pockets of his overcoat. Morgan might have changed her mind, he knew, but he hoped not. He did not want the deep obligation he felt toward her. Her acceptance of his invitation for a drink would in part mitigate his debt to her, making it possible for him to avoid the long ritual of repayment.

A few minutes after eight the door opened, and a bush of curly brown hair stuck itself around the door. A face appeared beneath it, adorned by a neat mustache and wire-rimmed glasses. "Oh." A smile spread over the wide-featured face. "I didn't see you there. Come on in, Charlie."

Charlie took the offered hand. "Thanks, Ced. I'm waiting for someone."

Cedric lifted a finger. "If you're staying for the stage show, I'll put a reservation on the center front table for you."

"Just the place for me," Charlie murmured.

"It's a good night tonight," Cedric went on after rolling his eyes upward. "Harry's on at nine and eleven, and Gene is on at ten and twelve." He tugged at his Magic Cellar sweat shirt.

"I'm looking forward to it. I'll be down shortly." Charlie nodded as he watched Cedric disappear down the steep stairs, passing under the huge poster promising wonders performed by Carter the Great. At the bottom of the stairs, Cedric turned back, saying, "Jan's working the door tonight, Charlie. I'll tell her you're here."

Charlie waved an acknowledgment, then stood back as five teenaged boys surged past him and down the stairs, their feet booming in the stairwell. One of the boys carried six large steel rings around his arm, and they clanged as he ran.

It was perhaps five minutes later when Morgan walked defiantly up to him, her practical raincoat wet at her shoulders. "The parking is terrible. I'm three blocks away. I might as well have kept the car at the office," she informed him as if it were somehow his fault.

"I know. I'm parked way down on Pine myself."

This seemed to mollify her. "It's all because they got rid of the on-street parking over on Broadway. It's impossible." She peered at him. "This is dutch, right?"

"That's what I said. So long as you let me buy you a drink," he agreed. Then he pointed her down the stairs. "This way."

"God, this is steep." She took a firm hold of the handrail and went down, Charlie walking beside her.

"Hi, Charlie." The woman at the desk was willowy, her face surrounded by a cloud of dark-blond hair. "Ced told me you were coming in." She smiled warmly as Charlie reached for his wallet. "Oh, no. Now, put that away. Look, you saved us all from having our cars towed away last month. Don't worry about the cover charge. This is on Ced and me."

Charlie lifted his brows as he turned to Morgan. "Do you still want to go dutch, or will you let me . . . pay . . . for this?"

Morgan glared smolderingly at him and took two bills

from her purse, offering them silently to Jan, who laughed easily and handed them back to her.

"Thanks, Jan," Charlie said, returning her smile.

"What now?" Morgan said in an undertone as she followed Charlie to the bar.

Charlie nodded to Cedric, who had taken up his post among the glasses, ice, and bottles. "Ced, this is my new associate, Morgan Studevant. She's never seen the Cellar."

"Good evening," Cedric said, making that formal greeting sound casual. "If you want a tour, Arthur can give you one after his close-up show."

"We'll look around for ourselves," Charlie said, then ordered drinks. As Cedric tossed his secret ingredients into the blender, Charlie asked, "What happened around the office today?"

"On the Trobridge case?" Morgan asked astutely.

"That is what I had in mind."

"Well," she said, raising her voice to be heard over the blender, "Cronin's ordered a full investigation of all salesman-distributed drugs at all the hospitals. Frank Shirer called and said they've got a lead on Sam Elgin's murderer. It looks like that salesman from the Mayling company was the ringleader of the operation. Wantage, one of the other salesmen, has said he'll turn state's evidence."

"Spelled plea bargaining," Charlie interpolated.

"Here you are, folks," Cedric interrupted, putting down two small brandy snifters full of what looked like orange slush with a half a banana in it.

"What is it?" Morgan wanted to know, looking at the glass critically.

"That, my dear," Cedric announced, "is my own invention. The house specialty. It's called a Levitation."

"Take the name seriously," Charlie recommended.

They took their drinks and drifted away from the bar. "How was the Board of Supervisors? Did the Guttierrezes get their new basement?"

Charlie chuckled. "It took forever. But they've got the basement, and the city is refunding part of their taxes because of the inconvenience brought about by the Department of Public Works."

"I'll bet they didn't like that." She tasted the drink. "This is good."

"That it is. No, Public Works was furious. But old Rocco Lemmini backed them up against the wall and nailed them to it." He chuckled again. "That old fox belongs back with the de' Medicis. What a terror he is."

Morgan had been looking around the club. "Not to change the subject, but what's all this stuff a copy of?"

"It's not a copy of anything. This is Carter the Great's own magical apparatus." He pointed to the bedsheet-sized posters on the walls. "Those are real, too. Ced has all the stuff."

"Did he buy it from Carter?"

"Carter died in India in the thirties. And the story is a long one. Get Ced to tell it later tonight." He led her past the levitation couch and the sawing-the-lady-in-half box to a semicircular table covered in green felt.

"What happens here?" Morgan asked as she took another sip. "Am I wrong, or is this drink a lot less innocuous than it tastes?"

"You're right about the drink." Charlie sipped cautiously on his. He treated all alcohol with great respect. "This is the close-up table. The magician sits there, and we sit here." He pointed out the close quarters. "And the magic is done under your nose."

"Oh, go on."

Charlie took a seat, pulling out one for Morgan. "Sit down, Morgan. Arthur starts his show in five minutes."

A slow drift of the other patrons to the close-up table confirmed this, and in a few minutes the Oriental rug that hung against the wall lifted at one end and a stocky young Japanese, built like a judo instructor and dressed like a banker—both of which he, in fact, was—stepped out and beamed at the audience seraphically.

"He doesn't look like a magician," Morgan said dubiously to Charlie, sotto voce.

"Just watch," Charlie said.

"Good evening, ladies and gentlemen, and welcome to the Magic Cellar. My name is Arthur Murata, and I'd like to show you something you might find kind of interesting."

Morgan shot Charlie a skeptical glance, then turned her attention to the four oversized cards Arthur Murata held in his hands. "Well, he can't palm something that big," she admitted.

But it was the balls in the cup that fascinated her the most. She turned to Charlie after Arthur had fooled her the third time. "Do you know how he does it?" she whispered.

"No," he answered truthfully. "That's not my field."

The cup which had been empty a moment ago was upended to reveal a turnip, which Arthur happily turned into an atrocious pun. The audience groaned. Arthur showed them that the cup was empty and put it upside down on the table. "I know," he said, grinning in anticipation. "You thought that joke was a lemon. Well"—he turned the cup up again—"here's the lemon," as the yellow fruit rolled out of the cup and across the table.

"Maybe I believe in magic after all," Morgan said, resigned to enjoying herself.

Arthur began to drop coins through the solid table into an old-fashioned glass.

Charlie looked at the coins, thinking of something else, his mind far away from the applauding nightclub patrons. As much to himself as to Morgan, he said, "There's all kinds of magic. All kinds of magic."